Simi

CHRONICLES
of NICK:
SHADOWS OF FIRE

SHERRILYN KENYON

OLIVERHEBERBOOKS

1

9527 BC

In a place the gods called Kalosis, Simi hesitated in the shadows of a small courtyard. Her big sister, Xirena, had told her this was a hell realm, but it didn't feel like hell to her.

It felt like home.

Maybe it wasn't as sunny and brights as wheres they used to nest, but still, Kalosis had her matera, her big brother and her big sissy, so to Simi it seemed very nice and special. Homey. Excepts for the fact that Simi couldn't find her matera at the moment.

Not anywhere she looked. Where could she be in this dark place?

She missed her mommy.

Her matera had told the Simi that she was going ons an errand and that she'd be right back. But right back was a long time ago now, and that made the Simi's heart hurt. It gave it a mighty pain that was only equal to the one in her belly that said it was time to eat.

And the Simi needed her mother. Not just because she was hungry and her heart ached. The Simi missed her mother's hugs and warm tickles. So she'd snucked away from her big sissy who was always watching her and fussy about everything and everyone, and came here to where the beautiful goddess paced in a wide circle around the dark, shimmering pond that let the goddess see other places and things.

Only it wasn't things the goddess looked at mostest. Mostest the goddess watched a boy Simi didn't know.

With long white-blonde hair and swirling silver eyes, akra-Apollymi was the Atlantean goddess of destruction. She was also her mother's bestest friend and Simi's second mama-akra. Though others called the goddess scary and mean, Simi didn't see that. Akra-Apollymi was forever nicest to her. She always had the bestest tasting treats and lots of toys and dolls.

And hugs. Lots of hugs.

Even when akra-Apollymi was upsetest, which the goddess seemed to be at the moment, she gave the Simi extra treats and warm, gentle hugs.

Maybe the goddess was missing Simi's mama, too.

So Simi stepped forward through the doorway, in the dark, pretty garden filled with black roses and dark green shrubs. "Where's the Simi's matera, akra?"

Akra-Apollymi stopped pacing and turned toward her. The beautiful goddess knelt down and held her arms out for Simi so that she could run to the goddess and gets a hug that Simi was missing from her mother.

"She's not back yet, sweeting. Soon."

Simi pouted before she ran to her and threw her arms around akra-Apollymi's neck. She put one small thumb into her mouth and buried her other hand deep in the goddess's white, silky hair.

While it wasn't quite as nice as her mama's hugs, it was enough to make her feel better.

Akra-Apollymi tightened her hold on her.

Simi laid her head on the goddess's shoulder as akra-Apollymi began to sing and rock her.

How strange, especially given that the goddess didn't seem to be in the moods to sing. "Why is akra so sad?"

Standing up with Simi in her arms, akra began to pace the garden again. "I'm not sad, Simi. I'm anxious."

"Is anxious like when the Simi eats too much and her stomach hurts?"

She smiled and kissed the top of her head. "Not exactly. It's when you can't wait for something to happen."

"Ooo, like when the Simi is hungry and she's waiting on her matera to feed her. Or like the Simi now wanting her matera to come for her."

"Something like that."

Then all of a sudden, Simi felt what she needed to feel. That slight stirring in the air that she'd been waiting for.

"Matera!"

Her beautiful mother flew in with her black wings fluttering. Like Simi, her skin was a swirling combination of red and white. The red of her skin matched her mother's hornays ...

Like Simi's.

But her mother didn't seem as happy as Simi was that she'd come back.

The goddess frowned at her mother. "What is it?"

Her mother, Xiamara, held her hands out for Simi. Without hesitating, she flew from the goddess to her to get the hug the Simi needed most.

But her matera was crying, and that confused her greatly. Why would matera's eyes flow with water? Simi had only seen that happen when her mama thought about her papas who'd died.

And only when her matera thought no one was around to see her tears.

"Xi?" akra-Apollymi asked gently. "Tell me."

"Why's Simi's matera so sad?" Simi asked, wanting to make her feels all warm like her matera did whenever the Simi had tears that flowed down her cheeks.

Rocking her gently, her mother clenched her eyes closed. "I don't know how to tell you, akra."

The goddess approached them fretfully. "Is he not well? I'm still a prisoner here, so I know he lives even though I can't see him in my mirror at the moment."

Her mother rubbed Simi's back. "He lives."

Who was *he*? Was it the boy the goddess sometimes watched? Simi wanted to ask, but she knew from experience that it would anger her mother if she interrupted her while she spoke to their goddess.

"Does he not love me?" akra-Apollymi asked with tears in her swirling silver eyes.

To her deepest sadness, her mother set her down. "Go find your sister, Simi. I need to speak with akra alone."

But why? Again, Simi knew better than to ask that out loud. Grownups often shooed her away, even when the Simi was trying to help them. And especially whenever she was trying to understand them.

Oh well ...

Sucking her thumb, Simi skipped away from the garden back to the path that led toward their home. Even so, she really wanted to know what was so important that it made everyone's hearts hurt.

Grown-ups. She'd never understand them and she wasn't sure she wanted to. They's all boring and bleh!

"Simi! Here! Now!"

Her eyes widened at the sound of her sissy's angry shouts as she left the goddess's temple. She removed her thumb from her mouth so that she could yell back. "What!"

Angry as always, Xirena rushed out of the shadows to scoop her up before she could even tell which direction her sister had come in from. Her sissy's skin was marbled red and black, and her yellow eyes were tinged with worry. "I've been looking all over for you! Where have you been?"

As always, Simi was where Simi was. She never understood that question, nor the anger that came with it.

"Simi wanted Matera. But she done told the Simi that she can't be with the Simi right now. She with akra-Apollymis so Simi had to leave and go away. Can we have food now, sissy? Simi's hungry."

Xirena let out a deep, aggravated sigh. The most frequent sound Simi heard from her older sister. "You're always hungry. I don't understand why you can never get full."

To be fair, that was true. Simi didn't know why either, but her belly constantly demanded food. So did her taste-buddies. They liked yummy things and in particulars *really* hot, yummy things.

But at least her sister didn't yell at her like normal. Simi was tired of that, even if her sister was her protector. Xirena wasn't her matera and she shouldn't have a right to scream at Simi all the time. For some reason, her sissy thought it was her job to boss Simi alls the times.

But right now, Xirena held her close as her sissy flew her toward their home.

It was a small cottage set off by itself, which Simi didn't understand as the other Charonte demons lived in a giant hall together, near the goddess. When she was littler, they had a much bigger place, but that was in Katateros—the heaven realm where the Atlantean gods all lived, and where akra-Apollymi had lived until the evil gods got together and cursed her here because she wouldn't let them kill her baby son.

So long as akra-Apollymi's son lived, akra-Apollymi couldn't leave their Kalosis and so the Charonte stayed with her.

Simi didn't blame the goddess for not wanting to leave.

She wouldn't let them kill her baby either. Or her sister, brother or mother. She would always protect what she loved. No matter what.

But it still didn't explain why their house was off all by itself.

"Why do we have our own place when the other Charonte don't?" Simi asked as they landed on the doorstep.

Sighing again in irritation, Xirena opened the door. "Don't ask those kinds of questions."

"But why?"

"It'll make Matera sad." Xirena set her down by her side.

Confuzzled by that, Simi skipped into the cottage to find their brother, Xedrix, leaning against the wall as if he was waiting on their arrival.

Xedrix jerked his chin toward Simi. "You know we're going to have to tell her one day."

Like Xirena, he had yellow eyes, but his skin was swirling blues that reminded Simi of a cloudy sky. But he could change that if he wanted. They all could. The one fun thing about being Charonte was that they could have any body color they wanted. And most of them liked wearing multiple, swirly colors.

Simi preferred looking like her mother the mostest. She had no idea who her brother and sister looked like or why they picked their colors. Those colors were pretty, but not Matera pretty. Just normal pretty.

Matera was extra special beautimous.

Xirena hissed at Xedrix. "It's not our place."

He shook his head before he scooped Simi up from the floor. "Hungry?"

She smiled happily. "Always!"

Xirena tucked her black, feathered wings down as she headed to the cupboard where they kept Simi's favorite foods. "She's an eating machine. I have no idea how she can stay so tiny and eat so much."

"Maybe we should turn her loose on the Atlantean gods."

Xirena hissed again. "Careful! What if one of them heard you?"

Opening the cupboard before Xirena could reach it, he scoffed, then moved aside for Xirena to pick through the icky healthy things to find Simi's snacks. "They're terrified of Apollymi. They don't listen to what we do here. They don't dare. If any of them showed their faces, Apollymi would rip their hearts out and feast on them. She's just aching for an excuse to burn the entire world down and especially *that* pantheon. Which will probably happen as soon as her son turns twenty-one and comes into his powers."

With a ragged breath, Xirena rubbed Simi's back while Xedrix held her, then handed Simi a piece of dried beef. "I don't understand Matera's loyalty to her."

"Because Apollymi is equally as loyal to Matera. And we're lucky for that. If she wasn't—"

Xirena placed a hand over his lips to silence him. "Stop it! Matera doesn't want our Simi to know."

"Know what?" Simi asked.

"Nothing," Xirena snapped.

Xedrix rolled his eyes. "She'll learn. They always do."

Simi frowned at her sissy and bro-bro. They often talked like this, but she didn't understand, and they always refused to explain it.

All she knew was that akra-Apollymi had a baby boy which was why the goddess lived here in Kalosis instead of their old home in Katateros. Them evil Atlantean gods had trapped her here because they believed the baby akri would kill them all.

They were scared, but it made no sense to the Simi. Who could be afraid of a tiny little baby? A baby, even a god baby, couldn't hurt a big god. It was stupid.

Them gods were silly things. Personally, she'd just eat the baby and not worry. But then, she was a Charonte and not a god. And while she didn't know any Charonte who'd ever eaten a baby, babies might be tasty to the tummy.

And speaking of tasty …

"Can the Simi have more?" She held her hand out to her sister.

Growling at her, Xirena handed her another piece. "Isn't it your bedtime?"

"No. It's eating time." Simi smiled at her so wide that she flashed her fangs.

That made Xedrix laugh.

Simi still didn't understand why her sissy was so angry all the time. Or why she didn't like akra-Apollymi who was always nice to Simi.

The world confuzzled her. But maybe one day, it might make sense.

Today, however, wasn't that day. Today was just another day where Simi would aggravate her sister, eat some meat and try to figure out why her mother was so upset.

2

Simi lay in her room with her feet propped up along the wall. She was watching shadows play across the ceiling when she heard Xirena cry out.

It was an awful, terrible sound. Like her sissy's entire heart had been shredded. The only other time she'd ever heard such a horrible sound was when akra-Apollymi had cut her baby boy from her own belly and handed it off to another goddess to be taken to the human world so that the Atlantean gods wouldn't kill her baby boy.

Worried that her sister had cut out a baby, too, she quickly rolled over and flew to Xirena.

Only Xirena wasn't the only one crying. Xedrix cried, too. Just as hard, but in silence.

Xedrix never cried. Not for any reason. Xirena said he hadn't even cried when their pappas died.

"What's wrong?" Simi asked, approaching them slowly in the air. "You gots aches in your hearts? Why?"

Xirena cried even harder. "I can't tell her, Xed. I can't."

Xedrix grabbed Simi out of midair and held her so tight against his chest that it hurt. Her wings were crimped against his muscled chest.

"Simi can't breathe!"

He only loosened his hold slightly. "Our mother's dead, Simi," he whispered in her ear.

Those words hit Simi harder than one of her sissy's blows as she tried to understand them.

Matera dead? No.

No!

It was a lie. It had to be. Their father had died long ago.

Not their mother. They were confused.

Matera wasn't dead. She wasn't allowed to be. Not when Simi needed her.

Akra-Apollymi needed her, too.

Unable to believe them, she teleported from his arms, into akra-Apollymi's garden. Sitting on the edge of her dark fountain, the goddess was crying even harder than her brother and sister were.

No. No. No …

No!

"Akra?" Simi asked as tears blinded her. "Where's my matera?"

The goddess pulled her into her arms just like Xedrix had done. "I'm so sorry, Simi. I wasn't able to protect her. I never meant for this to happen. It wasn't supposed to be like this."

Squeezing her eyes shut, Simi wailed at the loss of her mother. How could she be gone? How?

Why?

The Simi was alone with no matera. The very thought of it caused a scream to echo through her soul.

Akra-Apollymi brushed the dark curls back from her red and white face. "It'll be okay, little one."

"How? I have no matera to hugs me and takes care of her Simi. Simi can't be alone. She a small simi. I need my matera!"

"You'll have a new father."

"The Simi don't want no new father," she wailed. "The Simi didn't even know her old one. Simi wants her matera! Make her come back to life! You a goddess. Bring her back to me!"

"I wish I could, precious. But I don't have those powers."

"Then find them!"

Akra-Apollymi sniffed back her tears. "It doesn't work like that, child."

"Then I hate you! The Simi hates you! I'll always hate you!" She left the goddess and returned home to where her brother and sister were hunting for her.

"The Simi wants to leave here!" she demanded, tugging at Xirena's hand. "Take the Simi to her old house."

Her sissy looked horrified. "I can't, Simi. We're not allowed to go there."

Simi cried even harder. She didn't want to be in the hell realm anymore. It was dark here.

Cold.

There was no matera to make it warm and homey. No more cuddles or kisses. How could her matera leave her like this? Didn't she know the Simi loveded her and needed her? That her Simi was losted with no matera to keep her safest?

She didn't want to be here with her Rik-rik and her sissy.

Covering her eyes, she screamed and screamed. But the pains wouldn't stop. They just kept hurting her and making her heart ache so much that she couldn't breathe.

Why was her mama dead?

Suddenly, she found herself back in front of akra-Apollymi who must have used her powers to drag Simi to her.

The goddess took Simi's hands and pulled them from her eyes.

"Look at me, Simi."

She didn't want to. She hated the goddess who'd hurt her matera. Hated the world. But when she hiccupped, her eyes opened, and she saw the mean goddess who had taken her mother from her.

"Listen to me, Simi. The evil Greek gods killed your matera. I hate them as much as you do."

She hiccupped again as those words chased through her mind. "The Greek gods?"

Akra-Apollymi nodded. "They are our enemies. Never forget that. And I have a favor to ask you."

That made no sense. Akra-Apollymi was a goddess.

What favor could a simi do for such a powerful goddess. "What?"

"I'm sending you to your akri. He will take care of you and love you just like your mother did. I need you to watch over and protect him. To love him as your family. Can you do that?"

How could she love someone she didn't know? "I want my matera!"

The goddess ignored her. "He will be waiting in your old home, and he will need you. I promise, Simi. Your akri will take care of you. He will be a good father for you."

Her breathing ragged, she looked up at the goddess. "The Simi can go home to her old house?"

"Yes. Back to Katateros. Would you like that?"

It was light there. Sunny. Unlike here where it was night all the time. Simi had been happy in Katateros with her family. Everything had been wonderful in the hall of the gods. Even most of the old gods had been nice to her.

And she wanted terribly to be happy again.

The Simi didn't want to feel like this. She didn't want to have the sadness in her heart or wetness on her cheeks. Simi missed smiling and laughing and playing chase through the old temples. "Please make the Simi happy, akra. Simi don't like this aches in her bellies and heart."

Akra-Apollymi cupped her cheek and nodded, then everything went dark.

Simi had no idea what was happening. Not until the light returned and she found herself inside a large room behind a huge throne made of stone.

She remembered this place from long ago. It was Archon's throne ...

Apollymi's mean husband who used to scowl at the Simi and her matera. Only the Atlantean god wasn't here to scowl at her now. The hall was eerily empty with no mean gods in it anywhere.

That made Simi afraid. Where had all the gods gone? Would they come back and hate her or chase her away?

She had no matera or sissy for protection and she was a little demon. Little demons could eats and fight, but that was nothing compared to what a big god could do.

Terrified, she tried to find a place to hide so that they wouldn't pull her wings off.

All of a sudden, a huge shadow fell over her.

No! They'd found her before she could hide. Eyes wide in terror, she looked up to see ...

Well, it wasn't Archon and for that she was mighty thankful. Confuzzled, she stared up at the boy-man who towered over her with a curious frown. Extremely tall and handsome, he had long black hair and swirling silver eyes just like akra-Apollymi.

The Simi smiled, hoping he wouldn't pull her wings off.

Not sure what else to do, she glanced to the huge staff he held. It was topped by Apollymi's sun emblem that was pierced by three lightning bolts. That gave the Simi some more hope. "Are you Simi's akri?"

Akri was the masculine term for 'lord and master,' though Simi and her family used it for akra even though she was more friend than someone who wanted to control them. She hoped her new akri was that kind of akri, and not the mean one.

His scowl deepened. "I'm no one's akri."

"Oh ..." That didn't help at all. She looked about for the one akra-Apollymi had sent her to find. If this wasn't her akri, maybe her akri was lost, too. "But akra sent me here. She said my akri would be waiting. The Simi is confuzzled. I lost my mama and now the Simi needs her akri or else there won't be anyone to take care of Simi." Frustrated and afraid that she would be forever alone, she sat down and started crying again.

What if she never found her akri?

Was she stuck here? With no Rik-rik or sissy? She couldn't imagine anything worse than being stuck in this place alone. Without anyone.

No. Simi needed her family!

The stranger laid down his staff so that he could pick her up. "Don't cry. It'll be all right. We'll find your mother."

That only made it worse! "Akra said the Simi's matera is dead. Them evil Greek people kilded the Simi's mama. Now the Simi needs her akri to love her."

She didn't have anyone else.

If he wasn't her akri, she was alone in this world, too, and she didn't know how to get back home to Kalosis.

He rocked her gently in his arms as akra-Apollymi's shady ghosty form appeared beside them.

Simi stopped crying as she saw her there. "Akra, he says the Simi's akri isn't here."

Akra-Apollymi smiled at them. "He *is* your akri, Simi."

"What?" her akri asked in shocked surprise.

"Her mother, Xiamara, was your protector. Like you, Simi is all alone in the world with no one to care for her. She needs you, Apostolos."

Now Simi understood. This was akra-Apollymi's son that her brother and sister had talked about in whispers. The Atlantean god they'd tried to kill. Only he wasn't a baby now. He was a growed up man.

"Bond with him, Simi, protect my son as your mother protected me."

But she didn't know how to protect anyone. She was only a small Simi.

And the boy god didn't look happy about having her with him. "I don't want a demon."

Tears stung her eyes at those words. She had no one? Simi didn't want to be here without someone.

"Would you cast her out alone in the world?" akra-Apollymi asked.

"No."

"Then she's yours." And with that, akra-Apollymi vanished and left her with a god who stared at her as if he didn't know what to do either.

And Simi definitely didn't know what to do. She had no idea how to get back to her brother or sister.

So, she stared at her akri, then snuggled against him and laid her head on his shoulder. "I miss my mama, akri."

"Where's your father, Simi?"

That made her even sadder. All she knew about her

father was whispered stories. And the warnings from her family that they weren't supposed to talk about him. "He died before the Simi was born."

Her words seemed to make her akri have hurts in his heart, too. "Then I will be your father."

Her lip quivered with hope that she wouldn't be all by herself in this place. "Really?"

Smiling at her, he nodded. "And I swear to you that you'll never want for anything."

"Then the Simi has the bestest akri-papa in alls the world." She hugged him tightly. "Simi loves her akri."

Wanting to show him just how much, she did what all Charonte did when they bonded to someone, she faded into a shadow and placed herself on his skin, just above his heart as a colorful dragon image. Because she liked dragons. They were strong and bright.

Here, she could reside for a time as a part of him. She could feel his emotions and the soothing beat of his heart.

He brushed his hand over her, and it made her laugh. More than that, it tickled. So, she moved up toward his collarbone so that she could rest in peace and let the sound of his heartbeat soothe her.

This was her father. She'd never had one before. Would her akri be as good as her matera?

Simi hoped so. Honestly? She was scared. The world had changed, and the Simi didn't like change. But she would trust in akra-Apollymi.

Most of all, she would trust in her new akri.

"Ow!"

Simi stared at her akri as he pulled away from her on the ground where they'd been sleeping. She licked at the blood on her lips, wanting to taste more of his hand. It'd been surprisingly yummy.

His swirling eyes were filled with shock. "You're not supposed to bite your father, Simi."

"But the Simi's hungry and akri was lying there all still and yummy looking." She smiled at him, hoping he'd let her have at least a finger.

He moved even further away. "Um ... let's find you something else to eat."

She pouted. "Now or later?"

"Yes. Now."

Wiping away the blood with the back of her hand, she sighed. "Okies."

"Hide your horns, Sim, and your wings. Humans won't respond kindly if they see them."

Akri always said that whenever they went around humans.

Especially given how many people were deads 'cause his mother had kilded them all over what the Greek god Apollo had done to her akri. She hated those Greek gods.

So did her akri.

They were mean and hateful. She hoped they all died one day, just as awfully as her mother had, especially Apollo.

And because the world was nothing like Simi remembered. They were in what akri called a Stone Age. All their technology and tools had been lost. And the island of Atlantis was no longer here. Akra-Apollymi had sent it to the bottom of the ocean when she'd found out what they did to her son.

All because the humans had hurt her akri. Personally, the Simi was glad akra-Apollymi had kilt them. It was only fair 'cause akri was a good Simi daddy.

Even now, he picked her up and carried her on his shoulders. It was why she made sure that she looked like his daughter. She just wished her eyes matched his. Sadly, she couldn't make them swirl. The closest she could do was a light blue.

But that was okay. They was close enough.

And after a while, they came to a broken village that had been abandoned like so many others. Only a few buildings still stood and they weren't fully intact. Whoever had lived here before the goddess's tantrum had run off, but they'd also left some of their foods behind.

Akri set her down so that they could both look through the broken things to find her food.

"Hey, Simi. I have something for you to eat."

She froze at a voice that seemed familiar. Oddly accented and deep. Her akri held her back from the stranger.

Simi didn't know why. He seemed friendly enough with his tousled dark-hair and thick beard. His skin was a bit darker than most of the Greek people.

But akri was tense as he faced him. "Who are you?"

The man stepped around a fallen column to kneel before Simi. He set a basket down at her feet and uncovered loaves of bread, fish and cheese. "I know you're hungry, sweet. Dig in."`

Delighted at the banquet, Simi let out a squeal before she set on the food with a vengeance.

The man stood up and offered his arm to her akri. "My name is Savitar."

Her akri hesitated before he finally shook Savitar's arm. "How do you know Simi?"

One corner of his mouth lifted. "I know lots of things, Acheron. And I've come to help you learn your powers and to understand your simi demon. She's too young still to be left to callous care, and the last thing I want is to see either one of you hurt because of it."

"I would never hurt her."

"I know, but the Charonte have special needs you must understand. Otherwise, she could die ... as could you."

"The Simi would never hurt her akri!"

Savitar laughed. "But you might take a finger or toe."

She licked her lips as she remembered how yummy akri's finger had been that morning. Savitar wasn't wrong. If she got hungry enough, she mights take a finger. Maybe a toe, too. But right now, the bread and fish were much tastier.

Acheron scowled at Savitar. "Are you threatening me?"

Savitar laughed. "I never threaten. I just kill whatever

annoys me. Stand down, Atlantean. I'm here as your friend."

And he was definitely the Simi's friend. She loved her anyone what brunged her food.

Buts it was weird that the men didn't speak while she ate. Akri picked through the rubble as if looking for something while Savitar sat near her, watching her eat.

Very strange, and yet not really. Akri didn't talk much to anyone. He was always guarded around others who weren't her. 'Course, that made sense given that the evil gods had tried to kill him.

And the evil Greek god, Apollo, had succeeded.

Which made Simi hurt most of all. While akri never spoke about it, she sometimes saw the handprint on his throat where that mean god had killst him.

Akri didn't deserve it, and she wanted to make sure no one ever hurt or threatened her akri again. Akra-Apollymi was right. Akri was the bestest father anyone could have, especially a demon.

Simi burped, then giggled as she finished her food.

Laughing, Savitar stood and picked her up in his arms to carry her while he and akri walked through the crumbled streets that showed just how angry akra-Apollymi had been when they'd hurt her akri.

His human death had freed akra-Apollymi from her prison in Kalosis. The goddess had taken out all her fury over losing akri and Simi's matera on the human world. Akra had almost eaten them nasty Greek gods, too, but Apollo's sissy, Artemis, had tricked akri into coming back to life so that his mama would be trapped again and unable to kill the ones who'd hurt akri.

Simi wasn't sure what she thought about the heifer goddess bringing back her akri. Other than she was glad she had her akri, even if he was sad lots of times because of it.

"She's impressive, isn't she?" Savitar asked.

Akri scowled at the question. "My mother or Simi?"

Savitar laughed. "Both, but I was speaking of your mother."

With a deep sigh, akri looked around at the destruction his mother had wrought. "Yes, she is."

She met akri's sad stare. "The Simi's seen akra make them Atlantean gods pee their dresses before."

Akri arched a brow. "What?"

She nodded. "They was very scared of akra-Apollymi. When she gave the stone baby to Archon instead of my akri, that mean old god of war they had peed on himself. Goddess Akra Bet laughed about his doing it, though. She thought it funny 'cause she said they deserved it for wanting to hurt a baby."

That made akri smile.

Until he suddenly stopped and looked at Savitar. "I can't hear your thoughts."

Savitar shifted her to his other side. "No, you can't. And you never will. You'll find that many of the higher beings of the universe will be silent to you. Some gods, demons, and other special creatures. We all have our secrets, but the comfort to you is that most won't be able to hear your thoughts either."

Like Simi. She never could hear akri's thoughts. She could only feel his emotions.

"Can you hear my thoughts?" he asked Savitar.

"The answer you seek is no, but the truth is, I hear you, Acheron, and yes, I know all about your past."

That made his heart hurt even more and Simi wanted to hugs him to make him feel better. "What of the others? Will they know my past, too?"

"Some will." Savitar stroked her back while he carried her. "I don't care about your past, Acheron. It's your future that matters to me. I want to make sure that you have one and that you comprehend how important you are to the balance of power."

Balance of power? Simi had never heard anyone talk about that before.

"I don't understand," akri said.

Neither did she.

"Apollo cursed his Apollite race."

Akri nodded. "I know, and my mother killed them all."

Savitar shook his head. "Many died when she destroyed Atlantis, but there are thousands of them who have spread over the Mediterranean and who live in many other countries now, including Apollo's own son, Strykerius. All of them have been cursed to die on their twenty-seventh birthday. *All* of them."

"Then how are they a problem? If they all die in a few years, they'll be extinct."

Savitar kissed Simi's head before he started walking again. "They're not going to die, Acheron. They will live and they will procreate many times over."

"How?"

Savitar let out a long sigh before he answered. "Your mother will lead them and show them how to prey on human souls to circumvent Apollo's curse."

Simi's eyes widened. Akra-Apollymi definitely liked her vengeance.

But akri seemed horrified. "I don't understand. Why would she do such a thing?"

"Because the universe is complicated, and there's a delicate balance in all things that must be maintained ... and mostly because she's angry, and it's a way to get back at Apollo for what he did to you."

Oh ... now Simi understood.

Akri was aghast. "Yes, but if you know these people will die, can't you stop her from teaching them?"

"I could. But it could unravel the very essence of the universe ... and make her even angrier." Holding her closer to his chest, Savitar picked up a random stone from the ground and held it in his hand. "Tell me what happens if I throw this with all my power."

Simi scratched her cheek. Well, if it hit someone, it would hurt.

Her akri gasped. "It hits a soldier in his shoulder, wounding him and making his arm lame. It would force him to become a beggar."

Savitar nodded before akri continued, "Eight score

people will die because the soldier can no longer protect them in battles that wouldn't even be fought for years to come. But out of those people who died ..."

"It goes on and on and on," Savitar said, interrupting him. "Do I throw the rock, or do I drop it? And a thousand lives are changed by one innocuous decision." He let the rock fall to the ground.

Bored by their discussion, Simi laid her head down and closed her eyes while she listened to them talk.

"You and I, Acheron, are cursed to understand how the tiniest decision made by every being can go onward to affect the rest of the universe. I know what should happen ... what needs to happen. And if I stop something as simple as a rock throw, it could cause catastrophic consequences. However, unlike you, I don't see the future until *after* I make a decision and act. The moment I do something, I then see everything unfold from that point on. You are lucky. You will always see the future *before* you act."

"But I didn't see my sister's death."

"No. The Greek Fates, when they cursed you, blinded you to the fate of those closest to you. Anyone you care about will always be your blind spot."

Simi bit her lip as she realized she would be her akri's blind spot, too.

"That's not right."

"Well, kid, brace yourself. This one's even worse. You also will never be able to see your own future or the future of anyone who seriously impacts your future."

Ouch. That had to be terrible for her akri. She couldn't imagine such a thing.

"Can you see it?" Acheron asked.

"It's why I'm here."

"Then tell me what you see."

Savitar shook his head. "Just because you can, doesn't mean you should. If you knew what was ahead of you, you'd avoid doing the very things you must do in order to have it unfold properly. One small innocuous decision and your destiny will be altered forever."

That scared her.

"But you can see your future."

"Only *after* I've set it into motion and can't change it."

Poor Savitar. Simi couldn't imagine which one had it worse. Both seemed awful to her. She was glad she didn't know the future at all.

Savitar clapped akri on the back. "I know how confusing it is for you to have all this power and knowledge and not know how to channel it. Or tap it."

"It is hard."

Savitar smiled. "That's why the first thing I want to teach you is fighting."

Didn't akri already know that? Simi had learned that before she was born. At least that was what her brother told her whenever he was mad at her.

"Why fighting?"

Savitar laughed as they walked. "Because you're going to need it. There's a war coming, Acheron, and you have to be prepared for it."

"What kind of war?"

Savitar didn't answer as he lightly shook her. "Little one, I need you to return to your akri and stay on him while he fights. Don't worry, though, it's only pretend fighting. No need for you to come off him to protect him."

Simi nodded sleepily before she obeyed. She drifted onto akri's arm.

"Move up, Simi," Savitar said to her. "Go to his neck where you won't be hit."

Good. The Simi didn't like to be hit.

"Can she feel a blow when she's on my skin?"

"Yes, she can. And if she's stabbed while she's there and it wounds you, it will wound her, too. Guard your demon, boy."

3

"Why is akri so sad, akri?"

He smiled as he adjusted the blanket around her while she was lying in bed with her legs propped up along the wall. Her wings were spread out and akri was careful not to hurt them.

"I just wish I had a better world for you, Sim. Most of all, I wish I could bring your mom back for you. I know you miss her."

"Does akri miss his matera? Is that why you're so saddest?"

Sighing, he took her hand and toyed with her fingers. She didn't know why, but that always made her happy. His hand was huge compared to hers, but then she was just a small simi and he was a grownie man. "No. Unlike you, I didn't have a mother to love me when I was little. The woman I thought was my mother was very cruel."

Simi sat up so that she could crawl into akri's lap. "The Simi is sorry, akri."

He folded his arms around her and held her close. "It's fine. I'm glad I have a mother now. I just wish I could really see her."

"We's can go see her. Just find an Apollite bolt hole, and we goes straight to her realm."

He laughed. "That wouldn't work out well for the humans."

She snorted at the very thought. "Pfft! They's dumb. What we care for them smelly things?"

He shifted so that he could hold her while he leaned against the wall. "I don't know, Sim. They weren't exactly nice to me, either. A part of me is just cruel enough to want to unleash my mother."

"Then what's stopping you, akri?"

"Ironically, you are."

Simi moved her head so that she could look up at him. "The Simi? How come?"

He cupped her cheek in his warm, calloused hand. "You remind me of what I was like as a boy. Back when I had a brother. And it makes me hate the people I was around so much, because I will never understand how they could be so cruel to me and Styxx."

Simi was aghast over something she never knew. "Akri have a brother?"

"Did. But things ... no, people, came between us." He let out a bitter laugh. "Then we came between each other."

She didn't quite understand what he was saying, only that it made him hurt deep in his heart. "Simi's sorry, akri."

Closing his eyes, he leaned his cheek against the top of her head. "When I see you, I think of all the other little children out there. I could never do to them what was done to us. Or allow them to be harmed. People should be protected."

"Even by Simi?"

"Especially by my Simi. You're very dear to this world, Sim. You are the only one standing between it and utter destruction."

Her eyes widened. "Me? But I's just a little Simi."

"And it's the little things that matter most. You keep me grounded and remind me of what's important. As much as I love my mother, I will never help her destroy a world that brought you to me."

Simi stood up in his lap so that she could hug her akri. Not just with her arms. She wrapped her wings and tail around him, too. "You's the bestest akri any Simi could have!"

"And you're the best daughter ever born. I will be forever grateful to your matera for being so kind to you and giving you a very special heart."

Simi buried her face in his hair so that she could feel like she did when her matera held her. Only akri could make her heart feel the way it'd felt when her mama helds her.

Safe. Warm.

Special.

"The Simi will never leave her akri."

"And I will never willingly leave you."

She sat back down and spit on her palm, then held it up toward him. "Always!"

Laughing, he spit on his hand and shook hers. Then, he tucked her back in bed and left her room.

Simi knew he was exploring the gods' temple. It was what akri always did while she slept.

Two weeks ago, they'd found the slumbering gods in the basement. That had made akri both mad and happy. Happy 'cause they were all gone, but mad that they'd cursed him for being born. That made her mad, too.

Even so, akri had been curious about the family he had been banished from.

So, one by one, she'd walked with him around the gods, telling him the names she knew. Some had been mean, and she didn't have real names for those. Instead, she made them up. Poo-poo Bottom was her favorite. It'd even made akri laugh.

But it was the one goddess who made her heart hurt like akri's.

Bet'anya. She had always been kind to the Simi. And just like akri, she had pain in her gold eyes that had always made Simi want to make the goddess feel better.

Sadly, the only thing that took the pain from her eyes was when the goddess had been pregnant.

While Simi understood the others being punished for their mean ways to akri, akra-Bet wasn't like that.

She should have been allowed to be happy.

Akra-Apollymi had never asked Simi her opinion and there was nothing a baby Simi could do. But one day, she'd find a way to make akri smile all the time and forget about the Apollite people who'd been cursed by the god what had killed akri.

And the one thing that made him saddest of all. The fact that his own matera kept the Apollites safe and let them loose to eats the humans.

"The Simi don't know why you did that, akra." Not when it made akri so hurts.

To her surprise, akra-Apollymi appeared in her ghosty form next to Simi on her bed. "One day, you'll understand, Simi. We all do things we wish we hadn't done."

"Akra is sorry she saved the Apollites?"

Shaking her head, Apollymi smiled. "No. I will never be sorry for saving the innocent victims Apollo and his pantheon condemned."

That only confuzzled her, as it didn't make much sense. "What about the innocent humans you kilted?"

"The Apollites didn't hurt my son. Not the way the humans did. Nor did I trust Apostolos to the Apollites for them to take care of him when he was a boy."

That made Simi's heart pound funny in her chest. "What of the Simi? You trusted akri to Simi."

"And you will always take care of him."

Simi sputtered. "What if akri trips and skins his knee?"

She laughed. "That's not what I mean. You would never cause him to be harmed, nor will you make his heart sad."

"Oh no! The Simi would never do that."

"Then he's in perfect hands." Akra-Apollymi rose. "Go to sleep, Simi. Dream of sweets."

Simi did like her sweets. But now she wasn't sleepy. Too many thoughts raced around her head as she watched the shadows play around her legs on the wall.

It was a scary world here. Far vastier than Kalosis was. Well, not here so much because they were in Katateros where the gods were gone and trapped.

The human world ...

It was gigantus! Akri had taken her places she'd never seen before. Wide open places where no one lived. And lots of places where humans had yummy food to feed her.

In spite of all akri's rules, she liked the human world. The Simi was just undecided about the humans them-selves. Some were very kind and others ... they needed manners and tenderer hearts.

In all the time with akri, she had yet to meet a human she wanted to be around for any length of time. And that was fine by Simi. She liked that it was just she and akri. Akri needed her and she needed akri. No one else was necessary.

∾

"What are you doing here, Charonte?"

Simi blinked at the short ... she wasn't sure what he was. Well, part god. She knew that much. But he was something else, too, and she wasn't sure what that other was. Not to mention, he smelled odd. Not bad. Just not right.

He was *other*.

Pursing her lips, she frowned at the handsome man with hazel gray-blue eyes and hair that was a peculiar shade of mixed browns. "The Simi fell into this place. It's not anywhere, is it?"

"It's in-between, and you shouldn't be here."

That caused her to frown. "In-between what?"

"Everything."

Simi snorted. "What kind of answer is that?"

"An honest one."

Maybe. And she was still curious about the odd god-not-god. Walking up to him in the dim, shadowy light, she sniffed at his leg.

He moved away from her. "What are you doing?"

"Trying to figure out what you are and why *you're* here."

That seemed to offend him. "I live here."

"Why?" Simi asked.

He stared at her as if in complete disbelief that she'd ask such a simple question. "Again, Charonte, you don't belong here. Where's the one who's responsible for you?"

"Akri asleep. He told Simi to stay in Katateros, but it boring when he's tired. So Simi went into the shadows 'cause they seemed interesting and the Simi was hungry."

A strange light darkened his eyes. "Katateros? As in the Atlantean realm of their gods?"

"Do you know Simi's home?"

His cheek color paled. "Where Acheron lives?"

She grinned, flashing him her fangs. "My akri-daddy! You know him?"

He turned even paler. "Akri-daddy?"

She nodded. "He loves his Simi and his Simi loves him. You know my akri?"

"Yeah. Little bit. Why don't we take you back to him?"

She pouted. "'Cause he's sleeping and Simi's hungry. Simi hates when she wakes him when he's sleeping. He don't do that much. It makes Simi all pouty and sad to make akri more tired." She pursed her lips even more. "You got any eats, god-not-god?"

"Shadow. My name's Shadow, and yes. I have food. Let's get some and take you home before your akri wakes up."

"Okies. Simi likes home. But can I ask you something akri-Shadow?"

"Sure."

"Why you want to live here where it's so dark and boring?"

He shrugged. "People leave me alone."

"But don't you get lonely?"

"Better lonely than abused or used."

Simi had no understanding of his words. "What's abused or used?"

He picked her up and held her in his arms. "You're very lucky, Simi, that you have no idea what that means. They're both terrible things that hurt and leave scars."

"Is that why akri has aches in his heart?"

"Probably."

She reached up to touch his handsome cheek. "And why you have aches in your eyes?"

"Definitely."

"Then the Simi's sorry you have that, akri-Shadow." She laid her head on his shoulder. "You can come lives in our house. No one would hurt you there."

He gave her a light squeeze as he smiled. "I don't know, Simi. I have a feeling Acheron might harm me if I tried to live there. From what I know about him, he doesn't like others any more than I do. Probably for the same reasons. I think it's best that I return you to your home and then come back here to live."

"But first we eats?"

"Of course."

Simi didn't say a word as akri-Shadow took her from the shadowy world she'd stumbled into out to the human one where there was always good things to eat. Like akri, he found a busy marketplace and bought her some of the grape leaves and rice, along with lamb and honey cakes that she really liked. For himself, he bought a jug of wine and set them at a table in a corner of the open market where they wouldn't be disturbed.

She was just starting on her third helping when a shadow fell over them.

Shadow looked up and froze in place.

But she smiled as she saw akri standing over them, even if he was frowning and looking all kinds of mad and mean.

"What is this?" akri demanded.

"Food. Want some?" she asked even though she knew he never ate anything.

Shadow shot to his feet. "She came into my realm and didn't want to wake you. I was planning to take her home the minute she finished eating. I swear it."

Simi had no idea why Shadow was so panicky. Although akri did seem a bit upset, and she didn't understand that either.

"Are you all right?" Akri grabbed her up in a tight hug.

"Why wouldn't I be?"

He held her so close that it was a bit painful.

"Akri!" She bristled in his arms. "Simi hurts! Please don't holds her so tights! Ouch!"

"You scared me, Simkey. I woke up and had no idea where you were. I told you not to leave."

"The Simi was hungry, and you said for the Simi not to nibble on your fingers or toes. So, the Simi went to looks for some eats."

He only loosened his hold a bit on her before he turned toward her new friend. "Thank you, Shadow."

"No problem." Shadow jerked his chin in her direction. "I had no idea you had a Charonte daughter."

"Not something I want bantered about with others either."

"Understood." Shadow stepped away from them. "She's a joy. Anytime you need a babysitter, let me know. I'll make sure and bring lots of food."

Akri scowled. "I'd never take you for such a baby person ... or in Simi's case, a toddler person."

"Me either, but it was nice to be around someone who was honest and not playing games with me. I'd forgotten what innocence looked like."

"I know. It's what I value most about her. I don't ever want her tarnished."

Shadow nodded. "That's the thing I hate most in life. When others kill that part of us."

Simi saw the sadness in akri's eyes. "I don't ever remember having it, and I will kill the one who takes it from her."

"I don't blame you." Shadow reached out and ruffled her hair. "I'll probably help you. It's a pity we all have to lose that part of ourselves."

Simi smiled at the god-not-god. "Thank you for the eats, akri-Shadow."

"Anytime, little one. Just next time, tell Acheron that you're leaving first."

"Okies."

Acheron held his arm out. "I owe you one, Shadow."

Shadow clasped his arm and shook it. "No, you don't. I'm just glad I saw her first. Whatever you do, make sure my mother never knows Simi has any ties to you or your mother."

Simi cocked her head at his peculiar words that seemed to confuzzle akri, too.

"What do you mean?" her akri asked.

"I know who Simi's real parents are, Acheron. Her father was an enemy to my mother. And Xiamara wasn't her friend, either. If Azura or Noir ever see your little demon, they won't hesitate to take her hostage and use her against you. Or as a tool to strike at your mother. You need to make sure your demon understands the dangers lurking for her and the enemies you have. While I'm with you and I would love to preserve her innocence, Simi needs to know that you have too many enemies who wouldn't hesitate to harm her. As does your mother."

"That's what I'm afraid of."

Simi hugged her akri. "Don't worry. Simi would eat any bad god who tried to hurt her."

"It's not that simple, Simkey."

She wanted to argue, but there was something in both their eyes that told her they were right. She needed to be careful. After all, her mother had been a very powerful warrior, and the gods had killed her. She was nowhere near as strong as her mother had been.

"Then akri will teach his Simi. She will be the bestest demon, and she will eats them heads and learnst to protect akri and herself from everyone. Even the meanest gods!"

Shadow smiled. "There you go. And whatever you do, Simi, stay away from Azura and Noir. They hate Charonte and all they want is to free Apollymi and unite their army with hers so that they can destroy the world."

4

Simi crept quietly through the dark lands. Not the shadowy place where akri-Shadow lived or the hell realm where akra-Apollymi was trapped. This was the forbidden place that would make akri extremely angry if he learned Simi dared visit here.

Azmodea. The home of Azura and Noir.

There had been a time long, long ago when akra-Apollymi had called this place home, too. When the angry goddess had lived here with her brother and sissy. Noir and Azura. Simi didn't know if they were older or younger than akra-Apollymi, not that it mattered.

They were no longer family because akra-Apollymi hated them with all her hearts. Simi wasn't exactly sure why, but it had something to do with a baby born before akri. A baby boy she'd heard her matera and sissy whispering about when they thought no one else could hear them.

A boy called the Malachai that akra-Apollymi had been forced by her brothers and sisters to curse. That was why akra-Apollymi had been so incredibly angry about losing akri. Her heart had already been broken by having to lose one son. The last thing the goddess wanted was to be forced to lose another.

"What are you doing here, Simi?"

Simi froze at the sound of a deep, accented voice that kind of reminded her of akri's. Only it wasn't akri. This one was deeper and with a gruffer accent that wasn't as musical and sweet as akri's.

Turning around slowly, she faced a tall, dark-haired man who had two different colored eyes. One was a deep brown that reminded her of the nuts she liked to snack on, and the other was the bright green of yummy mint.

"Who are you?" she whispered, not sure if she was in trouble or not for her snooping.

His features softened. "Jaden."

Ah. This being was definitely a god and a powerful one at that. His powers were old and extremely strong. He reminded her a lot of akra-Apollymi. Only he was a lot sadder ...

Like akri. He had tons of aches in his eyes and heart.

Simi stepped closer to him so that she could stare up and the giant god who no longer scared her. "Hi, akri-Jaden." She held her hand out to him. "The Simi's pleased to meet you."

That made him smile as he knelt down so that he could take her hand and kiss her knuckles. "You shouldn't be here, Simi. It's not safe for you in this realm."

"I know, but the Simi wanted to see the dark gods."

He frowned at her. "Why?"

"Well, akra-Apollymi is a dark god, but she's very kind. Simi knows she doesn't like her brother and sissy, but Simi was wondering if maybe they're not so bad. Maybe they's just been misadjudicated."

He chuckled at her words. "I wish they were misadjudicated, Simi. They're not. And they're nothing like Apollymi. She has a heart where they don't. Not even for their own children."

"Then that is very sad indeed. How can someone not love their simis?"

He scooped her up in his arms and stood. "I don't know. Sometimes it seems like people don't love their babies when they do."

"You have simis?"

"Yes, I do and I can't be with them. That is its own kind of hell."

She could only imagine.

Jaden let out a tired breath. "Then there are gods like Noir and Azura who really don't love their children, and they don't care what happens to them."

"That's so awful!"

"Indeed."

Simi sighed heavily as she tried to imagine having parents who didn't love her. It was impossible in her mind, especially given how much akri loved her. "Why would they have simis if they don't want to love them?"

"So many reasons, little one. Some for power. Sometimes they do it to have control over another person."

There was a note in his voice that made her achy in the heart. "You have a simi for that reason?"

"Their mothers had them for that reason. They wanted to control me. Even so, I still love them both. It's not their fault their mothers lied to me. But I haven't been the father they deserved. I didn't dare let anyone know that I care about them because it would have made it worse on all of us."

She didn't understand that. Not even a little tiny bit. "How can loving someone be a bad thing?"

"Love isn't easy, Simi. It'll be a long time before you understand what I mean. It's the greatest feeling in the world when you have it, but it's one that leaves you more vulnerable than you've ever been. So long as the person you love loves you, you're safe. But when they don't love you ... it's the worst thing you can imagine. Truly, there's no greater hell."

Like akri and Artemis. Now, she understood. Akri had loved the goddess more than his life, and she had betrayed him horribly and left him to die. Hurt him in a way even worster than Apollo who had killed her akri. That pain never left akri's eyes or his heart.

It was why Simi hated the ugly heifer goddess so much. No one should be so very mean to the person who loved them. Not for any reason.

And as she brushed her hand over Jaden's back, he flinched. Gasping, Simi realized her hand had blood on it. "Akri-Jaden is bleeding?"

A deep grimace marked his handsome features. "It's fine, Simi. I bleed so that my children don't have to bleed worse."

Still, she stared at the deep red color against her skin. It reminded her of her mother whenever she returned from battle.

I fight so that my children won't have to.

That was what her mother had said, but it had never been that simple, and Simi knew her brother had fought battles even while their mother protested.

"Why do you live here, akri-Jaden?"

"Like Apollymi, I have no choice."

"They made you a prisoner, too?"

He hesitated before he answered. "Something like that."

Feeling terrible for him, Simi did what she'd been told never to do ...

She healed his wounded back.

A look of extreme disbelief came over his features. "You're a *fide iuvit*?"

She put her finger to her lips and shushed him. When she spoke, it was in the lowerest of whispers. "We never speak of such a thing. They don't exist."

Because it was a very rare thing, and her mother had schooled her well on what could happen to her if others learned what she could do. They would covet her powers and take her away. She didn't want to be taken from her akri or hunted.

Not even her brother or sissy knew what she could do. She'd promised her mother to keep it secret, but akri-Jaden seemed to need it.

And he was just as stern when he spoke as her mother had been. "Never let anyone know of your powers, Simi. Not even Acheron."

"Akri would never hurt his Simi."

"Never let anyone know," he repeated.

That only confuzzled her more. "But why not akri?"

"Because there are others who can read his mind and learn what he knows. Those people might want to hurt him, and the best way to do that is to hurt his Simi."

"Oh." That was a terrifying thought. "You won't hurt Simi, will you?"

He hugged her close to his side. "I will never harm you. Just be careful and stay away from this realm."

5

JULY 10, 8649 BC

Simi sat at a corner table in a market, waiting for more beef to come while akri was off, speaking to a friend. It felt like it'd been forever since the waiting lady had tolds her she'd be back, and her stomach was rumbling something fierce.

She was just about to go tell akri she wanted to find more food, or eat a human, when she saw a warrior entering the marketplace near her.

At first glance, he looked like a young, handsome teenager. But he wasn't what he seemed.

No ...

He was a demon god, yet not one like her. No, he was something else entirely, and she had no idea what. And he made all the human people around them quake in terror at his lethal approach. They seemed to know him.

She could tell he liked their fear. Something in his soul ate it up the same way she guzzled sweet cakes.

Until he neared her.

"Rawr!" he sneered at her, trying to put a scare in the Simi's heart.

She laughed. Like he was really scary? The demon-boy had no idea of the scary things she'd seen.

Or the scarier ones she'd eaten.

And her humor didn't please the warrior at all. "You dare laugh at me?"

She cocked her head at his words as she tried to understand his anger over something so silly. "Well, what were you trying to do?"

"Scare you, little girl."

The Simi was not a little girl. Even though she was thousands of years old, Simi knew she appeared to others around the age of six or seven. It was a Charonte thing. Since they lived for so long, they aged very, very slowly.

The thought of him thinking she was a little girl made her snicker again.

And that, too, made his hazel blue-green eyes flare with fury. He took a step toward her only to have akri appear between them. The tip of akri's staff glowed so that his sun symbol was apparent to all.

The warrior drew up short. Respect replaced the meanness in his eyes as he recognized her akri. "Acheron."

"Prince Leucious," akri said in the same sharp tone the warrior had used.

Leucious's gaze went past akri's shoulder to where Simi continued to sit. "She's with you?"

"Always and is very dear to me."

That took all the anger from his eyes. "Then forgive me. I can see why she laughed at my inept stupidity at trying to intimidate her when she's used to you."

Simi stood up then and moved closer to the demon warrior. "Why you want to scare a little girl?"

Akri answered for him. "He can't help it, Simi. His people are known for their cruelty."

Another warrior walked up behind Leucious. "I believe Acheron just accused you of having no home training, my prince."

Simi didn't like the newcomer. His armor was made from the skeletons of humans, and it smelled as awful as the creature's body odor.

Akri smirked at him. "Don't try and cause a fight between us, Mot. Your lord knows better."

Leucious inclined his head to akri before he turned a fierce, angry sneer to the smelly one and shoved him away. "Learn your place, Grim. You're a fallen god. I know you're not my equal in battle, even though we're allies." With those words spoken, he headed off to scare the serving lady who was bringing Simi her food.

Unlike Simi, the serving lady actually screamed.

Mot continued to glare at akri. "I rode with your brother, long ago."

"And you betrayed Monakribos. You're lucky my mother didn't destroy you for everything you've done."

"She's too afraid of my parents to even try."

Akri laughed at that. "You keep telling yourself that lie.

One day, you might come to believe it. Now trot along after your master. Your stench turns my stomach."

There was raw fury in Mot's eyes, but he was smart enough to do as akri commanded.

Simi didn't move until he drifted off, after Leucious. "Who was that, akri?"

He took her hand and led her back to the table where the lady had placed her platters of beef. "My cousin, Mot."

Her eyes widened at that. "Cousin?"

Akri nodded. "His mother is Cam and his father the god, Set."

Stunned by the knowledge, she stared up at him. Set and Cam were the brother and sissy of his mother, akra-Apollymi. "Why don't he smell like a god, then?"

"He no longer has the powers he used to. He turned against his parents and sided with Noir and Azura in the First War of the gods. Now, he's left to serve as a lapdog to Noir's bastard child."

"Leucious?"

Akri nodded as he cut her meat for her. "Unfortunately, Leucious doesn't know all that yet."

His words confuzzled her. "How he not know who his daddy is?"

Akri took her hand and placed it on his cheek. The moment he did, she saw akri-Jaden in the horrible realm where she was forbidden to go. The sad god with mismatched eyes stood before Noir's bony throne where the dark god gave him a sneer. Not because Noir was angry at Jaden. Rather, the meany god always looked like that.

"Paimon will be my surrogate to carry my seed, and when my son is born, he will rule the human realm and find a way to free me. Make the deal with the human woman for his birth."

Akri-Jaden bowed and left to do as he'd been bidden.

Simi gasped as she pulled her hand away and saw akri's grim frown. "Why does evil Noir think Leucious will free him?"

"Because of how vicious Leucious's adoptive father is. He's given that same cruelty to Prince Leucious."

She suspected there was more to it than that. "What do you see, akri?"

"I see Leucious turning against Noir and beyond that ... I don't know."

Simi chewed at her beef as she considered his words. "How can you not know?"

Akri poured himself a goblet of wine. "You know my limitations, Simkey. I don't know if Leucious will become my friend, or if he'll somehow impact my future. Or maybe it's because once he realizes Noir is his father, he becomes a full god, and I lose the ability to see anything about him. Take your pick."

Perhaps. Any of those would make it so that akri wouldn't see anything. It was unusual and interesting. Simi continued to think about it while eating.

All of a sudden, Leucious appeared beside their table again.

Akri scowled at him. "Is something wrong, Your Highness?"

Leucious scratched at the neck of his leather armor. "I ..." his voice trailed off. He seemed to go between anger and some emotion Simi couldn't name.

Finally, he put a small rag doll down on the table beside her. "Never let anyone scare you, girl. Not because of Acheron. Because you are unique." And then he rushed off even faster than the first time.

With a frown, akri picked up her doll to look at it curiously. "I think you made a new friend, Simi." He held the doll out to her.

Simi took it, then put the doll's hand in her mouth to taste it.

"No!" Akri pulled the doll away. "It's not food, sweetie."

"Then what do you do with it?"

He smiled gently at her. "You play with dolls."

"Play? The Simi doesn't understand."

He returned the doll to the table. "I guess Charonte don't have human dolls, do they? Human girls pretend the dolls are their babies and they practice being mothers with them."

That didn't make sense. "Why?"

"The same reason little boys play with soldiers. So that we can pretend to be grown up for a little while."

Simi was trying hard to understand. But it seemed silly to her. "But why?"

He shrugged. "It's what kids do. It comforts them."

"Human children are very strange, akri. Why won't you let me eat them?"

Laughing, he shook his head. "Eating humans is wrong."

"Not what my matera said ... or yours."

"It's what your akri says."

Simi let out a long-suffering sigh. "Fine. Not kiddy eats. Or grown-up eats." She chewed on another piece of meat. "Moo-moos are good, though."

She paused as she caught another whiff of Mot. Turning her head, she tried to find him in the small human crowd, but there was no sight of him anywhere.

Even so, a chill went up her spine. Mot didn't like akri. He wanted to hurt him. She knew that with every part of her being. And the best way to hurt her akri was to hurt his Simi.

I better watch for the evil.

Mot wouldn't be happy until he made akri cry.

LEUCIOUS WAS furious as he made his way back to their horses. He still didn't know why he'd bothered to try and apologize to a little girl, even if she was Acheron's.

His father would beat him for such rancid stupidity.

For such weakness.

He was seven-and-ten. A man. No, a ruthless warrior who'd proven himself in battle. Even his father, King Tesiah of the Brakadians was proud of him and that was no easy feat.

Tesiah was a brutal warlord who had murdered all four

of Leucious's older sisters for no other reason than they'd been born daughters.

And I'll kill you too, brat, if you disappoint me.

That was no idle threat. Just a promise made by a man who looked for any reason to beat his son.

If his father ever learned he'd purchased a doll for a little girl, there was no telling how badly he'd be punished for it. Knowing Tesiah, he'd probably make him eat the doll.

Why did I do such a thing? One moment he'd been walking past the female merchant selling them and the next …

He bought one because he'd wanted to see Simi smile.

It'd been stupid really, but Leucious couldn't help it. Simi had been absolutely adorable in her reaction when he'd growled at her. Utterly unexpected. And her laughter had been infectious and heart-warming.

At least, he'd realized all that after his initial anger had faded.

As he neared his black warhorse, his servant bowed low enough that he almost touched Leucious's boots. He barely gave it a thought as he swung himself up into the saddle. The moment he did, his men came rushing from all areas of the town so that they could ride with him. Not out of loyalty but rather fear of what his father would do to them should they lag behind.

Maybe he should be as cruel. It was what his father preached relentlessly. Some days, he was tempted. But unlike his father, he didn't really enjoy hurting others.

Rather, he saw it as an unfortunate necessity that came with war and power.

Because sadly, there were those who only responded to threats. Or violence.

As typical, Grim pulled up the rear of their army with the swagger of someone who begrudged Leucious the summoning. Leucious was well aware of how much the former death god hated him even though they were allies. It literally bled from every pore of Grim's body. At any moment, he expected the former god to try and slide a blade through his back.

Honestly, he had no idea why Grim traveled with them. Grim was one of the generals who had served the original Malachai—a demon so fierce and angry that the Malachai was feared by all of its kind and most of the gods. Which made sense as the Malachai was descended from Apollymi—the first goddess of death and destruction.

Leucious had only gone up against the current Malachai as a child, when he was serving in his father's army. Thankfully, he'd been too young to fight the demon who had laid waste to ninety percent of his father's troops. Even his father had barely survived and had lost an eye for his effort.

It was that battle that had caused Grim to defect to their side. He'd saved Tesiah's life, and Leucious's father had granted him amnesty for it. Not that anyone really trusted Grim.

How could they?

Once a traitor, always a traitor. Only a fool would forget that, and Leucious was never foolish.

"Where are we riding to, my lord?" Grim asked.

Leucious glanced at him over his shoulder. "Ledea. My father is already there with a contingency of men. We're to combine forces and take on the Ikkidians." Provided their king didn't surrender as soon as he learned of their approach. It was what anyone with a brain would do.

But there were still enough brain-dead kings who wanted to fight. Who thought they could win against Tesiah. And they might have stood a chance had Leucious not been born. For whatever reason, he'd yet to fail in battle. Seldom had he been wounded and even then, only a minor scratch or bruise. For whatever reason, Leucious appeared invincible. So much so that even their own troops were beginning to fear him.

They believed him to be a demigod or demon. But no one said that out loud. To disparage Leucious's mother was a crime he punished personally and violently.

Still, he heard their fearful whispers.

Evil bastard. He reveled in the title as much as his father did. Better to be feared than respected.

And he *was* feared.

Except for an adorable little girl with black pigtails who'd laughed in his face.

Even now, the thought of Simi made him smile ... something his father would punish with a backhand. Men didn't smile. It was a woman's trait.

And yet he kept seeing Acheron's daughter and her

impish, adorable courage. Which made sense given the unholy power of her father. No one was quite sure who or what Acheron was. Tesiah called him a necromancer who'd come to their court when Leucious was a young boy. He still remembered the first time he'd met the giant Acheron who'd towered over everyone, even their tallest warriors.

And those swirling silver eyes ...

They said he was of an unnatural origin.

Which made him curious.

Leucious slowed his horse's pace so that he rode beside Grim. "What do you know of Acheron?"

Grim narrowed his gaze on him as if he were trying to understand Leucious's sudden curiosity. "He's the son of gods."

That made sense. "Which ones?"

"Apollymi and Archon."

Apollymi ... she was Braith after Braith had forsaken her siblings and gone to live among the Atlantean gods after the Primus Bellum. Archon was the king of the Atlanteans. At least until Apollymi had destroyed him.

And if that was true ... "He's half-brother to the Malachai?"

"To the original one, yes. The latest ... he is an uncle many times removed."

"So, he's cousin to you, then?"

Grim nodded.

Well, that explained Acheron's innate hatred of Grim. Nothing like family to stoke the flames of hatred. And who could blame him? Grim was the reason all the Malachai had been cursed to be conceived in violence to do violence, and to die violently.

But that left him wondering about Acheron's innate secrecy over being a god. Everyone Leucious knew would revel in that fact and exploit it. Not hide it. "Why doesn't Acheron tell people who he is?"

Grim let out an evil laugh. "Acheron was cursed by the gods when he was born. The Atlantean pantheon did their best to kill him."

That was an interesting tidbit to know. "Obviously, they failed."

"No, they didn't. He was killed by a Greek god and brought back against his will."

Leucious gaped, then quickly caught himself. Rule number five of his father's lengthy dictates, never let anyone know they surprised him. Always appear calm and decisive.

Brutal, in all things.

"I assume his mother brought him back?" After all, Apollymi would make sense.

Grim shook his head. "She's a goddess of destruction. Those powers aren't hers."

Good to know. "Then who did it?"

"Acheron."

Now Leucious was completely confused. "Acheron brought himself back?" That was unheard of. "He's that powerful?"

Mot nodded. "Beware his powers. He's not just a god. He's something more."

"And that is?"

"A god-killer."

Leucious snorted in denial of something that was impossible. "You can't be both."

"You sure? Because *he* is."

Again, it was impossible. Forbidden by the oldest and highest powers. God-killers had been created to make sure no god abused his or her power. Whenever they did, a god-killer could end their lives and absorb their powers to ensure the stability of the universe. A god with those powers ...

It would be disastrous.

"How can he be both?"

Mot's grimace turned intense and warning. "That is the question, isn't it?"

Yes, it was. "And the answer is?"

"No one knows. Not even Acheron. He's a strange anomaly." And with that, Mot turned his horse away.

Leucious didn't bother to call him back. He was too busy digesting those words.

Acheron was a Chthonian god-killer. Those were a small handful of creatures who'd been born randomly from anyone, other than the gods, so that they could destroy gods who abused their powers and preyed on humans.

Or others.

Because of that, no god was allowed to be both. So how could Acheron?

Did it even really matter?

Acheron wasn't his target. His father had always been clear on the matter ... Prey on humans and ignore those with more power lest they decide to prey on them.

Leucious wasn't the bully his father was. There was no honor defeating those who were weaker. He preferred to fight those who were his equal or better. It was how he stayed honed and ready.

Because the one thing he knew to be true.

Everything changed. And the things that changed someone the most were those that they never saw coming.

6

JUNE 19, 8655 BC

Leucious paused as he heard a noise in the stable where he'd gone to get his horse. Instinctively, his hand went to the hilt of his sword. If it was an enemy, they'd be sorry ... "Who's there?"

A soft giggle answered him.

That was no enemy. His first thought was that it came from the cute barmaid who'd made eyes at him.

Until a sneeze sounded and was followed by a small, "Uh-oh!"

He knew that adorable voice. "Simi?"

She popped out of a bale of hay a few feet from him. Straw was stuck in her black pigtails and she gave him an impish smile. "Hello, akri-Leucious!"

Shaking his head at the little girl's infectious exuberance, he had to smile. And he was grateful his father wasn't here to see it.

Or hers.

"What are you doing?"

She plucked at the straw, then made a face at it. "Simi heard today was special."

"Special? How so?"

She nodded so hard that her pigtails bobbed. "Akri-Jaden done told the Simi that today was the day you were born. Only not today, obviously, because then you'd be a baby. But years ago ... you was born. So, happy baby birthday, akri-Leucious!"

How strange. No one had ever remembered his birthday, and why would Jaden know what day his mother had birthed him? His people didn't celebrate such things. The only time his father had ever remarked on it was the day he turned ten-and-four.

"You're a man now, Leucious. Do me proud." Then Tesiah had backhanded him so hard he'd almost lost his front teeth.

But as his father intended, he remembered that day well.

Simi dug her way out of the straw and moved to stand in front of him. She held a small basket out toward him. "The Simi wasn't sure what you liked, so I gots you something sweet, something spicy and some of the mead drink Simi knows you like."

Leucious didn't know what to say. It seemed like there ought to be something people said when they were given an item. But his people didn't give gifts to each other.

Unless you counted insults. Those were given freely.

But as for real gifts ... they only took. With swords or blows. No asking. Definitely no giving.

Simi scrunched her face at him. "This is the part where you say *thank you, Simi!*"

He laughed and then froze as he realized it was the first time since his early childhood that he'd had a real laugh. One that felt good and wasn't borne from mockery or cruelty. "Thank you, Simi."

She clapped him on his arm. "See how easy!"

For her maybe. For him ...

Impossible was the word. And yet somehow, she made it simple. What was it about her? She was ...

Words failed him.

She poked gently at the basket she'd given him. "Aren't you going to look and see what the Simi brought you?"

Biting back another smile, he pulled the cloth from the top to see honey cakes and the salted beef they used to sustain themselves on their marches. They were nestled around a small jug of the promised mead. "It's wonderful, Simi. How did you know what I liked?"

"Well ... you always ask for mead whenever we're with you. The Simi has seen them meat sticks in your pack, though the Simi isn't sure why you eat them. I mean, they's okay. But not like them big juicy nummies akri gets for his Simi. And the cakes ... that's birthday food. Everyone loves birthday food."

The light in her eyes warmed him. What a beautiful soul. Until her, he'd never met anyone who was kind.

Giving ...

Sweet.

Was that the difference between having a father capable of kindness versus having a father who only doled out violence?

For the first time in his life, he wondered what he might have been like had someone like Acheron been his father. Stupid really, but he'd never given thought to such a thing before.

Would it have made a difference in his personality?

Tesiah had power. They had wealth and lands. His father believed that was enough.

Everyone feared their army and their wrath.

But was it the best way? People respected Acheron. They adored Simi.

Neither Acheron nor Simi had to beat anyone into submission to get their respect.

Of course, Acheron could do that without even trying. Still, the Atlantean god didn't use force to coerce or even intimidate others. People simply respected him.

His father would call Acheron weak.

But not to his face, and no one else would dare.

Nor would Leucious ever be that stupid. Acheron was anything but weak. In truth, Leucious didn't think he'd ever met anyone more powerful.

Or even more intimidating, and Acheron didn't try to intimidate.

He chose a different way to lead and inspire others.

Was that better?

Leucious didn't know. Maybe both were correct.

Or worse ... what if they both were wrong?

It was all very confusing for someone who'd been trained to never question his father or their way of life. But the truth was, he didn't like anyone who was on their side. Not his men or their allies.

Least of all his father.

And no one meant as much to him as Simi did.

"Where's Acheron?" he asked her.

She shrugged. "Akri was talking to Savitar so the Simi snucked off while he was ignoring me."

Those words sucker punched him. Was she serious? Had she any idea what she'd done?

"Acheron is with Savitar?" Savitar was one of the Chthonians who protected mortal creatures.

Were they supposed to talk to gods? Was that allowed?

How weird. Chthonians had been created to police divinity. He'd never heard of them associating with gods before.

She nodded. "Sometimes they talk for hours. Get so excited they forget the Simi's there. It gets so boring that the Simi wanders off." She grinned even wider.

Um ... yeah.

"Simi, your father doesn't forget you're there." How could he? "He's probably looking for you right now." No doubt he was frantic, too. "I'm sure we need to get you back to him." Because every minute she was gone, Acheron would be ready to gut someone over her absence.

And he definitely didn't want to be that someone.

She made a buzzing sound with her tongue. "Pffft!

Why you take all the joy out of my life, akri-Leucious? Don't you know the Simi was bored? All they do is talk about stuff the Simi don't care about. It so boring!" She threw her head back and groaned.

She was so adorable, but it didn't change the fact that Acheron would be worried sick.

"The last thing I'd ever want to do is take the joy from your life, Simi. I'm more concerned about Acheron taking the life from me if he finds you gone and blames me for it."

She laughed. "Don't worry, akri-Leucious. Akri knows how the Simi slips off sometimes. He don't like it, but he can't stop his Simi from being a bad girl."

"You're not bad. We just need to return you to your father before he starts pulling body parts off others."

Simi made a face at him. "If we must ..." She was adorably put out.

"We must," he insisted. "How do I get you home?"

With a long, heavy sigh, she approached his horse that rested in a nearby stall. "I've never been on one of them horsies before. Would you take the Simi back to her akri on that?"

"If you like."

"Simi would like very much."

"All right." He gently picked her up and put her on his saddle, then he pulled himself up behind her. "Where am I taking you?"

She pointed at the door. "That way!"

He laughed again. "And after we go through the door?"

"Oh. They in a village thingie. Meyash new ... yah?"

Leucious scowled at a name he'd never heard before. "Where?"

"It was Me-something."

There was only one place he knew that began with *Me.* "Miadan?"

She nodded. "That's it! Me-something."

At least that wasn't too far away. A couple of hours out of his schedule.

Or so he thought.

They had barely cleared the yard when Acheron appeared in front of him. Lightning flashed over his head and struck the ground so close that it caused his horse to rear.

Simi whooped as she clung to Leucious. "Go horsey, go!"

That made Acheron even angrier. "What is going on here?"

Leucious had never tasted fear before, and he wasn't quite sure he felt it now. But there was a lump in his stomach that made him dread facing the older god. "I was taking her back to you."

Acheron's eyes turned blood red and the air itself pulsed with his fury. "Why is she here?"

Simi vanished from his lap, then reappeared next to Acheron. "Akri! Be nice. This is akri-Leucious's birthday and the Simi wanted to give him prezzies like akri gib the Simi on her special day."

That had the same effect on the angry god as it had on him. Acheron softened immediately and picked Simi up in his arms. His red eyes faded back to their normal swirling silver color.

Leucious would never forget the look of love on Acheron's face as he tightened his arms around his young daughter. "Sorry, Leucious. I panicked."

"Understood."

Simi turned around in his arms to look back at Leucious. "Akri-Leucious said you'd do that. You were right. Akri did miss his Simi."

Of course he did. If Simi was his, Leucious would never let her out of his sight.

Acheron walked slowly toward him. "Thank you for bringing her back to me."

As Acheron approached him, his horse became skittish. No doubt it sensed Acheron's inhuman powers. Leucious patted his horse to settle its nerves. "Any time."

He shifted her to his other side. "As long as you take care of her, you'll always have a friend in me, Leucious. You ever let harm befall her ..."

"You don't have to threaten me, Acheron. I'm not my father. I don't prey on those weaker than I am."

Acheron let out a sinister laugh. "Trust me when I say this, even though she looks like a little girl, Simi is *never* the weaker creature. But it's not just physical pain. I take it personally whenever someone hurts her feelings, too."

"Note taken. And don't worry. She's too precious to harm. Like you, I hope no one ever taints her ... uniqueness. Or dampens her smile."

Acheron held his hand out to him. "Sorry to be such an

ass, Leucious. Trusting others doesn't come easy for me. And when it comes to Simi, I tend to be rabid. I've already lost one child I loved more than my life. I don't want to lose another. I'm not sure I could survive it."

Leucious shook his extended arm. "I've never lost anyone I was close to." Because he wasn't close to anyone. "And in spite of my upbringing, I don't enjoy causing pain."

"Says a warrior renowned for his brutality."

"War isn't pretty, but it's my mother and my mistress."

Acheron snorted. "Maybe you should think about breaking up with them."

It was a thought. However ... "And do what? Farm?"

"It's a noble occupation."

"Not for a prince who will one day reign over a vast empire."

"Will that satisfy you?"

Leucious wanted to say yes, but why bother? Acheron could sense the truth he didn't want to say out loud. Or even admit to himself.

He would never be satisfied. Just like his barbarian father, he would always want more.

And there was no telling where that would take him. Or who he'd end up hurting in order to get more.

7

JUNE 19, 8645 BC

Leucious had awakened to a peculiar feeling. Not one he could easily explain. Just one of deep unease. Similar to the feeling he had right before battle. That moment when the war drums became his heartbeat and the stench of sweat, fear and anticipation hung heavy in his nostrils.

Not his fear, but that of the troops who had no idea if they'd live to see another day.

Had he valued his life even a tiny iota, he might have shared their fear. But death didn't scare him. Living was far more traumatic.

At least death would bring peace, and though he'd never known that word, he liked the sound of it.

Peace.

Yet this wasn't a day for tranquility. He didn't know why he believed that. It was merely a premonition he couldn't escape. A deep sense of foreboding.

Didn't help that Mot gloated over something the idiot god knew that he refused to disclose. That only added to his deep sense of dread. When the loquacious Mot drew silent, hell usually followed.

"Leucious?"

He paused on his way to the stream where he'd planned to take a bath while his army continued to sleep after their victory celebration the night before.

Last thing he expected to see in the woods was Jaden Al-Baraka—the demon broker. They had met years before when his father had conjured the creature in order to strike a bargain for victory.

Jaden had refused. "*You don't need me, Your Majesty. Your army is more than capable of laying waste to your enemy without any demon interference.*"

His father had been furious.

Secretly, Leucious had laughed at Jaden's audacity. Not many creatures said no to his father and lived. But then Jaden was stronger than most.

And Leucious had no idea why Jaden would be here in the early morning to see him when he hadn't summoned the creature. It made no sense. "Is there a problem?"

"Not per se. But I know it's your birthday. Your twenty-first birthday."

He'd given that no thought. What difference did such a day make? "And?"

Jaden became somber. Silent.

Which aggravated Leucious. "Are you here to spy on my bath, or do you have a real matter to discuss?"

He snorted. "I have something to tell you." Seconds ticked by as Jaden said nothing more.

"Still waiting."

With a heavy sigh, Jaden glanced away. "Have you ever noticed that you're a little different from others?"

Where was this going? "More intelligent? Taller? Better looking? Wealthier? Meaner? Yes. I've noticed."

Jaden rolled his eyes. "Stronger. More resistant to bleeding."

That sent a chill down his spine. Of course he'd noticed. Everyone commented on the fact that he'd never once been seriously hurt in battle. Even blows that should have laid him low had been deflected at the last minute. It was as if something unseen protected him. "What exactly are you saying?"

Jaden let out a tired breath. "Right now, Mot is telling Tesiah about a bargain I struck for Veru approximately twenty-one years and ten months ago ... give or take a day or two."

Leucious froze as those words sunk in. Veru was his mother. And that timeline coincided with ...

"My birth."

Jaden nodded slowly. "Your mother was terrified for her life. Tesiah had told her that if she birthed one more daughter, he'd kill her along with the baby."

That sounded like his father. The man had bragged endlessly about killing Leucious's sisters and threatening to do the same to him when he displeased him.

I didn't murder four innocent babes to be stuck with a

useless, mouthy whoreson! Do as you're told, boy, or join your sisters in their graves!

How could anyone forget a tirade that had been shouted at Leucious for as long as he could remember?

"So what? My mother bargained with you for a son." How could anyone blame her for that when she was married to a brutal lunatic who would have murdered her had she disappointed him again? "What's the harm in that?" His father had wanted a son, and she'd given him one. If anything, his mother should be applauded for her ingenuity.

At least that was his thought until Jaden spoke again. "Tesiah isn't your real father."

Those words slammed into him like a fist. That changed things drastically, and not in a good way.

If Tesiah wasn't his father ...

What did that mean?

Nothing, he decided. It meant absolutely nothing because he knew the truth. Jaden was lying. "Tesiah is my father."

Jaden shook his head. "No, Leucious. I made the bargain with your mother myself. I know exactly what happened."

Was he saying what Leucious thought he was? *"You're my father?"*

The color faded from Jaden's cheeks. "What? No. No! What would make you think ...?" He paused as if running his words through his head, then nodded. "Let me rephrase what I said. I made the bargain with your mother for her to have a son for your father. The son she was desperate for."

This was getting tedious, and it was making him furious. "Who's my father, Jaden?"

He hesitated a moment before he answered. "Noir is."

Leucious stood there unsure of how to react.

Noir. The darkest god of them all. The one who'd cursed Mot and that Mot had talked about with utter contempt and hatred.

His mind reeled at the implications and the horror. Noir ... His father.

"How's that even possible?"

Noir was condemned to a hell realm. Locked there. He couldn't leave it to impregnate his mother. It made no sense. Even for a god, how would that be possible?

"I don't think you want the gory details since we are talking about your mother. Suffice to say, he used the demon Paimon as a surrogate. I arranged the bargain. Paimon fulfilled it."

Curling his lip, Leucious let that seep into his soul. A demon had impregnated his mother. A demon. Everything he'd thought about himself was a lie. Everything. "Why are you telling me this *now*?"

"Because as soon as Tesiah is told the truth, he will lead his army out to destroy the bastard he didn't father. That means you. He will want your head over the lie he's been told all these years."

Of course, he would. Leucious knew that better than anyone. His father would never allow the son of someone else to sit upon his throne. He'd rather leave it vacant and let the others fight it out rather than see Leucious take it now.

The worst part? His mother was already dead. She would have been Tesiah's first victim after the news. And hers would not have been an easy or merciful killing.

That made him sick to his stomach.

But there was nothing he could do to save her.

No wonder he'd been anxious all morning. Leucious turned and headed back toward his men in the camp. He needed to sober them up and be ready to route his ... Tesiah. He had no idea what to call him anymore since he was no longer his father.

Although in all honesty, he'd never really been a father to him. Just someone who scowled and cursed at whatever weakness he perceived.

The heavy fist that beat the weakness out of him.

Still ...

It'd been all Leucious had known.

And if Tesiah wasn't his father, he definitely wasn't his king.

Where did that leave them?

Enemies. What else? And Tesiah had taught him that all enemies must be dealt with and eliminated with extreme and bloody prejudice.

He started for his camp.

Jaden caught his arm. "Wait, Leucious. You need to understand why Noir fathered you."

"I don't care."

"You will. Noir wants an army and a conqueror. In you, he has both. It's why he agreed to your mother's request when he normally turns such things away."

Just like Tesiah. No one had ever wanted *him*. They only wanted his sword arm.

And Leucious had never been keen on being used. Not by anyone, and especially not by a creature who'd never had the decency to tell him he existed. That he was Leucious's real father.

Instead, Noir had played a game with him and that he resented all the more. Because unlike Tesiah, Noir had plenty of human and demonic lives to play with. Plenty of other demons and warriors he could use.

"Why does he need me when he already has the Malachai?"

"The Malachai doesn't serve Noir, and he doesn't trust him. Noir wants someone whose loyalty he can believe in."

That definitely wasn't Leucious. Tesiah had only taught him betrayal. How to hold power by making everyone fear him.

All that mattered was power and control. It was one of the reasons why Tesiah had kept him on the road with his army.

Leucious was less likely to betray and attack Tesiah for his throne if he wasn't at home to take it.

Now ...

"I have to rouse my army."

Jaden smirked. "Trust me, Noir isn't going to let him hurt you."

Leucious scoffed. "I'm not afraid."

"I know. But the question is, which side are you going to land on?"

LEUCIOUS STOOD ALONE on the hill, overlooking the bodies of allies and enemies. This was the part about battle that he'd always hated most. When the fight was over, and the grieving began.

Yes, there was celebration over the fact that he'd won. That he was still standing. That most of his army was still alive.

But that couldn't compensate for the horrors of watching others die. For knowing that his own life had been bought at the price of theirs. It was a steep price, especially given the fact that he didn't really value his own existence.

More times than not, he wished himself dead and out of this misery called life. Why should he want to live? He had no reason to. And yet those men below had given their lives for an ungrateful ass.

Suddenly, someone touched his hand.

Leucious curled his lip until he turned to see Simi standing beside him with a frown on her adorable little face.

Tenderness flooded him and wiped away his anger.

"You got hurts in your heart, akri-Leucious. Why you so sad?"

He brushed his hand over her soft cheek. "I killed the man I thought was my father today, Simi."

Tears welled in her eyes. "Oh, the Simi's sorry. Did you want to eat him? Was he good tasting?"

Leucious scowled at her. "What?"

She clasped his pinkie in her tiny hand. "Is that not why you kill things? To eat them when you's hungry?"

God, how he loved her innocence. She couldn't conceive of all the horrible things people killed for. To her, you killed for survival and no other reason because nothing else was worth killing for.

"No, Simi. Sometimes people kill to protect themselves."

"Like the Simi's matera who died protecting Acheron."

He picked her up and held her to his side. "I'm sorry you lost your mom. No child should be motherless." And he should know. He'd rarely seen his after she'd birthed him. His "father" had forbidden her to cuddle him or act as a mother in anyway. As soon as he'd been weaned, his war training had begun.

And he'd made good use of that today.

"That made you even sadder, akri-Leucious. Did you know Simi's matera?"

Sighing, he rubbed her back. "No. I lost my mother today, too." He wasn't quite sure why it hurt so much. Tesiah had made sure that he spent very little time with Veru for fear of it making him soft. Womanly.

You're a warrior, boy. Not a nursemaid.

And today, Tesiah had reaped the full harvest that

came from making Leucious as harsh and unfeeling as Tesiah had been. For killing the heart that beat inside him. It was nothing more than a cold organ that had no feeling for anyone.

Especially not the man he'd thought was his father.

And he would never forget the shock in Tesiah's eyes as he killed him. Or the lack of satisfaction he'd felt afterward.

Truthfully, he was numb over that part. What hurt inside him was the needless lives that had been lost over all this. And for what? Because his mother had been so terrified of one monster that she'd made a horrible bargain with evil to birth another.

In truth, he hated her, too, for giving him this existence that he wished to the gods he wasn't forced to endure.

"Life is so unfair, Simi."

"That's what akri says. That and that life is hard and unforgiving."

Leucious agreed.

"But akri says that's why we have hearts ... so that we can love good-quality people who's there to help when it hurts. Their hugs makes it all betterer."

Placing her arms around his neck, she gave him a big hug that actually made him feel a lot better or betterer. "Thank you, Simi."

She ruffled his sweaty hair. "You're very welcome, akri-Leucious."

And as Leucious held her, he wondered something. "Why are you here alone, Simi?"

She pulled back to stare up at him. "The Simi felt your sadness. It said, 'Hey Simi, I needs help 'cause I's having a bad, bad day.' The Simi don't want akri-Leucious to have them bad days. You should have happy ones."

"You keep an eye on me?" He wasn't sure how he felt about that. Not until she smiled.

"'Course. You're Simi's friend and friends always stay together. Watches each other's backs and fronts. The Simi will always be here when you needs her."

In spite of the horror of this day and the nausea he felt inside, he truly appreciated her company.

She was magick. Stronger than anything he'd ever known.

But the problem with magick was that it, like everything else, never lasted.

And friends were only an illusion. Because the one thing he'd learned in his twenty-one years was that friends eventually turned into enemies.

If Simi ever became his enemy, so would Acheron. While Leucious knew he had never been defeated in battle, he had never gone up against a god as powerful.

Honestly, he never wanted to, either.

And the last thing he wanted was to lose the only friend he had.

An adorable Charonte demon who had no concept of the evil that had birthed him. Or, more to the point, the evil that had fathered him because it wanted to destroy the world Simi loved so much.

8

OCTOBER 31, 8630 BC

Simi paused as she saw the awful, big bird-like creature fly way over her head. That was the kind of scary thing that made the humans scream and run. Part of her wanted to run, too, but not out of fear.

She wondered if they'd be good eats.

If it wasn't so high, she'd be even more tempted. But while she liked to fly, she didn't want to fly up there where it was really, really scary.

And mostly because akri would be mad if he knew she'd come here. Not that she'd told him she wouldn't.

Shadow be mad, too.

They both had warned her many times not to venture here. Not for any reason.

But she'd heard akri talking to Shadow about akri-Leucious and how he'd lost his minds and decided to make peace with his nasty god-daddy.

That made her worried about akri-Leucious. She knew

how he felt about the ancient evil god, and it explained why Simi hadn't been able to check in on him. He wasn't in the human world anymore. He was in the icky, scary place akri didn't like for her to visit.

So, she pushed open the door to the dark creepy obsidian palace where she felt akri-Leucious's presence. He was sad. Hurting. She could feel it with every bit of her heart. Now, she had to find him in this big old empty castle.

"Akri-Leucious?"

"It's Thorn now, Simi. I don't use Leucious anymore."

Simi didn't like being startled. But his deep voice made her jump as it came out of the darkness in the big room with a weird fireplace. He was sitting alone in the corner, near that fireplace, drinking. "Why are you here, akri-Thorn?"

He laughed bitterly. "I don't know."

Slowly, she crossed the cold empty room to the wooden chair where he sat with a goblet in his hand. She saw all kinds of other drink vessels on the floor around his chair. Akri-Thorn had been drinking a lot.

He wasn't his usual selves. For one thing, he stank awful. And his long hair was tousled, and a gross beard was growing all over his face. He was still handsome, only he was messy handsome not the clean, neat handsome she was used to. "What happened to you? You lose your comb and razor?"

He laughed at that. "No. Something much more important. I lost my way, Sim. I don't know who I am or why I'm here."

"That's easy. You akri-Thorn. Though Simi's not sure why you changed from akri-Leucious. But that all your business. Change your name if you wants. Akri does. He Apostolos to his mama. Akri to his Simi and Acheron or Ash to others. Though some of them call him other names that make the Simi mad sometimes. They don't seem to matter to him though. But that's side the pointy. You the little boy who tried to scare the Simi, only you made me laugh insteads. That's who you is."

Thorn winced at that. "I wish I were that boy again, Simi. He knew what he wanted. What he was supposed to become. I don't know me anymore and it hurts. I miss who I used to be."

Putting her hands on her hips, she stared up at him. "Well, that's just silly. Akri-Leucious meet akri-Thorn. See how easy that is? Now you know yourself."

With a sigh, he drained his cup, then let out a belch like the Simi did whenever she eated too much moo-cow. "Leucious was a prince. He was going to rule his father's people and conquer anyone who threatened his empire. Thorn ... has no father. He has no purpose and no reason to be here or anywhere."

"You gots a daddy. He's in that other big place across the way. Not a nice god. But ... we don't gets to pick our daddies. Sometimes we just get stuck with them."

"He doesn't want a son, Simi. Anymore than Tesiah did. All he cares about is a tool to further his agenda."

"Well, you not a tool, akri-Thorn. You not brainless. You gots a big heart." She flew up so that she could sit in his lap. "Tools don't have hearts."

He smiled as he allowed her to perch on his thigh. "I don't feel like I have a heart."

She put her hand on the center of his chest. Through the dirty linen of his tunic, she could feel the strong beat. "'Course you do, silly. It's right there. Thump-thump. Thump-thump." She pulled his hand up so that he could feel it, too. "See?"

He took her hand into his and brushed his thumb over her fingers. "I wish I saw the world like you do, Simi."

"That's what akri says, too. Though the Simi don't know why you can't. It's easy to do."

Taking her hand, he held it up so that he could study her fingers. Akri also did that sometimes whenever he was saddened.

"You are very precious."

"Thank you, akri-Thorn. You're precious, too."

He laughed bitterly. "No. I'm a product of an evil god who wants vengeance on the world he hates."

"You sound like akri. He worries about his mama getting out and hurting everyone."

"At least she would kill them. Noir wants to enslave the world and unleash his demons for the sake of havoc and cruelty. No real reason. He's just an ass."

"Havocy demons can be fun. They taste good, too. And akri don't mind when Simi eats them. So let them out, I say."

He laughed at that. "I've never tried to eat one."

"You should. But not their bones. Those are hard on your teethies."

He let go of her hand, then tossed his cup across the room. "I shouldn't feel sorry for myself, should I?"

"Maybe. That's up to you. Akri say a pity-party can be soothing to the soul. But Simi never does that. It not producive."

"You mean productive?"

"No. Producive. It don't produce anything but achies. Sad things happen and they shouldn't. People are mean and they shouldn't be. The Simi would like to eat all the meanie people, but akri say I can't. He say that meanie people are mean 'cause no one taught them right. And that when they aches, they want to share their aches. But wouldn't the world be so much better if people shared their happies, instead?"

He nodded. "Yes, it would."

"Then Simi will always share her happies with you, akri-Thorn." She stood up in his lap and took her thumbs to make the corner of his mouth turn up into a smile like she did with her akri.

And just like akri, he laughed, then pulled her against his chest so that he could hug her. "You're amazing, Simi."

"No ... the Simi's just making sunshine on a rainy day like her matera taught her. She said that rain has to come to wash away the ick in the gardens and water our soil so that good things can grow. *Don't fret the rain, Simi. Think of the harvest to come and celebrate what it'll bring us.*"

"I never thought of it that way."

She lifted her head up so that she could see his pretty eyes. "So, what harvest will you bring, akri-Thorn?"

"Hope. That'll piss off my father and give me something producive to do."

She clapped her hands. "There you go. We can both be producive."

THORN STILL WASN'T sure why he'd moved to Azmodea.

Other than the fact that he didn't have a place in the human world anymore, and he'd enjoyed throwing Paimon from the palace before claiming it as his own. Bastard deserved it for "fathering" him, and Thorn was going to make sure the demon regretted his part in Thorn's conception.

For eternity.

Though to be honest, his heart wasn't in conquering humans, and it didn't seem fair to fight against their armies given that he wasn't one of them.

Unlike his real and adoptive fathers, he didn't find honor in taking advantage of people who couldn't fight back.

He wanted a challenge.

And so here he was, leaving his new home and walking into Noir's palace to make a deal with the devil.

Mostly because he was bored, and there was only so much drinking anyone could do, especially when they were immortal and couldn't die from excess. And as much as he might want to, he knew he couldn't spend eternity in a bottle.

Simi was right.

Sooner or later, he'd need some kind of purpose.

"What are you doing here?" Paimon asked as he met him at the end of a long hallway in Noir's palace.

Thorn's reaction was swift and decisive. He punched the weasel who'd helped create him. The weasel who kept pretending he was Thorn's father.

And Thorn gladly took the modicum of satisfaction he felt as Paimon doubled over and whined before dropping to the ground at Thorn's feet.

Another demon came forward from the shadows. It took one look at Paimon and was then more circumspect. "Can I help you, my lord?" Much better tone.

"Where's my father?"

Paimon continued to wheeze. "His throne room. But—"

"Thanks, Dad, but I didn't ask you." Thorn kicked him, cutting off his words. Arching a brow, he turned to the other demon. "Show me where he is."

The demon quickly obliged.

Stepping over Paimon, he followed the demon to a room in the back of the massive palace Noir called home.

When they reached the tall, heavily carved black doors, the demon withdrew. There was no missing the fear in his eyes as he slinked away.

Fine. Thorn didn't need anyone to announce him.

Using his powers, he threw open the doors with hurricane force.

That succeeded in getting everyone's attention, including his aunt, Azura, and his father who sat on his throne while Azura appeared to be frozen in the midst of pacing in front of it.

Tall and with hair as dark as the beast's brutal heart, Noir was a handsome monster. One complete with sharp features and long hair he wore tied back from his face.

Azura was freakishly blue. Except for her white hair and eyebrows. She looked as frigid as the coldest ice storm. And Thorn knew from others that it wasn't just her looks. She was cold through and through.

"What is the meaning of this?" Azura demanded.

"Hold, sister." Noir's words were low and feral. "This is my son."

She scoffed at that. "He's not the only son you have."

That was news to Thorn. He'd had no idea that he had any brothers. Interesting that Grim had failed to tell him *that*.

All Grim had ever talked about was Thorn's half-sister, Laguerre who was also Grim's wife.

Of course, Grim said very little to him these days given that Thorn had betrayed him by refusing to help Noir. They were now at war, and honestly, he didn't care.

Noir cut a menacing glare toward her. "Yes, but this one hasn't disappointed me ... yet."

Thorn scoffed. "Far be it from me to stop a family tradition."

That made his father stand up. "Careful with your next words, boy."

He had planned on being careful.

And duplicitous.

"I'm going to reassemble my army."

Noir smiled proudly at those words. "Good. Take whatever you need from my demons."

"I was hoping you'd say that. Thanks, Gramps." But what Noir didn't know was that Thorn planned to use those soldiers to protect the humans, not harm them.

There would be hell to pay once Noir learned what Thorn was going to do, but he'd cross that bridge when his father dragged him over it to beat him.

For now ...

Like Shadow, he preferred to move sight unseen.

9

___

SIX MONTHS LATER

Still dressed in his bloody black spiny armor, Thorn stood in front of his fireplace, pouring himself a well-needed drink.

The doors behind him swung open so forcefully that they rattled on their hinges and preceded a wind sweeping through the room with such ferocity that it put out the fire and froze his armor.

There was only one person he knew who would have that audacity. "Something wrong, Father?" He turned slowly to confront the angry giant.

"How could you!"

Thorn set his frozen wine and goblet on the mantle, and prepared to be dragged across the proverbial bridge. "I asked your permission."

"To assemble an army. Yes. To use that army to fight my soldiers ... you knew I'd never agree to such."

Thorn shrugged with a nonchalance that was probably

suicidal. But really, he didn't care. "You're the one who failed to ask questions."

Noir drew back to hit him.

Thorn caught his wrist before he could complete that blow. "Think before you strike. I'm not one of your demons, and I don't take a hit without dealing one back in turn. Father or not."

That caught his father off-guard and was enough that Noir dropped his hand. "Your audacity is without equal."

"I'm the product of my breeding. If you have issues with it, perhaps you should look inward."

"You are a cheeky bastard."

Rolling his eyes, Thorn turned and headed for his own throne. "Do you have something more productive than insulting me?"

Noir's nostrils flared. "I want my army back."

"I like them where they are. I find that a private army suits me."

"Of course, you do, you brat. You were supposed to be your sister's general. Not off on this ... I don't even know what to call it."

"Youth rebellion. I'm told it's natural for a child to refuse to follow in the footsteps of their parents. Especially when they don't agree with them."

That made Noir's eyes turn a vibrant red. "You are a warlord."

Thorn steeled himself at something he'd once taken pride in. But those days were gone. "*Was*, Father. I *was* a warlord."

"And what are you now?"

"The thorn that nettles you every time you move." He recklessly smirked. "I want your agreement that in the future I'm able to redeem the soldiers I pick for my army."

Aghast, Noir's jaw dropped. "You want *what*?"

"An out for those who've been damned. Not just here in Azmodea, but in other hell realms, too."

"Are you out of your mind?"

"Given my relationship to you and Azura, it's a good bet."

Noir shook his head. "I don't have the authority to grant you that."

"Yes, you do. You have diplomatic agreements with other dark gods and Chthonians. I want your word that you'll back me for negotiating redemption for my people."

"Why would I do such a thing? They were damned for a reason."

"True. But it seems to me that if a single act could damn someone to hell, then an equally good or decent act should be able to save them."

Noir crossed the room to tower over him. An act of intimidation that only served to solidify Thorn's resolve. "I curse the day I created you."

"Makes sense, I've hated every day I've been alive." And the fact that he was immortal infuriated him all the more. It wasn't fair that death would never spare him this misery.

Noir's eyes turned red again. "Do you know what I do to those who cross me?"

"Given that one of my brothers is enslaved to the

Malachai and the other cursed by you, I have a pretty good idea."

"And they are full gods, like your sister. You ..."

"Half human. Did you think that would make me weaker?"

By the light in Noir's eyes, Thorn would say yes.

Fine. Half human or not, he refused to cower. "If you want me dead, old man, kill me. Do us both a favor."

Noir's eyes glowed infernal in the dim light. "Why have you chosen to live here?"

Thorn started to lie or answer to aggravate him. Instead, the truth was out of his mouth before he could stop it. "I don't belong anywhere else." No one had ever wanted him.

His mother had looked on him with fear and Tesiah had viewed him as a legacy.

As for Noir ...

He scowled as he considered Thorn's words. "You came seeking a father?"

That was a bitter truth that stung them both. "Yes," he whispered.

"Then why won't you obey me?"

Thorn let out a ragged breath. "Grown children don't obey. Besides, because of you, everything I thought I was and everything I thought I knew has been stripped from me. All I have left is my integrity. If I lose it, then I'll lose me, too. And that I don't want to do."

That seemed to confuse Noir. "You don't hate me?"

"I don't know you, Father. But I was hoping to learn something about you other than rumors and lies."

"So that you can hate me?"

Thorn shook his head at Noir's insistence that Thorn would find nothing redeeming in his sperm donor. And maybe he wouldn't. Only time would tell. But Thorn at least wanted to learn something about the creature who'd donated his DNA to his existence.

"That wasn't my plan. I never hated Tesiah, until he turned on me. Now I hate them all."

Noir considered that. "He abused you horribly."

That was putting it mildly. "He was my father. Love and pain are rather synonymous to me. Hatred I reserve for those who earn it. Since you haven't turned on me, I don't hate you ... yet. Insults and hostility don't matter." They were all he knew and they meant nothing.

Noir paused as he let those words sink in. All his children hated him. Dagon cursed him constantly and justifiably so given what he'd done to the god. Falcyn had turned on him centuries ago.

Laguerre ...

She might serve him, but she held no love where he was concerned, and he knew it. Her heart was too cold. Just like her mother's.

But Thorn was another matter. Was it because his mother had been human? Did it give him a greater capacity for love?

What do you need with such a petty thing?

He didn't. He was an all-powerful god. And yet as he

watched his son, he felt a peculiar sensation in his chest. A kind of pain, and something more. He couldn't really describe it. Could it be paternal affection? To his knowledge, he'd never had that before.

Even though he was angry at Thorn, he didn't have his usual need to beat or destroy him. Noir had never in his existence allowed anyone to speak to him the way Thorn did.

He had no idea why he put up with Thorn's attitude or rebellion. Really, it made no sense at all.

Unless it was the mysterious emotion called love.

"If it makes you feel better, Father, I'm pissing off the Naṣāru more than I am you by redeeming the damned."

Actually, it did make him feel better. A *lot* better. "Are you?"

Thorn nodded. "They despise the idea that someone damned might be able to escape their punishment."

A wave of ... happiness? Yes, it was actual enjoyment that swept through him. "I like that."

Thorn winked at him. "Knew you would."

Noir took a second to reevaluate his fury at his child ... a child he shared with no one.

There was another thought he'd never had before. His other children were born from goddesses. Each of their mothers had an equal sway with them. Even if they hated their mothers, their mothers were still there.

Forever.

But Thorn's mother was dead.

This child belonged exclusively to Noir.

For the first time in his existence, he felt a peculiar need to protect someone.

Thorn is mine alone. But the last thing he could afford was for Thorn to know that he held any tenderness toward him. That would make Noir weak.

Vulnerable.

Clearing his throat, he stepped back. "Very well. I'll allow you to continue angering the Naṣāru."

Thorn bit back a smile at his father's surly tone. He'd seen the look in his father's eyes. It was the same one Tesiah held whenever he came home victorious after battle. A subtle pride that would never be acknowledged.

Strange how similar the two of them were. Noir thought himself a monster and in many ways he was. But there was something beneath the beast that neither of them wanted to acknowledge.

Like Thorn, a creature of his birthright and environment. Even though Thorn hadn't spent much time with his mother, she had still taught him things Tesiah never had. Morality. Justice. Strength.

Not just physical brutality. The ability to show mercy on those he defeated. On those who were weaker.

While Tesiah had done his best to beat those traits out of him, he preferred to see the world through the eyes of his tiny mother.

So, he did what would have made his mother happy, he held his hand out to his father. "Friendly enemies, then?"

Noir took his arm and jerked him forward. Quicker than Thorn could blink, Noir hugged him, then shoved him away. "We never speak of this. It didn't even happen."

Stunned, Thorn had no response or reaction before Noir vanished.

Okay, then.

Had his father really hugged him, or had he hallucinated the whole thing?

He'd taken enough hits in battle that he could be imagining it. Anything was possible.

But one thing he was rather sure had happened. His father had approved his army of Hellchasers.

If for no other reason so that Thorn could anger both their enemies.

He was now free to find damned souls in need of redemption. Those who'd been good people forced by others into a bad situation.

They deserved that chance to save themselves and not be damned by circumstances.

And deep down in a place he didn't want to look, he knew exactly why this was so important to him. Because he was hoping that someway, somehow, he might be worthy of forgiveness one day, too. That maybe, just once, he'd be able to sleep without hearing the screams of the innocent lives he'd taken.

For Tesiah, he'd committed unspeakable acts that would have damned him had he been mortal.

My soul is too black to be redeemed. But maybe the others might find the salvation he knew he'd never be worthy of.

10

7382 BC

Bug-eyed, Simi stared at the strange human ghosty man akri had brought home with him. For her life, she couldn't imagine why akri would let someone come into their home. It didn't make sense. "Why he here, akri?"

Akri smiled at her as he ruffled her hair and tugged playfully at her red hornays. "Alexion ... meet Simi."

Almost as tall as akri, Alexion had blond hair and blue eyes, and he stared at Simi as if she were something annoying that was stuck on the bottom of his foot. "What is she?"

"My daughter," akri said with a note in his voice that told the human ghosty he would kick his butt if he hurt her feelings.

Simi wrinkled her nose. "What is he?" Let him see how that felt.

"Our new ..." akri scowled at Alexion as he walked toward his throne. "Steward."

That only confuzzled her more. "What's a steward, akri? Do they cooks?"

Taking a seat on his throne, akri arched a brow at Alexion. "Do you?"

"I have. Never said it was edible."

Flying, Simi went rushing to the throne so that she could tug at akri's black formesta robe. "Why's he here?" she whispered, only it must not have been quiet because the ghosty looked a bit perturbed.

"Why *am* I here, Acheron?"

Akri let out a long, tired sigh. "I don't know what else to do with him, Sim. I made a mistake, and he's stuck like that. It's all my fault."

"Then send him home."

Akri toyed with her hair. "This is his home now. He can stay with you while I'm ..." He didn't finish his sentence.

Which meant there was one thing he was thinking. "With the heifer goddess?"

That made akri's eyes twinkle. He always liked whenever she called Artemis the heifer goddess, which she was. "I don't like leaving you alone. Now you'll have company when I'm not here."

Simi looked back at Alexion, not sure about that. While he might be nice, he wasn't akri and she didn't really like the idea of sharing her space with someone she didn't know. "But Simi don't know about being lefts alone with him. What if he a murderer?"

"He won't dare harm you, Simkey. I'd gut him."

Alexion arched a brow at that. "I won't hurt you, Simi. I love children, and I would never do harm to a little girl."

Simi frowned at the way he said that. The words gave him a pain in his heart. "You have a little girl?"

A deep, awful sadness made Alexion's eyes droop. She knew that look, too. It was one akri had whenever he thought of his sister and nephew who had died.

"I thought I had a daughter."

She hated that she'd made him feel bad. Scooting off akri's lap, she flew back to Alexion. "Simi sorry you lost your little girl. I'm not her and you're not my akri, but if it makes your heart less achy, Simi coulds pretends to be your little girl, too."

That made him smile even as a tear slid down his cheek. "Sure, Simi. I'd like that."

Taking his hand, she looked back at akri and flicked her tail. "Okies, akri. Simi won't eat the ghosty. But he needs his own room. Simi don't want to share. Does Simi have to?"

Akri laughed. "No worries, Sim. He'll have his own place that won't interfere with yours."

Rising, akri moved to pick Simi up and hold her in his arms. "Come, Alexion. I'll show you your new quarters."

Simi wrapped her arms around akri's neck as he led Alexion in the opposite direction of her room and akri's. She loved her room. It was down the hallway from where akri ... well, she didn't know what he really did there. He seldom slept. Never ate. Yet he had a room there where he sat up late at night.

Alexion's room was on the other side of the temple where the Atlantean messenger god used to sleep and have big parties. Simi had never really liked that mean old god. But he did have a big room that made Alexion gasp when he saw it.

"This is bigger than my entire village." He walked around the ornate bed and gilded chest and table.

"Do you need anything?" akri asked.

Alexion shook his head.

Akri grimaced in that familiar way Simi knew so well. He was being summoned.

"Heifer goddess?" she asked.

Akri didn't answer. Instead, he sighed again. "I need to go commune with Artemis. Keep Simi company until I return."

Before either of them could say anything, akri vanished.

Alexion stared at Simi who stared at him in turn.

"What do you do for fun?" he asked.

"Eats."

"Is there anything here for you that you like to eat?"

Simi left him and went to the room where akri kept her food. She opened the cupboard so that she could look around for her favorite snacks. They was all there, like always. Her jerky and honey. Some bread and cake. Akri took good care of his Simi.

Alexion's shadow fell over her. She looked up to see him staring at all the food. "How long will that last?"

"Depends on Simi's belly. Maybe an hour ... could be two days at mostest."

He laughed. "Then I'm glad I don't eat food. I'd hate to deprive you of anything."

And as he started helping her prepare her snack, she decided she liked the ghosty human. "Thank you, akri-Alexion. You good quality people ghosty."

"Thank you, Simi. You're a good quality ..."

"Charonte."

"Is that what you are?"

She nodded as she climbed up the chair so that she could sit at the long table where she normally ate her food. "We quality demons. Much better than the others."

"I will definitely give you that." He placed her food in front of her, then brushed his hand through her hair. "And I promise I'll be a good surrogate demon-dad for you."

Smiling, she dug into her eats.

TIRED AND ANGRY, Acheron came home to find his temple eerily quiet. That was concerning.

Normally, Simi would greet him with loud complaints over how long he'd been gone. But as he walked over his seal in the entry and his clothes changed to his flowing black Atlantean formesta robes, there was no echoing Simi call. She didn't teleport to greet him.

Glancing into his throne room, it was empty.

He immediately teleported to the dining hall. Simi's favorite place.

Also empty.

Panic began to surge. While she was free to leave, Alexion wasn't. Because of the mistake Acheron had made in bringing Alexion back to some semblance of life, Alexion was trapped here in a limbo existence.

What had happened to the man sickened him.

Artemis was using Acheron's stolen powers in order to bring the dead back to life so that she could use Acheron's guilt to control him. To make him responsible for the men she was enslaving to serve her selfishness. Her army of immortal Dark-Hunters.

Unable to stop her, he'd come up with a bargain. Those she enslaved could earn their souls back provided a person who loved them was willing to restore their soul to their undead bodies.

What Artemis had failed to tell him was that the soul medallion would scorch the flesh of any human who touched it. Burn them deep enough to cause a permanent scar. That was how Alexion had died.

Staring into the eyes of the woman he loved while she told them both that she'd never loved Alexion, and that the children he'd been desperate to protect had been fathered by the man who'd killed him.

Acheron had done everything he could to save Alexion from dying a second time.

Nothing had worked. He'd been powerless as he

watched the life Artemis had returned to Alexion fade from the man's eyes. Only this time, Alexion had died with no soul. The only way Acheron could make his mistake right was to bring Alexion back as a soulless shade.

Damn me.

He still couldn't believe he'd screwed up so badly. First, his stupidity had cost Simi's mother her life, and now, Alexion existed as a ghost with no soul.

All because of him.

Sickened by his ineptitude, Acheron started past Simi's room, then froze.

Simi was asleep on her bed with her legs running up the wall while Alexion sat by her side, watching over her.

As soon as Alexion saw him, he got up and moved silently across the room. "You're home."

Acheron frowned at the sight of his daughter in blissful slumber. "What happened?"

"I fed her, then started telling her human stories. She was curious until she fell asleep."

That made him feel better. Normally, Simi fretted whenever he was away. And by the time he returned, she was agitated and anxious. It was nice to see her calm and resting, and not venturing off on her own to places he didn't want her to go.

Alexion inclined his head to him. "Thank you, Acheron."

"For what?" Ruining his life and his screwing up his death?

Alexion glanced back over his shoulder to where Simi

lay sleeping. "I've been at war for so long that I forgot how much I missed being a father. It was good to spend a night with a child again. She's quite remarkable."

Yes, she was. "She saves my sanity ... and drives me crazy."

Alexion laughed. "Fatherhood. The scariest adventure of all."

Especially when it involved an amoral demon. Even one as sweet as Simi.

Acheron cleared his throat. "I'll be in my room if you need anything."

Alexion looked down at Simi. "Will she be all right if I leave her alone?"

That was an interesting question. "Simi's actually several thousand years old, even though she's still a small child. Charonte age a lot slower than other species. So we need to keep an eye on her only because she's mentally young. Even so, she's remarkably self-sufficient." And at least she couldn't take a bite out of Alexion if she became hungry.

That was a big bonus.

Even three thousand years later, Acheron remembered the pain of the bite she'd given him. But it was nothing compared to the pain he felt at the thought of something happening to the only person he'd ever known who didn't judge him. In Simi's eyes, he was perfect. She didn't see the mistakes he'd made or curse his birth the way his own twin brother had done.

Simi only saw her father. There was no purer love than

that, and he was so grateful to her for it. For the first time in his extremely long life, he felt cherished and valued. Not pitied as his sister had done.

Or controlled like Artemis did.

Simi looked at him and smiled, and all the pain of his past was gone.

His heart warming, Acheron moved to the bed so that he could stroke her soft cheek. "She is perfect, isn't she?"

Alexion chuckled. "Our daughters always are. She is funny and remarkably sweet. Thank you for sharing her with me."

Acheron stepped away and nodded. "I really am sorry about what happened to you. I wish I could make it better."

"You have. This makes the horror bearable."

Nice way of putting it. "Simi has a way of doing that."

"Peoples ... stop talking. The Simi sleepy! Go to your rooms or bring eats."

Acheron smiled. "Sorry, Simkey. Have a good sleep." Leaning over, he kissed her forehead and left.

Alexion followed him out of the room, then headed toward his section of the temple.

Acheron wanted to say something, but he'd never really had a friend, and he was still uncomfortable around others. Too many years of being beaten and tortured. People had never been kind to him and as such it left him antisocial.

Even though he was currently a god, he continued to avoid others for fear of being harmed. While no one could physically hurt him anymore, his feelings were another matter entirely. Those were far more fragile than he wanted anyone to know, or even admit to himself.

And it was why he was determined to make sure no one hurt Simi's. Or harmed her in any way. No one had ever been there to protect him.

But he would always protect her. No one would ever make her feel as low and base as others had made him feel. She was not insignificant, and he would kill anyone who made her cry.

You know that's irrational.

He did, but it didn't matter. After all, he was his mother's son. Apollymi had destroyed the world as he'd known it over what had happened to him. While he appreciated the thought, it didn't change the fact that she hadn't been there when he'd needed her most.

When he needed anyone to reach out and tell him he wasn't worthless. Or alone.

Simi would never have those feelings. She would always have him here to defend her. Here to tell her how wonderful she was.

And now she had Alexion, too. Together, they formed a weird family. But family, nonetheless.

A god, a ghost and a demon.

He wouldn't have it any other way.

11

5656 BC

"There's a new Malachai."

Thorn looked up from his desk to where Shadow stood across the room from him. "Don't you knock?"

"Not when it's something this important."

Fair enough.

Thorn sat back and crossed his arms over his chest. "Have you seen him?"

Shadow nodded. "Adarian Malachai. He slaughtered his father more brutally than any Malachai before him."

Given the atrocities Thorn had seen from a Malachai, that was quite a feat. "Dagon?" he asked, wanting to know where his half-brother stood on this matter.

"Still serving the beast."

That was unfortunate. But then his brother had spent the entire Primus Bellum—first war of the gods—serving as one of the Malachai's best generals. Made sense he'd still be on the wrong side.

"Do you think this is the Malachai who'll break the cycle?"

Shadow shook his head slowly as he moved closer to Thorn's desk. "I think this Malachai will be the worst one ever."

"How so?"

"His mother was a demon."

Thorn sucked his breath in sharply between his teeth. Ouch. "How is that even possible?"

"Ask your father. He's the one who sent her in to attack Adarian's father."

Thorn cursed under his breath. Of course he was.

This was an awful turn of events. And it was the last thing mankind needed. A Malachai birthed by a demon. "Guess you're here to figure out what your mother and my dad have planned for our new king of demons."

Confirmation burned in Shadow's eyes. "A little backup would be nice."

Great. "Inviting me to the suicide, huh?"

"No one I'd rather jump into the pit with than you."

"I do have a sister, you know? Why don't you ever bother her?"

"I'd rather walk into battle with scorpions strapped to my groin than hold a single conversation with Laguerre."

Thorn flinched at the thought. Although, to be honest, he understood that sentiment as well. "Should I grab my armor and sword, or just wing it?"

"It'll be easier to run away without the extra weight."

Stifling a snort, Thorn gave him a droll stare. "I don't run."

"Good to know. I'll shove you at the enemy as I make my escape."

It figured. But at least he knew where he stood where Shadow was concerned. "So why do I put up with you again?" Thorn asked.

"I'm entertaining. Now c'mon. I don't have all ... day or night or whatever it is here."

Thorn would correct him, but honestly, he didn't know either. The worst part about Azmodea was the lack of sunlight. There was no way to tell the time.

Shadow opened a portal for them, so that they could easily access their parents' dreary castle without trudging there like human pedestrians.

They stepped out of the shadows into an eerily quiet residence. Weird. Normally, there was at least one or two demons screaming in agony.

Today, nothing. Tomblike.

Exchanging scowls, they looked about.

"Where is everyone?" Shadow asked.

"How would I know?"

"You visit here more than I do."

Thorn gave him a gimlet stare. "Not in the last thousand years or so. I tend to avoid it."

"Really?"

"Yes, really. I don't make stopping in for a visit a habit any more than you do."

"What are you doing here?" a voice growled from the darkness.

They turned in unison to see Paimon in the doorway.

Thorn curled his lip. "Well, if it isn't my least favorite hemorrhoid."

"I'd pick another almost adjacent body part."

Screwing his face up, he turned his head toward Shadow. "Seriously?"

"Sounded better in my head."

"Enough!" Paimon shouted. "Why are you here?"

Shadow arched a brow. "I didn't know he had a repeat function. Did you?"

"I don't think it's that so much as he's broken. Maybe a thump to the head might get something else out of him."

Shadow nodded. "Hit him hard enough, and we could get brain matter."

"Nah. He'd have to have brains for that to happen."

Paimon let out a long, aggravated growl. "If you're looking for Noir, he's busy in the dungeon. If it's Azura, she's busy elsewhere."

Thorn didn't want to think about what *elsewhere* meant any more than Shadow did. So, he closed the distance to Paimon.

"What do you know about the new Malachai?"

Paimon paled. "Nothing."

Yeah, right. He exchanged smirks with Shadow. "You're lying." He pushed Paimon toward his cousin.

Shadow caught the demon about his arms. "Tell us what you know, or we'll interrupt my mother and blame you for it. Because the one thing I know about her is that she never wants to be interrupted when she's *elsewhere*."

Thorn winced at the very thought. "Hate to be you, buddy. Azura isn't known for forgiveness."

Paimon let out another growl before he shrugged off Shadow's grip and motioned them closer. "They're going to capture the Malachai and use him to fuel their powers. They're hoping if they have him here, they can get Apollymi to contact them or build up their powers enough that they can escape."

That made no sense to Thorn. "But the Malachai isn't Apollymi's son." Why would she care after all these centuries?

Paimon gave them a droll smirk. "He's descended from Monakribos. They're hoping it'll be enough to sway her."

It was a stupid idea. But Thorn wasn't about to tell them. "What if they can't capture him?"

Paimon shrugged. "Then this one will destroy the world."

~

Four months later

Simi knew something was wrong, and it wasn't just because akri was off with the heifer goddess she hated. Artemis was a terrible goddess. Even if hating was wrong, she didn't care. The moo-moo goddess needed to be added to the Simi's menu. Why wouldn't akri let her to that?

But what she felt wasn't akri needing her.

So, she went to akri-Alexion.

He was sleeping in his bed, with a pillow pulled over his head. So he didn't need her neither. Hmm ...

Confuzzled by her feelings, she flew back to her room and frowned.

Something was wrong. She listened intently for a clue.

All of a sudden, she heard the voice in the ether and knew who was illing.

Akri-Thorn. He was awful hurting. His voice was faint, but she could tell he was having trouble breathing.

Before she could think better of it, she left and headed to the human world where she heard him whispering.

When she found him, he was lying in a field with what looked like hundreds of other soldier men all around him. This was a battle site.

Most were dead.

The rest were dying. It looked like those who were able to leave had done so and not cared about the other poor people who were trying to move away from the bodies. The able-bodied survivors had been out to save themselves.

Tears filled her eyes at the horrible sight. She could feel the pain of the dying as if it were a living, breathing creature. One that suffocated her.

Then she heard it ...

The sound of Thorn attempting to crawl on the blood-soaked field. He was whispering the name of his horse as he tried to get to it.

Rushing toward the sound, she found him on his stomach, breathing heavily. "Akri-Thorn?"

Thorn froze as he heard the last voice he'd ever expected, especially after the day he'd just had. "Simi?"

Suddenly, she was there. No longer a little girl, she'd grown quite a bit since the last time he'd seen her. So much so that he barely recognized her.

Had it not been for her wings and red eyes and horns, he might not have known her at all.

"Akri-Thorn ... you got lots of aches. You needs help!"

He wanted to argue, but she was right. In a horrid ambush, the Malachai had not only torn his army apart, Adarian had left him in figurative pieces. Never in eternity had he hurt so badly. Every breath was a struggle, and he really thought he might be dying. "Can you get me home?" His pain overrode his powers to such an extent that he couldn't teleport on his own.

"Simi can try."

Thorn began coughing up blood.

Simi gasped as she wrapped her arms around him and held him against her. Closing her eyes, she did what she was never supposed to do. What her matera had told her to *never* do.

She tapped her powers to heal him.

But they didn't work. Nothing changed. Thorn was just as ill as he'd been when she arrived!

"This isn't good, akri-Thorn."

He wanted to respond, but all he could do was cough and gasp for breath.

Until everything went dark.

Simi panicked as she felt akri-Thorn go limp in her arms. How could her powers not work? They always worked. She was a Charonte. Their powers weren't dependent on others. "No! No! Wake up, akri-Thorn!"

He didn't move.

Terrified that they both were broken, she called out to akri even though she wasn't supposed to bother him whenever he was at that mean old Mount Olympus. "Akri, your Simi needs you. I gots a problem."

Akri answered immediately. *I can't leave, Simkey. Artemis won't let me. Ask Alexion for help.*

That wouldn't do no good. Akri-Lexi couldn't just leave their home, and he didn't know anything about saving demons or gods. Akri-Lexi was wonderful, but not at this.

She tried again to use her powers to heal him.

Again, they failed.

Terrified, Simi could only think of one place to go. Wrapping her arms around akri-Thorn, she took them both to akri's mama who spent most of her time in her dark garden in Kalosis.

As soon as Simi appeared there with akri-Thorn, akra-Apollymi rose from her perch on the side of her fountain. "What is this, Simi?"

"Akra, the Simi needs your help. Please. Akri-Thorn is illed and the Simi can't help him."

"Get that creature out of here! Now! I don't want it near me!"

Those words startled her, as did the venom in her tone. Simi couldn't remember the last time akra had yelled at her, and she had no idea what she'd done wrong. "Please, akra! Please?" Covered in akri-Thorn's blood, she stood up to confront akri's matera. "He a friend to the Simi and akri. We both would be so sad if he died."

Indecision weighed in the goddess's swirling silver eyes. She turned back toward her fountain as if looking for something. "You would dare ask me to help the son of Noir —the beast who condemned my innocent child and his father? Why would I ever help a child of his?"

"But akri-Thorn didn't do that, akra. He helps akri, and he keeps the Simi safe. Akri would be very sad if something happened to his friend."

The goddess moved toward them slowly. There was no pity on her face as she glared at akri-Thorn. "I should throw him to my Daimons. Let them feast on his worthless soul."

Akri-Thorn opened his eyes and looked up at her. "Way I feel right now, it'd be a relief. Put me out of misery, Auntie. I need it."

A strange expression flicked across her features. "Apostolos is really his friend?"

Simi nodded. "Akri lubs him like a brother."

She hesitated a moment longer before she nodded. "So long as you're not lying, Simi, go to my garden and see my dragon, Sarraxyn. Tell her I need the elixir. She'll know what to send."

Nodding, Simi laid Thorn down very carefully, then flew to the garden as fast as she could. But there was no dragon there. Only a flame-haired woman with green eyes and pointed ears. She met her in front of the falling water that bubbled and hissed.

"Can I help you?"

Simi pressed her lips together as she looked around for the dragon. "Akra sent me to find her dragon, Sarraxyn. But the Simi don't see no dragons."

The woman smiled. "I'm Sarraxyn. What do you need?"

Oh, she was one of them shifty people dragons. That made the Simi feel better. "Akri-Thorn is illed and we needs the licksy that'll fix him."

The dragon hesitated until her eyes widened. "I'll be right back." Sarraxyn headed toward a copse of trees.

Simi hovered over the ground, waiting most impatiently.

It seemed like forever and then some afore the elfy dragon girl came back.

She handed Simi a bottle of something that didn't smell particularly appetizing. "This is what you need."

She wasn't so sure, but ...

Thanking her, Simi flew with it back to akra who was standing over akri-Thorn and not looking very pleasant about it.

"Here, akra." She handed the vial to the goddess.

The goddess took it and hesitated. "I'm not sure if I believe you, Thorn. Don't make me regret what I'm doing. If you do, my wrath will be immeasurable."

Thorn had no idea what she meant by that. Or why she was so angry at him for being his father's son. Not like he had any say in the matter. It was odd to be hated for something he hadn't done when his sins were so great. This was a first.

Apollymi knelt and handed him the vial.

It smelled like something that had grown out of his father's armpits. Nasty.

Maybe death would be preferable, after all. That was his thought until another wave of pain washed through his body. Yeah, fine. Either this would heal him or kill him. Either way, he'd be happy.

Holding his breath, he swallowed it whole.

Then cursed as he realized it tasted even worse than it smelled. That was bad. Worse? It went through his body like a lightning bolt. Or fire. Every part of him burned.

Until suddenly all the pain stopped.

Every bit of it.

Thorn lay there, waiting for it to assault him again. There was no way so much agony could just go away. It didn't seem possible or right.

Yet as he waited, he felt stronger. Then stronger still.

Rolling to his side, he pushed himself carefully to his feet.

Simi was there, helping him to stand.

"I'm too heavy for you, Sim."

She blew him a raspberry. "You not heavy, akri-Thorn. Friends help friends."

Not in his experience. God, he loved how she viewed the world so clearly. What he wouldn't give to have her abilities.

Just as she opened a portal for them, Apollymi's voice intruded. "Be glad, Leucious."

He frowned at her tone. "Glad of what?"

"Had you harmed Adarian, I would have killed you. While he might not be my Monakribos, he is still my bloodline. And in my eyes, blood is blood."

"I'm your nephew," he reminded her.

They, too, were blood.

"Son of a traitor who condemned my children. If I ever have the chance, I will kill Noir and Azura for what they've done. And if you get in my way, I'll kill you, too. They are not to know where I am or how to travel here. If they do, my wrath will be absolute."

"Noted, Auntie."

And with that, Simi took him through the portal to his home in Azmodea. Not to his formal room where he normally sat. She actually took him to his bed chambers.

Using his powers, he removed his armor. "Thank you, Simi."

"I would say any time, akri-Thorn, but the Simi hopes you don't get so hurts like this in the future. It's not a good thing be so badly wounded, and the Simi might not hear you next time you fall down. So don't do this again."

She had a point with that. "Well, I appreciate you. I don't know what I'd have done had you not shown up."

"Probably bleed some more and that would have made Simi even sadder. Goodnight, akri-Thorn. Gets some rest." She flew up and kissed his cheek, then vanished.

Stunned by her sweet actions, Thorn waited a few minutes in his room before he decided to return to the battlefield.

He was hoping to help his men.

What he found there was that the Malachai's army had returned while they were gone and finished off any survivors. The sight that greeted him would haunt him for eternity.

But not nearly as much as the fact that if Simi hadn't come to him when she had, he'd be one of the desecrated bodies lying on this field. He owed her much more than someone who'd simply helped him.

He owed his life to her.

And that was a debt he'd never forget.

12

———

JULY 20, 5654 BC

Thorn knew the minute the Malachai entered Azmodea. There was a disturbance so profound that it felt as if the entire realm had been ruptured. It shook his castle like an earthquake.

Before he could rethink his actions, he went to his father's palace.

Sure enough, he heard Adarian's shouts and demands for release long before he reached his father's throne room.

Somehow, they'd done it. They'd captured the uncapturable.

And the Malachai's full powers were on display. Demons were dropping dead all around while Azura and Noir did their best to corral the beast.

Falling back into the shadows, Thorn knew better than to make his presence known at this time. Having gone up against Adarian already, he had a healthy respect for the demon's abilities. Simi wasn't here this time to pull him out of the fire. And he had no desire to be beaten that badly ever again.

While he might not care if he lived or died, he definitely didn't want to be in pain.

"I won't serve you!" Adarian growled at Noir and Azura.

Thorn could respect that.

Noir cracked his whip at the king of demons. "You will do as we say."

He'd give it to his father, he was …

Remarkably stupid.

And it took an entire team of their demons to get the Malachai out of the throne room to where they intended to keep him stashed for the rest of …

Eternity.

Unless the Malachai had a son who would replace him, he'd live here in their dungeon forever. That was the theory, except for a prophesy that said there would be a Malachai born one day who would destroy the world.

Or one who might save it.

Competing prophesies because the gods never made sense, and they never wanted to make anything easy on anyone.

All this because his father and Azura were jealous over Apollymi. Jealous because she'd been lucky enough to find someone to love her in spite of her flaws. For that alone, they'd sought to punish her by killing her husband,

Kissare, and cursing their son Monakribos—the first Malachai.

Adarian was an innocent victim of that curse.

As were all the Malachai. Conceived in violence to do violence and to die violently. All cursed to die by the hand of their own son once he reached adolescence.

The only way to avoid that fate was to kill the son before he hit puberty. What an awful fate to be condemned to.

Thorn couldn't imagine anything worse. And all caused by his own father's jealous cruelty. The fact that he was descended from that beast wore at him.

How could anyone be so vicious?

No wonder Apollymi had hesitated to save him. It was a wonder the goddess was even sane after everything they'd put her through.

"What are you doing here?"

He jumped at Jaden's whispered question. He hated whenever someone snuck up on him.

And honestly, he hated the god who'd bargained for his birth. Just being this close to Jaden made his skin crawl. But at the moment, he had more important things to concern himself with. "I'm spying. You?"

Jaden snorted at his honesty. "Wondering how long it'll be before the Malachai escapes and what the fallout for this travesty will be."

"That's easy. Bloody."

Jaden nodded. "I don't know what they're thinking. This won't endear Apollymi to them, and even if she could leave her prison, she'd only come here to kill them for what they did to Kissare and Monakribos."

"Sounds about right."

"So, what's their purpose?"

Thorn arched a brow. "You're asking me? You're their brother."

"If I could understand them, I wouldn't be enslaved here, and my child wouldn't be cursed."

Only it wasn't really his child who was cursed. Jared was his grandson. Shadow had told Thorn of the farce that Jaden created to protect his son, Xev, who had an illicit affair with Jared's mother.

Not that it'd been enough to save her or Xev for that matter. Xev was enslaved for eternity to the Malachai while Xev's wife, Myone, had been killed in battle.

Their son, Jared, had been tied to the Malachai's life. Damned to live out eternity with the knowledge of what he'd done and that his life had been bought in blood. All because of Noir's cruelty.

Everything came back to his father's insanity.

"Such a mess," Thorn whispered.

Jaden nodded. "They won't stop until they rule the world and we're all subjugated under them."

"I've never understood that mind set."

"Because you're not insane."

Maybe. But it seemed like there ought to be more. What was the purpose of ruling over those who hated you?

Jaden met his gaze. "Look, kid. Nothing that came out

of the Primus Bellum was good. We were all scarred by it. And that's the saddest part about war—"

"No one walks away unscathed," Thorn finished for him. "I was a warlord. I know that better than anyone."

"Exactly. Most learn that lesson while some, like your dad and Azura, just never seem to get it."

How could they not understand something so simple? But then his father could be a bit thick. "Where does this leave us?"

"I don't know. Noir is always scheming. They think the Malachai will feed their powers. Even if he does, it won't be enough to let them out of here."

That left him with one basic question. "What could release them?"

"Lilith has the ability, but that'll never happen. She hates them even more than I do."

Thorn appreciated his conviction, however he knew one universal truth. "Never say never, Uncle."

13

APRIL 19, 411 AD

Simi sat with akri-Thorn in his dark hall, playing chess and munching good eats when all of a sudden, a loud screech sounded.

Eyes wide, she looked at him, then toward his doorway. "What was that?"

He shrugged. "Not sure. Since all my body parts are still attached, I know it's not your father upset that you're spending time with me in a place he told you not to visit."

She rolled her eyes at something he said a lot to her. "Pish! It was a terrible sound. Should we look-see?"

"I don't know, Sim. It came from my father's side of things. Might be something we should ignore."

"Might be something we shouldn't ignore, too."

Another scream echoed.

The Simi definitely didn't like that. "Someone needs help, akri-Thorn! We gots to go help them."

"That was a demon."

"More reason to go see."

Akri-Thorn gently took her wrist in his hand. "Sim ... these are not the Charonte. The demons over there are vicious and mean."

"Don't matter, akri-Thorn. We should see about them. Just because someone's mean doesn't mean we should be mean to them. See?"

"Not in this case."

She pulled her hand away and left him. Honestly, she didn't think he'd come with her, but she should have known better. Akri-Thorn was a good demon in spite of what he thought or said. He actually sprung out his wings so that he could follow her over to his daddy's side of the ugly woods and into Noir's scary palace.

Simi didn't like coming in here, even to see akri-Jaden. She much preferred seeing the demon broker whenever he visited akri or when they's in the human realm.

But this seemed necessary.

Akri-Thorn pulled her toward a shadow and shushed her kindly.

They were hidden deep in the shadows as a group of blue demons went by them carrying another girl demon in the middle.

"She dead?" Simi whispered.

Akri-Thorn nodded. "It's Teras."

"Who that?"

"The current Malachai's mother."

Simi gaped. She hadn't realized the Malachai had a matera. Though she should have known he had to have one. Most beings had a matera at some point, or they weren't born. Still, the evil Malachai acted like no matera had ever loved him, so she'd never thought about him having one. "What do you think happened to her?"

"Not sure. But if Noir allowed her to die, I can only think of one thing. Come with me." He took her hand and teleported them to where akri-Jaden normally rested and read. Simi hadn't visited here much, but it was her second favorite place in this realm.

Not because it was pleasant. Because it had akri-Jaden in it, and she liked akri-Jaden. Granted he weren't as nice as akri-Thorn, still ... he was good quality people.

But he seemed a bit upset right now.

And the moment he saw the two of them, akri-Jaden was even more upset. "What are you doing here? Do you know how dangerous it is right now?"

Akri-Thorn released her hand. "I just saw Teras's body being carried out. What happened?"

"Adarian escaped."

Akri-Thorn cursed under his breath. "How?"

"Seth helped him."

Simi's jaw fell open at the mention of the last person she'd expect to help the Malachai. Seth was the Guardian for Azmodea and was supposed to help keep things in this place, not let them out. "Why he do that?"

"Idiocy," akri-Jaden said with a sneer. "He trusted Adarian, and he's paying the price for it."

Akri-Thorn winced. "Is there anything we can do?"

Jaden shook his head. "You know better than to ask.

Last time I tried to intervene to help him, I made it so much worse. Poor kid. He should never have been brought here."

"Why they hates him so?" Simi asked.

Sadness darkened Jaden's mismatched eyes. "His father is our brother, Set. They hate Set, so they punish his son in his place."

Ouch. Simi remembered that scary god Set who had only liked his daughter, Bet'anya. Whenever akri had gone near him, she made sure to be a tattoo on his body 'cause Set was terrifying. And not terrifying like akri or akri-Savitar or akri-Thorn.

Scary on a whole different kind of level.

Akri-Thorn ran his hand through his hair. "So Adarian is loose in the human world. I'll let my Hellchasers know to beware of him and watch out."

"And tell them Caleb's now enslaved to the Malachai, too."

"What?" Thorn gasped.

The Simi had the same shocked reaction akri-Thorn did.

Akri-Jaden nodded and there was no missing the aches he had in his heart over his son being tooken by the Malachai. "Adarian's striking back at all of us. Lashing out at anyone he can as retaliation."

Pain went across Thorny's face to say that he felt akri-Jaden's pain. "I'm sorry."

Akri-Jaden didn't respond to akri-Thorn's words. Instead, he jerked his chin toward Simi. "You'd best get her home. Protect what you can until we know what Adarian has planned."

"I will."

Simi pulled away from akri-Thorn and went to akri-Jaden. "The Simi's very sorry about your babies. But they's very strong demons and gods. The Simi has faith they'll be all right."

"I hope so, Simi. Xev's been trapped a long time. There's no telling if he's even sane anymore. And even if he's not, I'm sure he hates me."

She gave him a hug, then went to akri-Thorn so that he could take her home to akri-Lexi who was no more thrilled to hear about the Malachai being free than akri-Thorn was.

Akri-Lexi inclined his head to Thorn. "I'll tell Acheron as soon as he returns."

"Thanks. I'm off to let my soldiers know before they get caught unawares."

"Good luck with that."

Akri-Thorn snorted, then vanished.

Alone in the throne room, Simi turned toward akri-Lexi. "Is it that bad that the Malachai is loose? Haven't they always been loose?"

"With the exception of the first Malachais, the rest of them had human mothers. While they inherited the strength of their fathers, the human blood of their mother's kept them containable. This one was created by Noir and Azura. They sent a demon out to be his mother and breed a whole new beast. He's stronger than many of his predecessors and we don't know how badly they tortured him while he was in Azmodea. Torture takes its toll on everyone."

"That's what akri-Thorn said. But no one was hurt more than my akri and he's not mean. He's still gots a wonderful heart, full of love."

"Acheron's special, Simi. Sadly, there are very few like him."

While she agreed, she didn't understand what made him special. "But why he different?"

"I don't know." Akri-Lexi pointed with his thumb toward the kitchen. "You hungry?"

"Always!"

"Let's get you some food."

"Okies." But as she followed after him, she couldn't help wondering if the Malachai would cause harm to those she loved. The last thing she wanted was to see akri-Thorn or anyone else harmed.

Something inside told her that the Malachai wasn't just tied to akri. He was tied to her, too. The Simi just didn't know how. But she had an awful feeling that it wouldn't be good.

14

JUNE 5, 720 AD

"You bastard!"

Entering his war tent, Thorn froze as he heard Brigid's furious tone. It was nothing compared to the slap she delivered to him as soon as she closed the distance between them.

The demon in him rose up, demanding her blood for the assault. But he tamped it down for one reason only.

He deserved it.

Her dark eyes flashed as she glared at him with the fury of her entire Celtic pantheon. Her breathing ragged, she struggled to control herself.

He licked at the blood on his lips from her blow. "I take it that you're upset with me, love?"

"Don't you even," she snarled in warning as she walked a circle around him, dragging her heavy brocade skirts in her tightly clenched fists.

Thorn arched a brow, still stunned that she was in his

tent in the middle of the war that was raging outside. More than that ... "I thought you swore that you'd never breathe the same air as I again." That was the polite version of her words, at any rate.

Two months ago, after she'd found out who and what he really was, and who he was related to, she'd broken his heart, kicked him from her bed, and banished him from the only happiness he'd ever really known.

"I'm pregnant!"

Thorn felt the color drain from his face as those words hit him even harder than she had. "What?"

"You heard me well enough!"

For one incredibly stupid heartbeat, he almost asked who the father was, but her fury answered that. It was obviously his issue she carried.

Joy tore through him at the prospect.

Never once since the day he learned who his real father was had he considered the possibility of fatherhood.

But that happiness was cut short the moment she spoke again. "You did this on purpose! What? Do you plan to offer him to your father as a gift?"

Was she serious? Why would she even think that?

He gaped at her insinuation. "You don't honestly believe that, do you?"

"You're a demon. What else am I to believe? All you've ever wanted was to get my father's shield. What better way to get it than to give me a child who can claim it?"

Wholly untrue. He'd never even contemplated that. But they'd already had this argument about Thorn wanting an enchanted shield he had no interest in. She refused to see him as anything more than his father's tool.

And that was not why he'd seduced her.

There for a time, in her precious arms, he'd almost been normal. He'd been in love and happy.

Too bad it wasn't reciprocal.

He wiped at his swelling lips. "It wasn't the whole reason. You are quite stunning when you're not slapping me."

She glared at him.

Thorn braced himself as he considered the implication of what they'd done. "So what are you planning to do with the baby?"

"I wanted it ripped from my womb the moment I learned of it, but I've been told that it would kill me in the process. With it being of conceived of your mixed blood, I have to deliver it."

Those words bit him to the core of his soul. Just once, he'd give anything to be something more than the despised progeny of his father. "The babe will only be a quarter demon." And that was only thanks to Paimon who'd mixed a part of his DNA with Noir's when he'd carried out his orders.

All thanks to Jaden.

"One drop is as good as total."

He winced. Of course it was. He should know that by now. "Then give him to me. I'll raise him."

Her eyes flared with angry passion. "I'd sooner cut his throat the moment he's born."

"Then you are planning to keep him?"

She shook her head. "I'm planning to put him where you'll never find him. Hopefully, he'll be mortal and will die quickly after his birth. If not ... I'll take care of it."

He glared at her. "That is your son you're speaking of!"

"What would you have me do? Suckle it on the milk of a goddess? To what purpose? To strengthen it?"

Those words cut him to the quick. "Brigid ..." He moved to touch her.

She quickly stepped away and raked him with a bitter hatred that scorched his soul. "Never touch me again. Go to Noir and tell him you have failed. Neither of you will ever take possession of this child."

And with that, she was gone.

BRIGID RETURNED TO her chambers as her fear and loathing warred with the love she felt for both the demon who'd seduced her and the child he'd given her.

How could she have been so foolish? But then that was Thorn's greatest power. The ability to deceive and to make his enemies trust him when they shouldn't.

Aye, he was a dodgy bastard. And she'd been so lonely these years since her husband had been slain. Her grief had made her weak. And she'd longed for comfort and companionship.

There for a time, she'd thought Thorn the most perfect man ever born, and he'd eased the constant agony in her heart. Had filled her days and nights with such great happiness.

Until she'd learned who and what Thorn really was.

Who he served.

Noir. The oldest, darkest primal power of evil. The essence of the worst of all kind. Closing her eyes, she placed her hand over her stomach where her son was barely the size of a bean.

"In your heart, you will have the ability to do the greatest of good."

Or the worst of all evil.

"What troubles you, daughter?"

She turned at the melodic sound of her mother's voice. In the form of a maiden, the Mórrígan was as beautiful as always.

Her raven dark hair was braided around her head in an intricate pattern.

Before she could stop herself, she ran to her mother and held her close. "What have I done?"

"What we've all done at times. You followed your heart, and it led you somewhere you didn't want to go." Her mother placed her hand to Brigid's stomach. "Breathe, daughter. All will be right."

"Do you know that, or do you believe that?"

"Is there a difference? We make our own truth with what we believe."

Brigid scowled at her. "As spoken by the goddess of fate?"

"Who better to know the truth?"

She was right, and Brigid loathed her for that. "No one can ever know who his father is."

"Then don't tell them."

Brigid nodded. Aye, she'd keep this secret. And she'd make sure that her son was forever safe from harm. Forever beyond the reach of all evil. He would be the last of her sons. She felt that with every part of her goddess being.

She'd buried one son already, she would not lose another.

"I shall name him Cadegan. The son of battle and glory."

And in addition to life, she would give him the one thing that she dared not entrust to any other. The one thing that would protect him from harm and keep him safe from all.

Her father's shield.

So long as Cadegan didn't shed human blood, he would be safe from his father's reach.

Her mother brushed her hand over Brigid's furrowed brow, smoothing it with her fingers. "Good and bad lives in the heart of us all. It is the choices we make, large and small, every day that determine our future. Have faith in your child, Brigid. For while he holds his father's blood, he also holds yours. Once he leaves you, his life will be his own. And as with all living creatures, he'll have to find the courage to face and battle what his enemies throw at him. Whether he stumbles, falls or ultimately triumphs is a decision only he can make. For there is no true failure in life, child. There is only giving up one day before we would have achieved success."

"But if he unites with his father?"

"His father was born of evil blood. Yet he spurned it and is now on our side."

"For today. What of tomorrow?"

"It will come, and we cannot stop that. But we don't have to fear the morrow. We only have to face it." Kissing her cheek, her mother left her.

She was right, and Brigid knew it. Whatever happened, she would do her best by her child and hope. After all, hope was the greatest gift and the single greatest curse of every living thing.

SIMI SAT ON THE FLOOR, listening to akri play his lute when all of a sudden, she felt a jolt go through her.

Akri-Thorn.

He had a great sadness in his heart like akri had whenever his thoughts went to his bitty nephew or his sister. It was so hurtful that it made her eyes water.

She could barely breathe.

But akri didn't like for her to leave on her own, and he would be angry if he knew she went to Azmodea. Whenever he went to visit the heifer goddess, he assumed his Simi stayed here with akri-Lexi and she let him think that. Akri-Lexi assumed she stayed in her room lots.

She never told him different either.

But now ...

"Akri?"

He looked up from his playing. "Yes, Simkey?"

"The Simi's tired. I go bed, okies?"

"You sick?"

She shook her head. "Just tired from all the good eats."

"Ah. Goodnight, then."

She went and kissed his cheek, then flew off to her room. As soon as she closed the door, she teleported to akri-Thorn's palace.

Only he wasn't in his throne room.

Still, it was easy to find him. He was throwing things in his bedroom. Lots of things shattered very loudly, like a scary thunderstorm.

For a second, she considered going back home. Maybe akri-Thorn needed to be alone for his fury.

Maybe not. Personally, she didn't like to be alone when she was angry. She preferred to have someone there to hear her howl in frustration.

So did akri.

Uncertain what to do, she crept slowly toward his room. It got worse. He was now shouting.

"I hate her! I hate everything! Damn you all! Damn me! Damn it!"

Eyes wide, she hoped he didn't hate her, too. Was someone else in the room with him?

If they were, they weren't saying anything.

Maybe he needed someone to shout with him like she did when she was furious.

Biting her lip, she decided to peek in and see what exactly was going on. So she teleported into his room, then drew up short at the last thing she expected.

Never before had she seen akri-Thorn as a demon.

Oh my!

He was incredibly handsome. Kind of like a Charonte except his eyes were more of a dragon's with their yellow hue and slit pupils. And his skin held a glittery quality to it. Still, she appreciated how beautimous he was in this form. Much betterer than his normal human body.

But the moment he saw her, he calmed himself.

"Simi ... what are you doing here?"

"You're hurts. The Simi felts it and was afraid the evil Malachai had bushed you again."

He scowled at her for a second, then smiled. "Ambushed me you mean?"

"That's what the Simi said."

Sighing heavily, he returned to his human form. "No, Simi. I wasn't attacked. At least not physically. My heart's been ripped out of my chest."

That made no sense to her. His heart was where it belonged. "Your heart's still in your chest, but it hurts." She could feel his pain inside herself. "What happened?"

He looked away. "I don't want to talk about it."

"Okays." She picked up a vase near her and threw it against the wall where it shattered into pieces and added more debris to the stone floor. "We'll break things, then, until you feel betterer."

Thorn laughed at her actions that mimicked what he'd

been doing on her arrival. He'd absolutely trashed his bedroom.

Leave it to Simi to make him smile given the severe heartbreak he'd just suffered.

She paused to look at him. "Why you stop, akri-Thorn? Aren't we going to break more things?"

He wanted to, but ... "It's not really helping." And it was making a huge mess in his room.

Hands on her hips, she pressed her lips together. "What can the Simi do to help if it don't mean breaking more stuff in here?"

Such an innocent question that it made pain, bitter and aching, tear through him. "There's nothing to be done, Sim. The woman I love hates me and wants nothing to do with me ever again."

The color faded from her face. "Oh akri-Thorn ... Simi is so, so sorry. That's the horriblest." Pouting, she stepped into his arms and gave him the sweetest hug he'd ever received. "Why she being so mean to you when you're so sweet?"

"Because I'm not sweet. I'm not even really kind. I'm an awful, horrific beast and she knows it."

"That not truth. The Simi know her akri-Thorn." She looked up at him with a sincere stare that cut him to the bone. "Simi's known you forever. You always the bestest. Only akri betterer and only because he's the Simi's akri."

How he wished that was the truth. But in his heart, he knew the angry side of him that he'd inherited from his real father. Even though he did his best to deny and ignore it, he was the son of Noir.

Evil through and through. There was no way around the truth. He might lie to others about his parentage, but he couldn't lie to himself.

Brigid had seen the beast and decided that he could never be trusted.

Worst part?

He agreed. There was a part of him that liked to dance with cruelty. It flirted with the darkness that had birthed him. And it was hard to resist.

Humans called him the son of Lucifer and he never bothered to correct them. Mostly because Noir was far more sinister.

Cruelty lured him like a siren. It wrapped its arms around him and made him want to hurt others. Some days, it took everything he had not to give in.

That was what had terrified Brigid. Honestly, what terrified him.

It was why she'd decided that she could never be around him anymore or share a future with someone who had his lineage.

"She's pregnant, Sim."

Simi cocked her head. "Your woman?"

He winced at her innocent question. "Not mine anymore. But yes."

"That's a good thing, right? Babies are always wonderful. Tasty too."

He snorted at the last bit, knowing she'd never eat a

baby anything. She just liked to tease about it because it got under Acheron's skin. "I'm not allowed to see him when he's born. She told me that she will hide my child where I'll never find him."

She blew out a long, disbelieving breath. "Then the woman be dumb. Don't know your powers neither. You could find anything. There's no place to hide your baby where you won't see him, and I know it."

He loved the way Simi made him feel.

If only Brigid could be so kind. Pressing the heels of his hands to his eyes, he let out a frustrated roar. "How can she take my son from me?"

Simi hugged him. "People are mean, akri-Thorn. Sometimes even meaner when they're hurt. Simi don't know why. But ... maybe she'll change her mind."

No. He knew better. It was over. He'd lost everything.

Even his mind.

How could he ever get past this? He'd loved her more than anything and she only saw him as a monster. She wouldn't listen to a word he had to say. He'd given her his best.

And she refused to see anything more than the worst in him.

It was awful.

Suddenly, Simi held an old doll up in his face.

Thorn scowled. "What are showing me?"

"It's what you gave the Simi when she was little. It makes the Simi feel all betterer when she's sad. I was hoping she'd make you feel better, too."

A foreign emotion choked him over something he'd completely forgotten about. He remembered that doll now. The day they'd met and he'd sought to scare a little girl.

The way Simi had laughed at his inept stupidity.

Amazed by the fact that she still had that rag doll all these centuries later, he took the doll that was remarkably well preserved. "I can't believe you kept this."

"Of course. The Simi keeps all her presents ... that I don't eat. It'd be ickiest to keep edibles. But the Simi loves her doll. Lucilu always makes me smile."

"Lucilu?"

"Named for akri-Leucious. You might have changed your name, but Lucilu hasn't."

He laughed in spite of his sadness. With a ragged sigh, he handed the doll back to her. "Thank you, Simi."

"You're very welcome, akri-Thorn."

He gently took her hand. "Seriously, Simi. Thank you. Your friendship means a lot more to me than you know. I don't have many friends. Or any, really. Trusting others isn't something I do."

"The Simi isn't others. She's Simi." Lifting herself up on her toes, she kissed his cheek. "Don't be sad, akri-Thorn. Things will get better. You'll see."

Then she was gone.

Thorn felt her absence more than he expected. How he wished he could share her optimism. But that part of him had been kicked out of existence when he'd been a boy.

He missed that part of himself.

There was a lot he missed, truthfully.

Sighing, he used his powers to clean up the mess in his room. But that only made it seem emptier.

Was this all there was to his life?

Loss?

Anger?

Betrayal?

Nothing made sense. Once again, he felt lost. Every time he thought he had his feet underneath him, something or someone came along and sent him careening.

"What am I going to do?"

This was just like the day he'd learned his father wasn't his father. That the world wasn't what he thought.

That everyone had lied to him.

How many times was he going to have to start over?

Sitting on his bed, he closed his eyes in an effort to get his bearings. He really didn't know what to do. Or what was going to happen.

But at least he still had Simi.

15

OCTOBER 8, 743 AD

"So that's your son, akri-Thorn."

Thorn froze as he heard Simi's voice behind him. Eyes wide, he turned toward her and motioned her to silence. "Careful, Simi. Cadegan thinks we're half-brothers. I don't want him to know the truth."

"Why not?"

Too many reasons to count, just as he wanted no one to know who his father really was, but the most prominent one was his own fear of how Cadegan would react to the fact. "He hates his father for abandoning him."

"That not your fault. The mean old goddess wouldn't let you visit. Can't you tell him that?"

How he wished. "It's not that simple, Simi. Emotions are complicated."

"That's what akri say, too. Emotions don't have brains. But I don't understand. Mine are simple. Hungry, I eat. Mad, I eat. Happy, I laugh. Angry, I eat. Simple."

He laughed at her childlike philosophy. While she was thousands of years old, she only looked like a young teenager. And Acheron had kept her so sheltered from the brutality of life that she had no real understanding of what the rest of them dealt with. To her, everything was good and easy.

No one dared teach her the hard lessons that had been shoved down their throats. Betrayal. Cruelty. Viciousness. Jealousy. Hatred. Those horrible emotions were unknown to her. How he envied her that.

Most of all, he wished he could have given the same gift to his poor son who'd been raised every bit as cruelly has he had.

No, Cadegan had it worse. At least he'd been able to fight back against those who bullied him. Cadegan had been forced to deal with cruelty and take it.

Thorn couldn't imagine anything more awful than to be forbidden to fight back. It was a wonder his son was sane.

And there was something even worse that both and Cadegan understood better than most ...

"You don't know betrayal, Simi. Be grateful. It's a hard thing to put behind you. If not impossible. The more brutal the betrayal the longer it takes to heal." Because betrayal began with trust. No one should be punished for trusting or loving someone else.

Of all life's cruelty, betrayal was the most vicious bitch.

Frowning, she turned to look at his son who was dressed in armor as he moved about the camp of warriors

Thorn had assembled to battle the demons and others set to prey on humanity. Cadegan was a handsome young man, and Thorn couldn't be prouder of him. But the one thing he never wanted was for Cadegan to curse Thorn's existence the way Brigid had.

And he couldn't blame the boy for hating him. Brigid had condemned his son to a wretched childhood. If only Thorn had been able to find him sooner, Cadegan would have been spared all that pain.

Even though Thorn had tried, he'd failed repeatedly. He'd never forgive himself for that.

But now that he'd found him, Thorn had no intention of ever letting Cadegan know he was his father. Cadegan pinned that blame on Paimon. And why should Thorn correct that misassumption? Paimon wanted to lie and pretend to be his father instead of Thorn. So be it.

Just like Paimon continually claimed to be Thorn's father. Sometimes he played along.

Other times ...

Thorn made Paimon pay for his part in his conception.

Even more ironic? The monks at the Cymara Clas monastery where Cadegan had been hidden had written down that Paimon had fathered the boy.

Imbeciles.

To a degree. They were right in that Cadegan's father was a vicious demon, but one much more powerful than Paimon. And Thorn was sure Brigid had done that as a way to slap at him. She knew exactly how he felt about that pathetic demon.

So be it. He could take her cruelty. He'd taken a lot worse. Besides, the last laugh was that he was grateful to them for blaming someone else. This way, Cadegan couldn't hate him for his mother's actions.

Simi turned toward him and made an adorable face. "Do he know what he is?"

Thorn shook his head. "I'm here to make sure he doesn't discover the addanc inside him." Because that was a terrible beast that the world was unprepared to fight.

"What if it gets out?"

Thorn didn't want to think about that. In truth, there were times when he feared his son might actually have more power than he did and in the form of the addanc, there was no telling how destructive his son could be.

If Cadegan turned against the humans ...

Acheron would be honor bound to destroy him, and he'd go after Acheron to avenge his child. A vicious cycle that wouldn't change anything.

Other than to make them both bleed.

Still, Thorn was going to protect his son. No matter the cost.

"I don't want to find out, Simi."

She smiled. "I trust you, akri-Thorn. If anyone can keep Cadegan on the right, it's you."

He loved her confidence. "I appreciate that." Thorn jerked his head toward the camp. "Would you like to meet him?"

"Of course I would. The Simi loves making new friends."

As they walked, he wondered what she thought of Cadegan. He was a tiny bit taller than Thorn, which nettled and at the same time made him proud. He had vivid blue eyes and dark blond hair that he kept a bit long for a knight.

But Thorn didn't mind. He wasn't one for short hair either.

Cadegan stood up from the table where he sat, eating alone. Like Thorn, he preferred solitude to bad company.

"Greetings, brother," Cadegan said in a heavily Welsh accented voice as he wiped off his hands. "You're the only man I know who could go for a walk and find such a fine young lady." Placing his hand over his heart, he bowed to her.

"She's the daughter of an old friend who was passing through. Simi, this is Cadegan."

"Simi? What a beautiful, unique name." Then he frowned. "But surely she's not traveling alone. Especially not with the demons we're trying to route."

Thorn silently cursed as he realized the mistake he'd just made. In the human world, women didn't travel about unescorted and definitely not ones who appeared around thirteen years old as Simi did.

Clearing his throat, he lowered his voice. "She's a demon." The last thing he wanted was for anyone else in their army to know that.

Cadegan's eyes widened as he stepped back and reached for his sword hilt.

Thorn quickly grabbed his hand. "Not the kind we fight."

"How so?"

"She's a Charonte and we're to protect her. Always."

His son's frown deepened. "I don't understand. We're protecting a demon?"

"This one, yes. With our lives if need be."

Suspicion hung heavy in his gaze as Cadegan moved his hand away from his sword. "If you say so, brother."

"I do. Simi's a very special heart. She knows nothing of cruelty."

Cadegan arched a brow. "Truly?"

Simi pursed her lips. "I know it hurts others, and the Simi doesn't like that. I particularly don't like the part where it keeps hurting long after the cruelty stops. It's not right for something to keep making someone ache. Watching someone the Simi loves suffer hurts Simi, too."

A range of emotions swept across Cadegan's face. "I've never heard anyone put it that way before." He met Thorn's gaze. "You're right, she is remarkable."

Simi looked at the table and her eyes widened. "Oh! Who got the funny hat?" She went to Cadegan's conical helm. "Simi's seen these. They so fun!" Picking it up, she ran her hand over the polished steel and felt the dents caused by battle. "May I?"

Cadegan nodded. "Sure."

Thorn was just about to stop her when she placed it on her head. As he expected, the helmet was far too large for her, especially without a coif.

"How you fight in this?" She turned her head inside it, but the helm stayed in place so that it covered her eyes. "The Simi can't see nothing!"

With a laugh, Thorn pulled his coif up and then took the helm from her and put it on his own head. "It's sized for a grown man, Simi, and to be used with an arming cap and mail. When you're older, it'll fit you."

She reached up to touch the edge of the coif that formed a U over his chest. "The Simi don't like this thing. I tried one on once and it snaggled all in the Simi's hair. Hurt my hornays, too!"

Thorn didn't speak. A peculiar tenderness swept through him at her touch. He'd never quite felt anything like it before, and he wasn't sure what caused it.

Simi didn't notice as she picked up Cadegan's gauntlets. "These are good though. Akri has a pair that Simi plays with, and they keep his little dragons from biting me. I like these a lot."

"Acheron has dragons?" Thorn removed the helm and placed it back on the table.

"Doesn't everyone?" Simi asked simply.

Thorn looked at his son who had no idea of his alternate water dragon form that Simi knew about. He wasn't sure how to answer that so he decided silence would be the most prudent response.

Thankfully, Simi didn't seem to notice. She pivoted around to face him. "Well, the Simi better get back afore akri wonders where I wents off to. Or akri-Lexi start looking for me." She smiled at Cadegan. "Nice meeting you."

"You, too, me lady."

She wrinkled her nose. "The Simi loves how you talk. I could listen to that all day!"

An unexpected wave of jealousy went through Thorn with such force that it actually startled him.

"Bye!" She vanished.

Cadegan returned to his food.

Still rattled by that unexpected jolt of raw emotion, Thorn took a moment to watch his son. How he wished he could tell Cadegan who he really was.

If only he had that courage.

For now, he'd watch his son closely and make sure nothing changed.

And that Simi stayed far away from Cadegan.

16

OCTOBER 13, 1045 AD

Thorn felt his own powers surging to fight as he saw the darkness within Cadegan. It was growing even before his eyes. His son had done the unthinkable.

He'd taken human lives. The one thing Thorn had forbidden him to do it.

The one thing Brigid had warned them all against.

Even though Thorn tried to stop it, his own eyes began to change. "What have you done?"

Ashamed, Cadegan looked away from him at the same time Thorn's demon servant, Misery, appeared by his side. While he didn't trust the sultry demoness at all, he knew she never lied to him. She didn't dare.

She only withheld the truth.

"He killed humans," she whispered in Thorn's ear. "Midlings who were trying to protect their sister he coveted for his own."

Thorn winced at the fear that his son had done the one thing he'd been forbidden to do. The betrayal and hurt cut deep. In all the world, Cadegan was all he had left.

All he loved.

Hoping, praying it was a lie, that Cadegan wasn't turning into the monster addanc he feared, Thorn glared. "Is this true? Did you take a human life?"

"Aye, but—"

Enraged as his own demonic blood ignited, he backhanded Cadegan.

His son knew their laws and why they had them. Theirs was a tenuous truce with the Naṣāru soldiers and others. One misstep and all of his Hellchasers would be banished back to the hell realms they'd populated with enemies who would do anything to lay hands to them. Enemies who would tear them apart and grow even more powerful. So powerful, the others would never be able to stop them.

Thorn didn't care what they did to him, personally. He'd more than earned his damnation, and he'd come to terms with that long ago, but the others who'd loyally served him ... They deserved the salvations they'd earned.

"There are no buts, boy! You swore to me that you'd never draw midling blood. Is this how you uphold your sacred oaths?"

Cadegan's eyes turned completely from human to demon. "They attacked me first."

Thorn winced as he felt Cadegan turning even more toward the darkness that flowed through their blood. Justification for cruelty was the slipperiest of slopes. Once begun, there was no turning back. Evil fed upon such blameless behavior, and it thrived with it in the heart of its tool.

"You are the blood of a demon! No midling can truly harm you. You know this! A bloody nose or black eye, you will survive."

Cadegan lowered his head. "Forgive me, brother. 'Twas a mistake."

Thorn wanted to believe him. He really did. But he'd been deceived too many times by those he'd put his faith in.

As much as he loved his child, he couldn't let this pass. He didn't dare.

Too many stood to suffer.

Tears choked him as he looked into a set of eyes that set him on fire and realized that Cadegan was his downfall. He'd allowed this child to come too close to his heart. That was how evil worked. Never from enemies you saw coming.

Only those closest to you could destroy you. The ones you mistakenly trusted.

The ones you allowed to mislead you because the pain of living without them was greater than the pain of tolerating the lie.

By forsaking his blood oath, Cadegan had taken that first deadly step toward the darkest forces. If he took one more, he'd be so powerful that none of them could stand against him.

None of them.

Thorn's gaze went to his desk, where the Malachai's name was carved in the wood as a reminder of how powerful a beast he was.

Should his addanc son merge with the Malachai ...

All would be forever lost. This world would be theirs and the only thing Thorn could do was stand back and watch it burn at their united command.

No matter how much Thorn loved Cadegan, he couldn't allow that to happen. Not after all the horrors he'd witnessed. And especially not after the promise he'd made.

Thorn shook his head. "Nay, the mistake was mine for thinking for one minute that you were something more than the mindless beast you were born to be."

Cadegan's entire face changed as the demon in him was ignited even more. Gone was any hint of compassion in his eyes.

Thorn curled his lip. "I can't believe I put my trust and faith in you."

Cadegan's face returned to its human appearance—as others before. A trick for compassion that almost always worked and weakened the fool who loved them. "Please, Leucious—"

Thorn grabbed his throat to stop those words before they succeeded in changing his mind and allowing him to forget how dangerous Cadegan was.

Not the innocent child he loved.

The monster that innocent child had foolishly

unleashed this night. A monster who hadn't been able to withdraw from those too weak to fight him.

Cadegan had bathed in their blood. He'd unleashed the inner demon at full wrath on those who couldn't fight back. Of all creatures, Thorn knew that euphoria much better than he wanted to. He couldn't allow Cadegan to become what Thorn had been.

A tool for his father who was more than willing to shed innocent blood.

No one would be able to reach Cadegan then. One man, even this beloved child, could never be more important than the welfare of the entire world.

Thorn tightened his grip and prayed this was the right decision. That Brigid would finally do what she should have done centuries ago.

Welcome her son to her realm where she could watch him and keep him from Noir's grasp.

"For crimes against Our Lord, for breach of my trust, I condemn you to the shadowed lands of your mother. No more are you to walk this earth as a living being. You will spend eternity remembering what you've done and regretting your actions. You are no longer one of us. For that, you are sentenced and banished from the world of man. Forevermore."

Cadegan tried to pry off Thorn's grip. For the merest instant, Thorn almost relented.

Until Cadegan's hand became a claw. Terrified of unleashing the addanc onto the world, Thorn threw him against the small mirror where Paimon had promised just the night before to devour the world through Cadegan's blood.

Cadegan went instantly into his mother's realm. He pounded against the glass, begging for release.

Thorn forced himself to show no emotion or mercy. To stand strong against the love that hated him for what he was doing. It must be done. There was no choice in this matter.

Unable to stand himself for his actions, Thorn turned away and covered the portal so that Cadegan's face wouldn't weaken his resolve.

I love you, child.

Unable to bear the pain of it, Thorn threw his head back and roared with agony ...

SIMI SAT up as she heard a loud, anguished cry. It echoed through her room.

At first, she thought it might be akri in the middle of another nightmare.

But this was worse than any sound akri had ever made.

"Thorny," she breathed.

Without a second thought, she teleported to where he was ... in his giant hearth room where he was on his knees in front of a mirror he'd covered with a black cloth.

She had no idea what was going on. Only that he was in absolute pain. Closing the distance between them, she knelt by his side. "Akri-Thorn?"

He pulled her into his arm and wept against her shoulder.

Simi wrapped her arms around him, trying to understand what had happened. He cried like she and her siblings had done when their matera died.

"It okay, akri-Thorn."

He shook his head. "It's not, Sim. I had to banish my son tonight."

"Banish him where?"

"His mother's realm. He hates me now."

She was confused. "Won't his matera take care of him?"

"I hope so."

"Then you should be happy. They don't know each other. This way, they will."

And still he wept against her shoulder. Simi felt so helpless. She wanted to make her friend happy.

Suddenly, akri-Thorn pulled away and changed into his demon form. And his demon armor. Though still extremely handsome, he looked scary now.

"Thorny?"

"I'm going to kill them. All of them. They did this. I will not choose humanity over my child. I won't!" He looked at her with a determination that was frightening. "If the humans are dead, it won't matter what Cadegan does."

Her eyes widened at the thought. "No. No. No. No. No!" She took his arm. "You can't do that akri-Thorn. The others, including akri will come for you. They'll kill you."

"What difference does it make?"

"The first difference is you'll be dead. That's not a good

difference. It's a bad one. Who will lead your Hellchasers then?"

"What do I care?"

Simi flew up so that she could cup his head in her hands. "Look at me, akri-Thorn. *You* care. You picked every one of them and gave them hope. Made them believe if they did goodst, they'd be saved. If you're not here, they'll all be damned again and there's nothing worsted than snatching back hope after it's been gived. It's cruel and you are not cruel or mean."

Thorn wanted to argue more. But in spite of the pain inside him, her words reached his bleeding heart.

"What kind of person chooses someone over their child?"

"Normally, the Simi would agree, but as you always tell the Simi, this isn't that simple. Akri-Thorn has many obligations than just Cadegan. Them Hellchasers are also your children. Like the Dark-Hunters are akri's. You have to protects them. They needs you."

"Cadegan needs me, too."

"But he not dead. He's with his matera. Right?"

Thorn nodded. Surely after all this time, Brigid would welcome him to her pantheon. "What if we're wrong, Simi?"

"What if you're right? Have faith, akri-Thorn. Trust yourself."

Easier said than done. He'd never had any faith in himself. Not even a little.

But Simi was right. This wasn't an easy thing. If

Cadegan fell into the hands of the Malachai, the dark gods would reign again. No one deserved that.

Everyone, including Cadegan, would suffer.

Have faith.

He would try and pray that this was the right thing to do.

17

AUGUST 3, 1753

Simi screwed her face up as she sat on the corner of a dirt road, watching the humans travel to and from a bustling port town called New Orleans. Akri had told her that the Adarian Malachai had chosen to call this place home, though he was hiding somewhere around the town.

"Sim?"

She looked to her right at the sound of a familiary voice. "Thorny!"

Akri-Thorn was up on a big horsey, dressed in clothes that reminded her of the pirates who haunted the street around akri's home. He even had on one of the funny triangle hats.

"What are you doing here?" they asked each other at the same time.

Laughing, akri-Thorn dismounted so that he could

stand beside her. "I left a group of my Hellchasers not far away, and I was coming to check on them. You?"

"Akri's putting a new Dark-Hunter here. Talon. Well, Talon not new. He an old Dark-Hunter. But he new to this place."

"Understood. Why aren't you with them?"

She made a face at him. "Boring."

He arched a brow. "Isn't sitting here, watching people ride by also boring?"

"Not if they're bringing food. You'd be amazed at the new spices the Simi has discovered by watching humans. Especially here. They have something called hot sauce. Simi has always loved her peppers, but this is something completely new and yummy! Have you tried it?"

"No, but if you recommend it, I will."

"You need to, akri-Thorn. It's amazing. The Simi is now putting it on everything." Cocking her head, she laughed at the waterfall of lace that fell from his neck. "Though it might be hard to eat it with all this material. You look like one of them ... what are they called?"

"Macaronis."

"That's it. Macaroni."

"Well, unlike your akri, I don't like dressing like a peasant."

She gaped at his words. "Did you really insult my akri?"

"No. Just the way he chooses to dress."

Simi tsked at him. "The Simi would be upset at you

excepting for the facts that I knows akri thinks it's funny when you say things like that."

"And speaking of peasants ..." Thorny's voice trailed off as he looked past her.

Simi turned to see what had taken his attention away. It was akri-Shadow.

That made sense. As did the comment about peasants. Akri-Shadow wore black knee breeches and a loose white shirt and open black vest. His hair was also loose around his shoulders. Unlike the other people around them, akri-Shadow reminded her more of someone who'd just woked up and rushed out of his house.

Simi, herself, was in a striped, yellow-and-pink dress and wearing a crisp kerchief. Akri always said she looked like a little doll when she wore these clothes. She wasn't sure about that, but the human peoples seemed to like it when she dressed this way, and they treated her well and gived her a lot of extra food. So while it wasn't her favorite clothes, she liked that everyone was nice to her.

"Did you lose a bet?" Thorny asked akri-Shadow as he joined them. "Or did someone steal the rest of your wardrobe?"

Shadow gave him a peeved glare. "Just don't. Have you heard what's going on?"

"If you mean that Adarian is loose here, yes. I heard."

"No. The Greek god, Dionysus has fathered a baby with an Apollite."

Thorn arched a brow at that. "Interesting. Why would he be so stupid?"

"That's the question, isn't it?" Shadow glanced to Simi. "Cam is also scheming to breed a new Malachai to kill Adarian, which is the main reason I'm here."

Simi widened her eyes at that. Cam was one of the original primal gods. Akra-Apollymi hated her awfully. Not that the Simi blamed her. Cam had done terrible things to akra's Monakribos. And Cam hadn't been particularly nice to the Simi's family either.

"Cam wants to kill Adarian?" Simi asked.

Akri-Shadow nodded. "She has some warped notion that she can breed a new Malachai who will break the cycle and usher in an era of peace."

"Or end the world," akri-Thorn inserted. "Let's not forget the other part of that prophecy."

"That's why I'm here to let you know. And why I'm planning to tell Acheron, too, as soon as I find him. We need to stop her."

"But can we?" Thorny asked.

Simi chewed her nail as she considered that. "Akri won't interfere. His whole life was made an awful big mess when them gods tried to stop the prophecy of his birth. He won't ever try to stop someone else's 'cause he says it makes everything messy and worser."

Akri-Shadow looked incredulous. "So, we do nothing and wait for a Malachai who is even more powerful than Adarian? Am I the only one who thinks that's a profoundly bad idea?"

Thorn let out a long sigh. "Simi's right. Everything I know about Acheron says he'll sit on the fence and do nothing to stop Cam's plan."

"What about you?" Shadow asked.

"Every time I've gone up against the Malachai, I've had my butt wrung out. Even with my army, I'm not strong enough to defeat him. Are you?"

Shadow shook his head.

"Then what do we do?"

"Tell the Malachai what Cam is doing?" Simi suggested.

Both men turned toward her with bugged eyes.

"No!" Akri-Thorn had the same tone akri used whenever she asked if she could eat a pesky human or the heifer goddess. "You can't go near him, Simi. He'll destroy you."

"What if he be reasonable? Won't he like to know that Cam is plotting evil against him?"

Akri-Shadow scoffed. "He's not reasonable. Trust me. Reasonable was never part of his genetic composition."

Thorn agreed. "What he said. Adarian is one of the most psychotic Malachai in history."

Simi wasn't so sure, but she wouldn't argue with them. The one thing she knew about male types ... they didn't listen.

Especially when they had their minds made up.

"Okies." So she left them to argue with each other while she quietly slipped away.

The smartest thing would probably have been to listen to them and go find her akri. Or go back home to their temple in Katateros where akri-Lexi waited.

But the Simi didn't really listen well, either. It'd always

been a flaw. She was what akri called pig-headed. And her pig-headedness tooked her to where she felt the big demons were nesting outside New Orleans in the bayou.

Ironically, not that far from where the new Dark-Hunter was planning to live.

Not that she blamed Adarian for picking this place. There was feeling here of something from another realm. Like Azmodea, only different, and it didn't have all them smelly demons flying around, either.

This would be the kind of power that could feed a Malachai and keep him strong.

Wrinkling her nose, she decided to use her wings even though akri didn't like for her to do so in daylight. Or in the human realm. But the ground here was squishy and wet. And the Simi liked her dainty boots. The last thing she wanted was to get them wet and ruin them.

Besides, things slithered in the brush. Snakes and other creatures that she wouldn't mind roasting and eating. Even the gators could be tasty if cooked right.

But for once she wasn't hungry.

She was just curious.

"Here, Mally, Mally ... Where you hiding?"

Fire blasted in front of her.

Simi pulled up short and blinked slowly. Was that supposed to scare her? If so, the Malachai had a lot to learn about Charonte demons. "That you, Adarian?"

"What do you want, Charonte?"

Simi froze as details about him came to her. It was something that didn't happen all the time. A power she'd inherited from her mother, but one she didn't understand. It was a broken power. Because her matera had died when she'd been young, she'd never learned to really use it.

But it gave her pieces of information about people or creatures.

Right now, it told her that Adarian already had a son ...

One hidden that he knew nothing about.

A Greek god one.

No ...

"Answer me, Charonte. Why are you here?"

Simi blinked at his ferocious growl. "The Simi was only curious. You're related to the Simi's akri. So the Simi wanted to see what you looked like. And so I see you. Now I go. Bye!" She teleported to her room in Katateros before he could do anything.

And there in her room, she sat on her bed as she tried to think about what she'd just learned.

The Malachai had a son he didn't know about.

A son akri-Thorn didn't know he had neither.

Should she tell?

Akri would say no. Leave things as they were because knowledge hurt people. Prophecy was bad. It'd caused her akri to be thrown out of his pantheon before he was born, and tortured horribly.

It'd killed her matera.

And all those actions had been for nothing. In spite of everything the gods had tried, Akri's birth had still caused them mean old Atlantean gods to die ...

Well, they weren't dead, but they were no longer alive

or in power. All of them were in stasis and gone. Akri had replaced them just as the prophecy said. His birth had been the end of them.

All their efforts to stop it had done nothing except hurt akri.

And her.

So, tell no one.

Because it would change nothing.

This would be her secret. She would leave the Malachai alone and hope that he would not harm anyone she loved.

18

OCTOBER 31, 1801

Simi sat at the ornately carved bar of the newly opened place called *Sanctuary* in New Orleans It was a fun restaurant where they served the best eats. Owned by a family of them BearWere creatures, Sanctuary was one of her favorite places to visit, she decided.

Even if the shape-shifting bear people weren't so happy that akri came with her.

And not just him. The Dark-Hunters in general made them Weres nervous.

Even so, they were exceptionally nice to her. Probably because akri spent lots of monies with them for her to eat as much as she wanted, and that was a lot.

"How are you doing, Miss Simi?"

Simi smiled at Nicolette Peltier or Mama Lo as she was generally known. Tall and blond, she was exceptionally beautiful and was dressed in a thin high waisted gown similar to Simi's except hers was a pale blue that matched her eyes. And it had little yellow flowers that were the same color as her short-sleeved jacket.

Mama Lo was the matriarch of the giant bear family who owned the place. But it wasn't just bears who lived and worked here. There were lots of other shape-shifters, too.

And they was all the nicest.

"The Simi's doing just fine, akra-Mama Lo. How is you today?"

"*Très bien, ma petite.* Would you like more chicken?"

"Please! And more of the hot sauce."

Laughing, Mama Lo motioned for one of the servers to bring what Simi asked for.

She patted Simi on the back and then gave her a kiss to each cheek. "*Bon appétit!*"

Simi smiled at her kindness. "*Merci, Maman.*"

Just as the waiter placed the food in front of her, a man sat down beside her. She paid him no heed as she started to eat.

Not until the human laughed. "You have quite the appetite, eh?"

Simi paused to pass an inquisitive stare toward the stranger. Older with a gray beard, he was decidedly human. Why he wanted to speak to her, she had no idea. "The Simi likes to eat."

"Indeed. Are you here alone?"

"She is not."

Simi looked over her shoulder at the sound of akri-

Thorn's deep voice. Not only was he angry, he actually placed his hand on the man's shoulder and lifted him up out of his seat.

"You should be going. Now."

The man took one look at the fury on akri-Thorn's face and quickly scrambled away.

Simi arched a brow. "Should the Simi ask?"

"The Simi shouldn't talk to strangers. I didn't like the way he was looking at you. Or the thoughts in his head where you are concerned."

Smiling, Simi licked the sauce off her forefinger. "It okies, Thorny-man. Akri says the Simi's allowed to barbecue any human man who tries to puts his hands on the Simi without her permission."

"Good." He took the seat beside her. "Nice to know Acheron has some sense."

There was a peculiar note in his tone that made Simi curious. "Akri-Thorn ... you're not jealous is you?"

"Of course not."

"You sound jealous."

Again, he scoffed. "I just worry about you."

"If you say so. But it didn't sound like worry to the Simi," she teased. "Sounded like jealousy."

To her amazement, he actually blushed. "Don't talk to strangers, Simi."

Before she could ask him about that, he excused himself and headed toward the stairs where a parlor was set up for card games.

Dev-bear came over to her. With long, curly blond hair

he wore pulled back in a queue, he frowned at Simi. "You know Thorn?"

"I do."

"Is he all right? He seemed a little flustered."

Simi held her hands up and shrugged. "Guess he didn't like the Simi teasing on him. Weird, right?"

Dev-bear tossed the white hand towel he was holding over his shoulder. "You want me to order you more food, Miss Simi?"

"Thank you, but the Simi's finally getting a bit full."

"I'll let the kitchen staff know they can slow down now."

Simi sat there for a few more minutes, thinking over Thorn's strange reaction. She wasn't sure what to make of it.

They'd been such good friends for so long.

But then akri was the same way. He never liked for unknown men to approach her. He got extremely testy whenever someone new came around, especially now that she was looking more like a young woman.

Simi wasn't sure what she thought about growing up. Charonte were very different than other species. Asides from being so slow to age, there were other things, too.

And it bothered her that she was the only one of her kind. She kept asking akra-Apollymi about her sissy and brother, but the goddess wouldn't tell her anything other than she was unique and akri's guardian.

Whenever she went to visit the goddess, there were never any other Charonte there like they used to be.

Simi was all alone.

Your job is to watch over Apostolos, Simi. He's your family.

But it was lonely being the only one of her kind. She missed being able to speak Charonte and laughing about silly humans with her demonic brethren.

While akri and akri-Lexi were wonderful and she loved them, she did want to see other Charontes. Though akri could look like a Charonte sometimes. He just very seldom did it and it wasn't the same as all time Charonte.

Simi turned her hand over and curled her fingers so that she could study her nails. They were actually more akin to claws. Thicker than human fingernails. Stronger.

Closing her eyes, she tried to remember what it was like to live in her nest, among her own. She could barely even remember what her brother and sister looked like.

Simi had long forgotten the sound of her mother's voice and that hurt most of all.

She missed her mother and her family.

Like the bears here. She saw Dev fighting with his identical brother Remi. They shoved and then hugged. That was family. You might fight, but you always came back together. 'Cause family was everything.

She believed that.

A sudden wave of sadness went through her. That wasn't like the Simi. She was always happy.

Well, she tried to be. There was enough sadness in the world. She didn't need to add more.

But that awful heavy feeling had moved into her chest. She didn't like it.

Was this what it meant to grow up? To stop being happy all the time? Most the adults around her carried awful sadness inside them.

She didn't want that. They all seemed to have a part of them missing. A part of their soul that was so scarred that it kept them from seeing the good things in their lives.

The little things that made her so giddy. Like hot sauce and music. A pretty sunset. Good eats.

Simi didn't want to fight or judge others. She just wanted to live in peace and find the unique beauty that surrounded everyone and everything.

What was it that killed hearts? Too much pain? Or living too many years? She wasn't sure. Whatever caused it, she just hoped that she never had it. 'Cause the Simi liked to laugh, and she wanted to always appreciate all the different kinds of people and creatures around her.

If growing up stole that from her, then she hoped she always stayed young. Maybe akri was right. She just needed to be a little girl longer.

At least as long as she could.

19

JULY 6, 1970

Simi paused as she saw akri-Thorn sitting alone in one of the booths in Sanctuary. It wasn't like him to hang out in the bear restaurant, as he preferred much swankier kinds of places. She very rarely saw him here.

And it definitely wasn't like him to be all mopey.

Hmm ...

Worried about her friend, she headed toward him and took a seat across the table. Without a word, she slid her bowl of ice cream over to him.

He looked up with a scowl that turned into a smile. "What are you doing?"

"You look like you could use some hot sauce covered chocolate magic. It never fails to make the Simi feel all better whenever she's feeling all bluesy."

Laughing, he pushed it back toward her. "While I

appreciate your thoughtfulness, I don't think this is going to help. I'd rather you enjoy it."

Simi pursed her lips. "You sure?"

"Positive."

"Okies." She took a bite while he returned to being fretful. "So, what's wrong, big guy? You look like akri when one of them Daimons eat too many human souls."

"I feel like Acheron when the Daimons eat too many human souls." Sighing, he rubbed at his forehead. "I just found out that Cam did what all of us told her not to do."

Simi licked the spoon. "She a goddess. She kind of does what she wants all the time. Isn't that the whole point of being a primal goddess?"

He didn't appear amused by her comment. "It's bad, Simi. There's a baby out there that Cam intends to use to birth a Malachai when the poor girl's old enough. None of us know where Cam's hidden that baby or who she is. It's an innocent child who's going to be used and abused and that's wrong."

Yes, it was. No one should be born for no other reason than to suffer. Yet, that did seem to be the fate of so many.

It wasn't right and she wished she could help.

"Can't akri find her?" Surely with all his powers, her akri could locate such a poor baby girl and save her.

Thorny shook his head. "None of us have the ability. We've all tried. So long as Cam is shielding the child ..."

That made her feel worse. "It just like akri when he was a baby. No one could find him, neither." Not until the evil Apollo god had kilt him and her matera.

He winced as if he had a bad headache. "There's something else going on, Sim. Something I can feel. A lot has been happening, and I can't figure it out."

"What do you mean?"

"It's like the universe is realigning." He looked up at her and his eyes turned a bright red. "Can't you feel it?"

"No. Are you sure it's not hunger pangies?"

"Definitely not. But I want you to promise me something."

His tone sent a wave of fear over her. "Okies."

"If I ever turn to my father's side, you won't hesitate to kill me."

Simi froze at the last thing she expected him to ask. "Wait … what, akri-Thorn?"

"I'm serious, Sim. It's hard to do the right thing. And it's getting harder for me every minute."

"Maybe you should move to another dark castle, akri-Thorn. Get away from your evil daddy."

He laughed bitterly. "I wish it was something that simple. Geography won't change anything. It's the part of me that I was born with. I can feel it growing stronger as I get older, and it scares me."

Simi covered his hands with hers. "But you not a demon, akri-Thorny. You are decent."

Thorn wished he could believe her. But a decent person wouldn't have condemned his son. More than that, he made hard decisions every day. Who to save. Who to cut loose.

Who to damn.

Every one of them took its toll and made him want to lash out, more and more.

He didn't know how much longer he could hold on. Or even why he bothered. Humanity was heading to a dark place. Maybe he should just sign on with Adarian and let him know what was already in the works.

Damn humanity.

But as he felt Simi's hands on his, he wanted to fight for all those like her.

To make it one more day.

Because she believed in him when no one else did. When everything was bleak, she was there.

He wanted to be the man she saw him as. If someone as pure of heart thought he was worthy, maybe he wasn't so bad, after all.

Simi squeezed his hands. "You'll be fine, akri-Thorn. The Simi knows it."

He could listen to her lilting accent and happy tone all day. There was something so infectious about her. Something that made even the worst day better.

"Don't ever change, Simi."

"Don't plan to."

Good because he'd lived through enough changes. Some things should be immune from the cruelty of time. He wanted Simi to be one of them.

Ageless. Timeless.

Eternal.

Unlike other immortals he knew, she had never lost

her faith or her child-like enthusiasm. She was as bright-eyed now as she'd ever been.

Being with her reminded him briefly of times when he'd been optimistic.

He missed that boy who had been obnoxious and cock-sure. So blind to the future that was barreling down on him. Maybe that was why people had children. So that they could be reminded of a time when life had been worth living. When every day had been miraculous instead of a never-ending trudge that just led from one tragedy and disappointment to the next.

Though, to be honest, he couldn't remember a time when he'd ever felt as if life had been worth living. It was what had made him such a fierce warrior.

Put simply, he'd never cared if he lived or died. It made no never mind to him.

Now ...

He still didn't know why he bothered. Except that these little snatches of time spent with his handful of friends made it bearable. Made him forget what he'd done to his only child.

Please forgive me, Cadegan.

He deserved Cade's hatred, and he knew it.

Taking a drink, he watched the way Simi ate her food. With gusto as if she'd never eaten before, and yet she was older than he was. How did she manage to keep her enthusiasm?

That was the only thing he'd ever envied.

Simi's happiness over absolutely nothing.

It was adorable.

"Do you ever worry about the future, Sim?"

She looked up and frowned, then wiped her mouth on a napkin. "I only worry about losing friends and family. Akri says that to lose things is just a dang shame. Losing people who lives in your heart ... that's tragic. Simi agrees. So long as my peeps are okies, Simi's okies. Lucky I have friends and family with lots of powers. So, the Simi tries not to think about a tomorrow where one of them might not be here because that's just too painful."

Because hearts always grew bigger to accommodate new family and friends. He knew her philosophy.

"Don't ever leave me, Simi. I don't know what I'd do without you."

She smiled at him. "You sound like akri. Don't worry. The Simi's not going anywhere. I likes my eats. Love my akri and am pretty fond of Thorny-man." She winked. "But you got to promise the Simi something."

"Sure."

"Don't go evil, akri-Thorn. The Simi and your Hellchasers need you. Pay no never minds to them awful Necrodemians who think you're evil. They just can't see your real heart. The Simi sees it, and I know how hard you're fighting. You can do this. The Simi believes in you."

Thorn just prayed that would be enough to keep him from following in the steps of his father and the demons who wouldn't let him live in peace.

20

NOVEMBER 11, 1993

Thorn headed for the table at the Café Du Monde where Acheron sat in a chair across from Simi. Tourists crowded the outdoor restaurant where it was unseasonably warm, even for New Orleans.

Simi had a plate of beignets she was eating while Acheron scanned the crowd from behind a pair of opaque Oakley sunglasses.

The Atlantean god paused when he saw Thorn in the shadows.

Without a word, Thorn headed for them.

As soon as he neared the small round table, Simi looked up and gave him a smile that was enhanced by powdered sugar.

Thorn had to bite back a smile.

"What are you doing here?" Acheron asked.

"There's a disturbance in the Force, Obi-Wan. Have you felt it?"

Grimacing, Acheron rubbed his forehead with his middle finger. "There's always a disturbance in the Force, Luke. I've learned to tune it out."

"This one is important. The evil beings have found Adarian."

Acheron sat up straight. "Is he captured again?"

Thorn shook his head. "Adarian was supposed to die ... something's changed that."

"What do you mean?"

"You know what I mean. Something has disturbed the timeline. I've no idea who, what or, most importantly, why. We both know that Adarian's death is a definite Pith point. If it's been delayed, we need to find out who did and what motivated them to do so." Pith points were specific events set in the timeline that nothing could change. Someone, even a god, might attempt to prevent or erase them, such as the gods did with Acheron's birth when they ordained him killed.

All their efforts did was delay the inevitable Pith that said Acheron's birth would be the end of the Atlantean pantheon. In the end, they were destroyed and Acheron survived.

Pith point.

And as the Atlantean considered that, he actually paled. He went completely still for several minutes. Because Acheron had the ability to see all timelines simultaneously—variants of the human world play out—it took a lot of concentration to weed through them, and by the expression on his face, Thorn would guess that each outcome was horrific.

Thorn didn't envy him that headache. And though it was a power that seemed interesting on the surface, he had no interest in developing or possessing it.

"Do you see Adarian's son?" Thorn asked.

Acheron shook his head. "I see nothing. He doesn't have a son."

Interesting, because the one thing he knew from his father was that the young Malachai was alive. Cam had succeeded in breeding Adarian's replacement.

"Would you see his son if the Junior Malachai's fate is tied to yours?"

Acheron cursed. "Of course not. Jeez! What do you know?"

"Not as much as I wish I did. I'm just spit-balling."

Simi wiped at the sugar on her mouth. "Want the Simi to—"

"No!" they both snapped simultaneously.

She blew them a raspberry. "Why you both so nasty?"

"We don't want you hurt, Simi." Acheron's voice was stern but loving.

"Yeah, exactly. You're powerful, but I've had my butt kicked enough by the Malachai to know to keep my distance."

She lifted her chin defiantly. "Malachai are nothing compared to Charonte. My peeps used to feast on them and their entrails in war."

Acheron shook his head. "On their species, Simkey.

None of the Charonte ever went up against my mother's son or his direct descendants. They weren't allowed to."

"Okies, that's true. But is he that much stronger?"

"Yes," they spoke again in unison.

"Well," Ash said with a smirk. "At least we're on the sane page."

Thorn scowled. "You mean same page?"

"No. The sane one that says to keep out of this."

"It's the Malachai," Thorn said slowly and with emphasis.

"I heard you, and you know I won't interfere."

Acheron was so aggravating. While Thorn understood, he didn't. He knew firsthand how hard it was to be torn by competing forces, but there was only so much neutrality anyone could adhere to.

"One day, you're going to need to pick a side, Ash."

"I have a side." He glanced toward Simi. "And it never wavers."

"You say that, but we've both lived long enough to know better. The only thing in life that's ever certain is change. It's inevitable. You can avoid taxes. We know plenty of people who've given death a middle finger. But the one thing none of us have ever been able to stop ... Change. And when it comes about because we fought it, it's brutal."

21

APRIL 17, 2004

Thorn paused as he saw Simi sitting at the bar inside Sanctuary, nose deep in hot sauce-covered chocolate ice cream. For the first time in his memory, she wasn't laughing or happy.

Fury went through him. He'd tear the head off whoever daunted her feelings.

Forgetting about his errand, he headed straight for her.

"Hey, pretty demon. What has you down in your ice cream?"

Simi sighed heavily. "You ain't even gonna believe this, Thorny-man. Artemis done gone and saved the Simi's life."

Was she serious? "Do what?"

Sighing heavily, she looked up at him with eyes full of conflicted misery. "Don't get the Simi wrong, I still hate the heifer goddess. But the Simi cannot make peace in her noggin why the heifer goddess would do such a thing?"

"I do, Sim. In her own twisted way, Artie loves Acheron

and doesn't know how to show it. She saved you because he loves you. It was the least she could do."

Simi looked up and scowled at him. "How you know about akri and the heifer?"

Thorn silently cursed as he realized what he'd just let slip. "Acheron isn't as good at keeping secrets as he thinks. I have a lot of friends in low places."

"You mean akri-Shadow?"

He laughed that she'd caught on so fast. "Among others."

"I see."

An adorable blond human waitress came over to them. "You need anything, Simi?"

"No, Ms. Cherise. Simi's all good for now. Twelve scoops seems to be my limit."

Cherise smiled, then looked at Thorn. "What about you, sweetie? You need anything?"

"I'm good. I actually came to meet another friend. But thank you, Cherise."

"Let me know if you change your minds." She wandered off.

"You know about Cherise?" Simi asked.

"Know what about her?"

Simi bit her lip as she debated if she should tell akri-Thorn what she knew. Cherise's son, Nick Gautier, was the Malachai they were all looking for.

Only Nick's granddaddy had restricted his powers and shushed his memories and replaced them with others. Nick had no idea who or what he was.

At least not yet.

No one was exactly sure how Nick would react once his memories came back, either. They were hoping for the best. But when dealing with a Malachai ...

Sometimes things went wonky.

"What about her, Simi?"

"She the mother of Kyrian's Squire, Nick."

"Oh ... no, I had no idea. Really?"

Simi glanced over to where Cherise was talking to a couple in a booth, then whispered, "But she don't know about us. Shh!" She placed her finger to her lips. "Nicky don't want anyone to tell her about our world."

"I'll keep that in mind. Thanks for the warning." He patted her on the arm and walked off to keep his meeting.

Simi watched Thorny go until she saw Nick playing pool in the back with the tigerwere ... Wren. They did that a lot. Mostly 'cause Wren didn't interact with anyone other than the monkey, Marvin, that was sitting on Wren's shoulder while he played.

It kind of hurt her tender feelings that Nick didn't remember their friendship. But she understood. Sometimes it was necessary to put the welfare of others above even the Simi's.

She also caught sight of Nicky's granddaddy, Xev, in the shadows were he and his brother Caleb kept watch over their charge to make sure no one unwrapped their bindings on Nick's Malachai powers. Though that sounded quite painful to the Simi. She wouldn't want anyone to keep those kinds of secrets from her.

Or to restrict her powers.

They'd all gone through a lot together. The only thing that made it worthwhile was that she knew they'd be together again.

The whole merry fun crew.

She couldn't wait for that day. Because honestly, she missed her friends, and she would love to have them back.

22

AUGUST 18, 2004

"You've been keeping secrets, Thorny-man!"

Thorn jumped at the sound of Simi's voice. "Shit, Sim! Little warning please." He was on the curb outside of Karma Devereaux's house where he'd just dropped off a present.

Simi's eyes glowed a faint red in the darkness as she glanced to the shotgun house behind him. "You got another little boy..."

"Shh!" Thorn gestured for her to keep her tone low. "Tell no one, Sim. I don't want him to grow up like Cadegan did." Hated by others and persecuted. He wanted to give E.T. a chance at a normal life. "Karma knows I'm not human, and she's okay with that."

"You love her?"

"What? No. No! It was a one-time thing that just kind of happened. I'm still not really sure how." He'd been in town to check on his people when she'd shown up at Sanctuary. They'd exchanged some witty repartee and the next thing he'd known ...

Yeah, the encounter had been a mistake, but he'd never regret his kid.

Thankfully, Karma felt the same way he did.

"I had no idea she'd get pregnant and neither did she. E.T. thinks I'm her friend and he calls me Uncle. I'm good with that." At least sort of.

To be honest, he'd rather be a father to the boy, but given that E.T. was part human, it wasn't worth the risk. Thorn had too many enemies who would use his son to get back at him.

Even though E.T. was still a toddler, he had yet to show any signs of having powers. Which meant the boy might never be able to protect himself from those who wanted to strike back at Thorn.

It was a risk Thorn wouldn't take. Besides, Karma's insane family had their own abilities ... mostly because they were descended directly from two of his Hellchasers who'd been called Deadmen in the eighteenth century.

Which made him feel so much better. What Karma and her sisters thought were an "aunt" and "uncle" were actually the progenitors of the entire Devereaux side of their family.

Uncle Jake Devereaux had been one of his original Deadmen and their aunt, Esmeralda, was Sancha Delarosa who'd married Jake in the eighteenth century after they'd earned their freedom and moved here to New Orleans.

The sisters had no idea.

That was okay by him, too. He liked the fact that E.T. would grow up surrounded by all of them. They would be watching and notifying Thorn if anything or anyone threatened his child.

Especially since Sancha and Jake were the only two besides Karma and Simi who knew E.T. was his son.

And he intended to keep it that way.

Putting her arms behind her back, Simi swayed in a very adorable way. "Would akri-Thorn minds so much if the Simi played with the baby sometimes?"

"Only if you promise not to eat him ... He wouldn't taste good, even with barbecue sauce. He has too much of his dad in him for that. Sours the taste."

Laughing, Simi let her horns show for a second. Like her eyes earlier, they glowed a low luminescent red in the dim light.

For the first time, he realized how much she'd grown over the centuries. Gone was the little girl he'd met in the market and scared all those centuries ago.

Gah, she'd appeared not much older than E.T. when they had first met. And over the years, he hadn't really paid attention to her growing up as she aged so slowly while he didn't age at all.

Now ...

She was grown. Physically, she appeared around the same age as Acheron.

It was hard for him to acclimate the Simi he'd known then to the woman in front of him now. Yes, she could be immature, but that was her innocent spirit. And that enchanted him all the more.

Stop.

She was completely off-limits. Acheron would tear him to pieces if he ever thought Thorn had these ideas in his head. When it came to his daughter, Acheron was insane and Thorn couldn't blame him.

Without a word, she hopped past him, toward Karma's door.

"What are you doing, Simi?"

"Going to say happy birthday to your little one and akra-Karma."

"You know her?" Why was he even surprised? Simi seemed to know everyone.

She smiled at him. "'Course, Thorny-man. Karma is Tabitha and Amanda's sissy. The Simi meeted her long ago."

And with that, she went and knocked on the door.

Thorn stood there, not sure what to think. Other than the fact that Simi was absolutely adorable.

Dangerously so.

And he needed to go take a long, cold shower before Acheron started ripping parts off his body he might miss.

23

CHRISTMAS 2004

Dressed like one of Santa's elves in a red Santa shirt with a short red miniskirt, and her favorite pair of scuffed-up black combat boots, Simi danced around the poor sick children in the hospital, singing Christmas Carols with them.

Akri sat on the floor, surrounded by children while he played his black guitar and sang chorus to the Simi's lead. They were right in the middle of *Put a Little Love in Your Heart* when she saw a tall, dark-haired man in the doorway.

At first, she thought he was Nicky until she realized that this was the Dark-Hunter akri had met a while back.

Jamie Gallagher. A former gangster in one of them big cities. Chicago, if she remembered correctly.

But he wasn't stationed here in New Orleans, so she couldn't imagine what had brought him here now.

Back in the 1930s gangster days, the poor man had been betrayed and then shot dead on his way to the hospital while his wife was having their baby.

She still remembered how sad akri had been on that day when he went to meet Gallagher for the first time after he became a Dark-Hunter. He'd felt so terrible for him.

And so did she. No one should die before they gots to see their simi. Just as no simi should ever lose a parent.

It was obvious by the Dark-Hunter's pained expression that the sight of all these babies upset him. No doubt he was thinking of the night he died.

Akri had his back to Gallagher and couldn't see the bemused expression on his face.

The nice, wonderful doctor lady came up behind Gallagher and smiled at Simi while she sang. "Now there's a sight you don't see every day, huh? Two punked-out Goths throwing a Christmas party for sick children."

Those words amused Simi. Dr. Wilson said that about them to everyone she saw. Simi wasn't sure why, but she enjoyed the fact the doctor thought they were strange.

"You've no idea," Gallagher said to the doctor.

She smiled. "I have to admit it took me some getting used to them when I started working here a few years ago. I thought the higher ups were joking when they first told me about the Goth Guardian Angel and his children's fund."

Gallagher arched a brow at the nickname. "So he comes here a lot?"

Yes, they did. It'd been something she and akri had done for as long as Simi could remember.

But not always this hospital. There were lots of them that they visited.

The doctor nodded. "Every few months or so. He always brings gifts for the children and staff and then plays with the kids for a while."

Gallagher appeared stunned by something that was second nature for akri. "Really?"

"Oh yeah. We figure he must be some rich kid with a need to do some good. The darnedest thing is whenever he comes, the kids become perfectly calm and serene. Their blood pressure goes down, and we never have to give them any painkillers while he's here. After he leaves, they sleep comfortably for hours. And best of all, the cancer patients go into remission. I don't know what it is about that young man, but he really makes a difference in their lives."

That's because the doctor didn't know akri was a god who cared about others.

And so did she.

The minute akri realized he was being watched by one of his Dark-Hunters, the light went out of his precious eyes. The humor faded and akri stiffened noticeably into that grim, take-no-prisoners leader that he always appeared as to his Dark-Hunter soldiers.

Still, he continued to play the guitar so that Simi could finish her song.

But once she was done, akri handed his guitar off to one of the older children on the floor and excused himself.

He stood up and left the room with a loose long-limbed, predatorial gait that made everyone around him so nervous. Akri's face was unreadable as he crossed his arms over his chest and approached Gallagher.

Simi stayed inside the room and showed the boy akri had given the guitar to how to play a couple of basic chords. While she was doing that, the cutest little toddler boy came over and squatted on her lap.

"Hello, little simi."

He smiled up at her. "Jingle bells?"

She laughed at the sweet cherub who kept saying that. So she began to sing it for him.

Simi didn't know why, but she really loved this baby. He was always so very sweet and cuddly.

Once akri was in the hallway and while she played with the baby, Gallagher let out a snide laugh. "St. Ash, who knew?"

Akri ignored his comment. "What are you doing here?"

Gallagher shrugged. "I was just passing through."

Cocking his head, akri grimaced. "Passing through? Last time I checked Chicago was north of Baton Rouge, not south."

"I know. But since I was so close, I just wanted to stop in at Sanctuary and wish everyone a Merry Christmas before I headed home."

As they talked, Simi remembered that this was the Dark-Hunter who'd broked their code last summer when his wife had died of old age. Against all their rules, he'd gone to see her.

Akri had been furious. So much so that they'd gone to him immediately so that akri could have words with Gallagher.

Only once they got there and akri saw how upset the Dark-Hunter was, he'd calmed down and decided to overlook the breach.

While akri may not have ever loved a human woman, he understood how hard it was to lose what you loved. And that always softened his heart.

Just like now. She saw the anger leave akri's eyes. "Tell you what, since you're here, why don't you just stay on until after the New Year?"

Gallagher scoffed at that. "I don't need your pity."

"It's not pity. It's an order. Since Kyrian retired, Talon could use an extra hand. Things get rather rowdy this time of year. Lots of Daimons head down south where it's warmer and people are out for New Year's."

Gallagher's gaze turned suspicious. "Are you full of crap or what?"

Simi came out into the hallway where they were, with the little boy, Ben, on her hip.

He was such a doll that she had one important question. "Akri, can I keep little Ben?" She patted the plump leg that was exposed from beneath his hospital gown. "See, he good eating. Lots of fat on this one."

Ben laughed at her teasing because he knew Simi would never really feast on someone so young. Especially him because he was so sweet.

"No, Simi," akri said sternly. "You can't keep the baby. His mother would miss him."

She pouted. "But he want to go home with the Simi. He said so."

"I do! I do!"

"No, Simi," akri repeated.

Simi huffed at him. "No Simi, no food. Nag, nag, nag. Does your daddy nag you too?" she asked the boy.

"Nope," he said as he pulled at one of the black-and-red horns on top of her head.

Akri sighed. "Simi, take the baby back inside."

Irritated, she moved to stand in front of her akri. It was time to pay him back for being so mean to her. "Okay, gimme a kiss and I'll go."

He looked extremely uncomfortable as he glanced at Gallagher, then back at her. "Not in front of the Hunter, Simi."

Shaking her head, she rolled her eyes at the Dark-Hunter. "The Simi wants a kiss, akri. I'll wait all century. You know I will."

To say he looked peeved was an understatement. He leaned over and kissed her quickly on the brow.

Simi beamed proudly, then trotted off with her newfound baby to sing another round of *Jingle Bells*. Even so, she could plainly hear the men in the hallway.

"Who is that?" Gallagher asked. "Or should I say, *what* is that?"

Akri's gaze turned angry. "In short, she's not your

concern." He rubbed his hand over his forehead as if he were in pain. "Where were we?"

"I asked why you were giving me temporary duty in New Orleans."

"Because Talon could use a hand," he repeated.

"I wonder what Talon would say?"

"He would tell you not to piss me off."

Gallagher gave a half laugh at that. "All right then. I'll take it under advisement."

Akri turned so that he could watch his Simi. "You can camp with the Peltiers at Sanctuary. Right now, I better go and help her before one of those kids ends up on a milk carton."

Simi snorted at his humor as she set Ben down and picked up an adorable little girl who wanted to dance with her while she sang.

Akri quickly took the girl away while the Dark-Hunter wandered off.

"What's he doing here, akri?"

"His great-granddaughter is in the hospital, and he's breaking rules again."

Simi widened her eyes. "What?"

Akri sighed. "Her friend was attacked, and Jamie saved her. They're about to meet even though I know they shouldn't." He brushed his hand through his long hair. "That's the hardest part for the Dark-Hunters. So long as they have direct descendants still living, it haunts them. And it's hard for them to resist the urge to check in on their family, even though it hurts them."

"You're not going to punish him?"

Akri shook his head. "You don't understand human pain, Simkey. It's horrible to lose what you love. I won't hold it against him. He deserves to be able to say goodbye to her."

That was why she loved her akri. His heart was one of the kindest she'd ever met. He always thought of others.

And she would keep an eye out for Mr. Gallagher because akri was right. No one should long for their family and not be able to talk to them. She couldn't imagine anything worse.

THREE DAYS *later*

LEAVING one of her favorite restaurants that had closed early, Simi was on her way to Sanctuary for their annual Christmas party when she saw Gallagher walking down Chartres.

Poor human. He looked terribly despondent. Kind of how she felt whenever she ate too much and there was still more good eats left that wouldn't fit in her belly.

Kind of like now.

It was Christmas Eve and the last thing she wanted was to see someone so sad on what was supposed to be one of the bestest holidays.

Obviously, he needed a friend.

"Hel-lo!"

He paused at the sound of her voice. Turning around, he scowled as she approached him. "Hi."

Simi bounced up to him. "What'cha doing out here all alone? Did you forget how to find Sanctuary?" Because he was headed in the opposite direction.

"No. I wanted to be alone for a bit."

That was terribly sad. She cocked her head and frowned. "Why? Were the bears mean to you? Mama can get a bit cranky whenever I play with the cubs. She thinks I'm going to eat one, but bleh! They're way too hairy. Now if she'd let me skin one first, the Simi might be interested."

He laughed. "Are you joking?"

"Oh no. I never joke about hairy food. It's disgusting." She looked up at him. "If they weren't mean to you then why did you leave when they have a party going on?"

"I don't know. I guess I didn't feel right being there."

That made no sense to her whatsoever. While Mama Lo could be a beast at times, the bears as a whole were wonderful. And so were the Dark-Hunters and others who came every year for the big bear party. "Why?"

He shrugged, then changed the subject. "What are you doing out here by yourself?"

"Not much. Akri is off with that red-headed demon, so he said the Simi could go play just so long as I don't eat nothing not cooked by a human. But all my favorite places are closed now, so I thought I'd go find the bears and see if Jose, since he's human, would make me up something good that wouldn't make akri mad if I ate it."

"Akri is Ash?"

It always amused her when others were confused by that. "Yes."

"And the red-headed demon?"

How could he not know who that was? "Artemis the bitch goddess. You know her. She's the one who stole your soul."

"She didn't steal it."

Pfft on that. Akri said that was all the heifer goddess ever did was steal the souls of desperate people.

So Simi blew him a raspberry. "Of course she did. She steals everything."

Standing up on her tiptoes, she stared into his dark brown eyes.

"Hey," she said, taking his chin in her hand so that she could move his head back and forth while she examined him. "You're hurting in there. That would make akri very sad. He doesn't like for his Dark-Hunters to hurt, and the Simi don't like it when akri is sad. Why are you hurt?"

"I miss my family."

That she completely understood, and it made her heart ache that he knew her pain.

Releasing him, she nodded sympathetically. "I miss mine too. My mama was good people. 'Simi' she would say, 'I love you.' Akri loves me too."

"I'm sure he does."

With a smile, Simi tilted her head down so that he could see her horns which were covered by her bestest gift.

"See, akri even gave me hornay warmers so my horns wouldn't get cold. You want some hornay warmers too?"

The look on his face said that this had to be the oddest conversation of his life. "I don't have horns."

"You want some?" she asked hopefully. "I could give you some real colorful ones. Akri has some black ones, but he doesn't let other people see them."

"Ash has horns?"

"Oh my, yes. They are quite lovely. Not as lovely as mine, but they are still very nice. The Simi would say she hopes you see them, but if you ever did, you'd be dead, and I think the Simi would miss you. You seem very nice, too."

And that made her want to make him happy.

She knew just the thing. Biting her lip, she rummaged around in her giant, over-sized, beaded purse that held the presents she'd brought for those at Sanctuary.

There were so many ...

Hmm. She knew the one she wanted, she just couldn't find it.

And then she did. Smiling, she pulled out an oven mitt that looked like a fish. Perfect!

She handed it to him. "That is quality. From QVC. My favorite place. Do you watch QVC?"

His frown deepening, he shook his head. "No."

"Well, you should. Akri says I watch it too much, but he never complains when I shop there. They like me, too. Put me on television and call me Miss Simi. I like that."

He handed her the fish back.

"Oh no, that's for *you*. Presents make people happy. The Simi wants you to be happy."

And still he looked a bit confused by her present. "Thank you, Simi."

"No need to thank me. See that's what families do. They take care of each other."

His eyes darkened with sadness. "I no longer have a family. I had to give them up."

Simi tsked at his untrue words. "Of course you have a family, Gallagher. Everyone has family. I'm your family. Akri your family. Even that smelly old goddess is your family. She's that creepy old aunt who comes around but nobody likes her, so they make fun of her when she's gone."

He laughed again. "Does Artemis know you say that about her?"

"Of course. The Simi say it to her face all the time. That's why akri told me to come play while he's with her. He don't like it when we fight." She took his hand into hers. "Now listen and I'll tell you what akri once told me. We have three kinds of family. Those we are born to. Those who are born to us and those we let into our hearts. I have let you into my heart, so the Simi is your family, and she won't give you up. If you are sad right now, then I'm thinking your family is still in your heart, too, and they are taking up so much room that you have no room for anyone else."

His lips trembled. "I can't give them up."

"And you shouldn't. Ever. No one should ever forget

those they love. But it's like with QVC—whenever the Simi fill up my room with too much stuff, akri builds me another room. Somehow there's always space for more. Your heart can always expand to take in as many people as you need it to. The people who live there, they don't go away. You just make room for one more person and then another and another and another. See how easy?"

With her arm in his, Simi walked him down the street. "Don't you want Simi to be your family?"

He paused as if he was thinking.

Simi leaned forward and whispered loudly, "This is the part where you say, 'Yes, Simi, I would like to be your family.' 'Cause if you don't then I'll have to take my mitt back and barbecue you. Akri is still upset about the last Dark-Hunter I barbecued and that was... oh, a thousand or so years ago. He part elephant when it comes to remembering things. So tell me, do you want Simi to be your family?"

Nodding, he smiled. "Yes, Simi, I would like to be your family."

She beamed. "Good. You're such a smart Dark-Hunter."

Without another word, Simi led him to Sanctuary.

She opened the swinging door and stood back, waiting for him to enter. Loud music thumped as they entered the bar and grill. There were four hawks lined up on one curtain rod, dancing in time to the rocking Christmas carols the Howlers—all in human form—were singing while Dev Peltier played the piano. A white tiger was lying on its back on the sofa while Marvin the monkey jumped up and down on its belly.

Aimee Peltier, who was in her large bear body, was feeding two baby cubs peanut butter sandwiches. Tabitha Devereaux, a red-headed woman with a scar on her face came up to them and grabbed Simi into a hug. "Hey little demon, where's boss man?"

Simi shrugged. "He off attending to Lord Queen Pain-In-My-Butt. How are you, Tabitha? Is your sister and Kyrian coming?"

"No, they'll be here tomorrow. Morning sickness hit Amanda as they were leaving, but Talon said he'd be here just as soon as he could."

Tabitha pulled her away from the Dark-Hunter so that they could do what Tabby called "girl chat."

Simi looked back to see Gallagher watching the revelry. There were all kinds of Were-Hunters, Dark-Hunters, demons, humans and even a Daimon.

All enemies and yet, for this one special night, they were all being friendly and nice. Because they were bound by something other than blood.

They were bound together by their hearts.

And Simi smiled as Colt, another bear Were-Hunter, went up to Gallagher. Unlike the other bears, he wasn't family per se. Rather the Peltiers had taken him in after his mother had been murdered.

He'd been here ever since.

With a cocky grin, Colt pulled a pineapple mitt out of his back pocket. "Man, Gallagher, you must really rate. You got one of the good fish. All I got was a lousy pineapple."

Simi laughed.

Gallagher scowled at his words. "Does she give one to everyone she meets?"

"Nope. Only family."

That was right. Simi only gave them to her family.

And that was everyone here.

They were one big, giant dysfunctional family that fought at times. But in the ends, they could always count on each other.

24

JANUARY 23, 2006

Standing in the throne room in Katateros, Simi stared at the other demon suspiciously as she moved her head back and forth, trying to believe what they'd told her. Akri-Lexi had brought another Charonte home along with a ghosty named Danger.

The Charonte's skin was marbled red and black, and she had yellow eyes. Simi looked at her closely as she tried to remember all those centuries ago when she'd been just a little demon.

Simi frowned at her akri. "What do you mean, she's my sister?"

With tears in her eyes, the Charonte stepped toward her. "Xiamara, do you not—"

Simi cut her off. "I am the Simi. Xiamara is my mother." Surely her sissy should know that?

Shouldn't she? If she was her sissy, she would!

Unsure of what to think for sure, Simi approached her

slowly and poked at her arm. It'd just been so very long since she last saw one of her people. Could this really be her sissy? "You look real."

Her lips quivered. "I am real."

That made the Simi angry. How could she be real and be her sister and leave her alone all this time? "Then why did you not come see me?"

"I couldn't. The bitch goddess wouldn't let me."

"Artemis?" Simi squealed. "The Simi hates her!"

"No," Xirena corrected, "the other bitch-goddess, Apollymi."

"Hey!" Simi snapped in synchrony with her akri.

Xirena looked even more confused.

Angry that this Charonte would dare disparage the one who'd given her such a wonderful akri, she glared at her. "She a goddess, that Apollymi. Don't you ever call her such a name! She always good to the Simi. She makes me hornay warmers to keep my hornays warm and she gives me lots of cookies when the Simi comes sees her."

Xirena's jaw dropped. "She does what? When have you been in Kalosis?"

Simi put her hands on her hips. "You heard me, deaf demon. She a good lady, that Apollymi, and the Simi will hurt anyone who says otherwise."

Xirena stepped forward and whispered loudly, "Will your akri let me talk to you alone?"

Simi blew a raspberry and waved her hand. "My akri don't control me. More times than not, he do what his Simi says. Mosty withs no complaints."

Xirena appeared horrified by her words. "He's your akri! Mind your tone!"

Simi blew her another raspberry. "He's my daddy."

"He's your akri," she said from between clenched fangs.

As if she knew anything about akris.

Looking at her akri, she scowled. "There's something seriously wrong with the Simi's sister. Why she keep saying you my lord and master when you're just my daddy, akri?"

He shrugged. "I have no idea, Simkey. You need to set her straight."

"Hmm." Simi considered that sharp barking. That rang bell as she remembered her sissy all the time fussy at her.

For everything.

Maybe this Charonte was her sissy.

If that was true …

Simi wrapped her arm around her sister's shoulders and led her over to the corner where she had her own television monitors. "See, in this world, Xirena, the Simi does what she wants and akri, he say, 'Okay, Simi, whatever you want, Simi.' Unless it involves eating people. Then he usually says no, but that's the only time. Other than that, he do what the Simi says. See how that works?"

Xirena appeared completely baffled by her words.

Simi popped her head up to look at her akri. "Where she staying now?"

"You could share a room with—"

"No," Simi said immediately as she realized what her akri was about to do. "The Simi don't share her room, akri.

Ever. You know this. I don't care that she is my sissy. My room has all my special mementos in there. I think you should make her one of her own."

The smile on his face said that her akri knew better than to argue with his demon. "Okay. Where do you want me to put her?"

She thought about it for a few minutes. "Kind of next to the Simi's room, but not so close that she blocks the view to my Travis Fimmel billboard that the Simi has on the great wall."

Xirena appeared horrified. "Your what? What's a Travis Fimmel?"

Simi's jaw dropped as she looked stunned. "You don't know about Travis Fimmel? Oh, sissy, you are deprived. He the finest man alive."

Xirena shuddered. "What have they done to you? You lust for men?"

"Well, I don't lust for women. They okay and all, if that's what you want, but that's not the Simi's interest."

"No," Xirena corrected, "I mean, you lust for humans?" The way she said those words sounded like it was the most horridest thing her sissy could imagine.

But Simi couldn't even begin to understand that. "Well, don't you?"

"Ew!" Xirena looked at akri. "What have you done to her? You have corrupted a perfectly good demon!" She looked back at Simi. "You need to see Drakus."

Drakus? "Who that?"

"He the finest Charonte demon to ever live. He can breathe fire out his nose and mouth at the same time."

That did sound like fun. The Simi could only imagine something so beautonius! "Ooo!"

Akri cleared his throat to get their attention. "Simi's too young for that."

"No, she's not," her sissy said in unison with her.

Akri-Lexi laughed. "I think you're outnumbered, boss."

Akri turned to see Alexion behind him. The ghosty Dark-Hunter, Danger, was entering the room just behind him.

He sighed as Alexion stopped beside him. "Forget Armageddon, this is the scariest thing I've ever seen. Two Charonte in one room."

Ignoring her akri, Simi took her sissy so that they could sits and compare notes on "hot" men and male demons. She wanted to know lots more about this Charonte that apparently were still around.

Okies, she'd be mad at Apollymi for that later.

Right now, she just wanted to hear more.

Akri-Lexi turned to Danger and smiled. "I think it's a good thing we have a woman in the house now. Maybe she can talk some sense into them."

Danger snorted. "The demons are your domain, not mine. I'm not even going there."

Akri actually whimpered as Xirena began telling the Simi so much about the correct mating habits of the Charontes. "This is going to get ugly. Thanks, Lex."

Simi rolled her eyes and ignored them completely.

This was her sissy! She wasn't alone anymore. It felt glorious to know that there were more of them.

She didn't know why akra had lied to her. It hurt so much to think about, but she wasn't going to hold a grudge.

Akri had given her the most wondrous life any demon could have hoped for. She would never faults her akri.

Especially given how much love she felt in her heart right now.

What was it that akri was always saying? Sometimes things had to go wrong so that they could go right.

This felt right, so she was willing to let it go and hold no grudges against anyone.

She had her sissy, her akri and friends.

What more could any demon want?

25

Furious, Thorn wanted to tear the wings off every demon in Azmodea.

"The Malachai?!"

Misery, his demon assistant, shrank away. "Are you all right, my lord?"

Of course not. He was vibrating with fury.

"Get out of my sight."

She vanished instantly.

Pain lacerated his heart. He hadn't held this much raw agony since he'd been forced to lock Cadegan away. How could this have happened?

He wanted to rip the head off Acheron particularly. How many times had he told the Atlantean to watch Simi?

But no ...

Ash knew best. He listened to no one.

Imbecile!

As Thorn threw his glass into the roaring fire, he felt

that familiar presence behind him. The one that normally comforted him, but today ...

He winced in excruciating pain. "What are you doing here, Simi?"

"I felt your achy heart, Thorny, and the Simi was worried. Has something happened to hurts you again?"

"Yes." He couldn't bring himself to look at her right now. Although they should be thanking her.

She'd caused Acheron to uncover and eliminate the new Malachai. At least until Artemis ignorantly brought the Malachai back to life because she thought she was doing Acheron a favor.

Oh the humanity.

Nick Gautier.

It explained so much. Why Acheron had always held such an affinity for the kid. Why no one could see Nick's future.

Damn you, Cam. She was the reason *this* had happened. Normally, the Malachai was a monster, easily spotted. One everyone knew to avoid and run from.

Nick was a good kid who hid the most frightening powers in the universe. Who would have ever suspected?

Cam had succeeded in one thing she'd set out to do. Nick was unlike any of his predecessors. Because of his innocent and loving mother, Nick understood love. Compassion.

Decency.

He wasn't a ruthless killing machine out to spread as much misery on others as he could.

But it didn't change the fact that Nick Gautier was the Ambrose Malachai.

The Malachai.

Simi walked up to Thorn and put her hand on his shoulder. "Can the Simi help you?"

Her touch broke him. It reached far beyond the physical and brought out the demon inside. The transition was so powerful and unexpected that it shocked them both.

"Why did you do it, Sim? What possessed you?"

She paled at his question. "Not you, too, Thorny. The Simi's already heard it all from akri. I was just curious. That's all. My sissy has gone on and on about how the Simi in't an itsy girl any mores. The Simi's all grown now."

Yes, she was. And like Acheron, he hated it. He missed that innocent little Simi who'd laughed when he tried to scare her.

In a life of brutality and agony, Simi had been the only pure angel to cull the misery of his life. The balm he and Acheron relied on.

But she was no longer that innocent little girl.

Simi stepped around him so that she could look up into his eyes. "Akri has been so upset at his Simi. Please don't be mads, too. The Simi didn't means to hurts so many 'cause she was curious about it."

Nodding, Thorn pulled her into his arms for a hug. "I would never hurt you, Simi. I'm sorry. It's selfish of me and isn't any of my business." The gods knew he hadn't been celibate.

But for some reason, this cut him to his bones. No one was supposed to touch their Simi. Never.

She hugged him close. "All good, Thorny-man. The Simi still loves you."

And he still loved her. "I don't know what I'd do without you, Simi. You've been with me for so long ... My best friend."

She pulled back to smile up at him. "You're mine, too. I don't ever want to lose my Thorny-man. So are we still on to sees our movie this weekend?"

Thorn laughed at her question. He hated movies. They bored him to tears, and yet he watched them at least twice a month with Simi because she loved them so much. "Sure. I'll start taking up a collection for the popcorn. Is Xirena coming?"

"Probably. Sissy likes to comes if there's free eats."

"Then I shall look forward to it." After all, those excursions were the highlight of his dreary existence.

Simi left and Thorn felt her absence like a physical ache in his chest.

She was a woman now. He still wasn't sure what to think about that. While she seemed the same, she wasn't.

Things always changed.

And he hated it.

His only comfort was that Nick was banished to Savitar's island. Because right now, Malachai or not, if Thorn had to look at the boy, he'd probably beat the crap out of that Cajun. Score one for Acheron for beating him to it.

It probably saved Thorn's life.

SIMI HEADED BACK to the temple in Katateros. Xirena was still watching QVC while akra-Danger and akri-Lexi lay on the couch with each other.

Akri wasn't here, and for once, she was glad. While she still loved her akri more than anything, he'd been in a terrible mood since he found out about her and Nick.

It made no logical sense.

And honestly, she was perturbed or preturbed or whatever turbed it was by his actions.

After all, the problem with Charonte was that they could take any form they wanted. It wasn't until her sissy came that Simi had realized she wasn't a little girl and allowed herself to show her real Charonte age. She'd been trapped in that form longer than she should have because no one had been around to remind her that she wasn't a girl demon anymore.

Because it made akri happy for her to be his little girly demon. And while she loved to make akri happy, she didn't want to sacrifice herself for it, either.

Why couldn't everybody be happy? Growing up was supposed to be a good thing. No one had ever warned her just how hard it was.

How confusing.

Most of all, they's never told the Simi that growing up would be harder on those around her than it was on her herself.

"Akra-Danger?"

The beautiful red-headed ghosty looked at her. "You want something to eat?"

Simi shook her head. "Do you think the Simi's selfish?"

Gasping, akra-Danger stood up immediately. "What? No! Why would you ask such a thing? Of course you're not selfish!"

Simi wasn't so sure about that. Because akri's pain made her feel like she'd put herself first over him. She'd never meant to do that. Had she any idea how akri would overreact, she'd have never slept with Nicky.

She'd not even thought about him being the Malachai. Just that he a longtime friend. That had made him seem safe.

But boy had she angered everyone around her.

What a giant mess.

"Is akri still mad at me?"

Akra-Danger wrapped her in a hug. "He's not mad at you, *ma petite*. He's afraid."

That only confused her more. "Afraid of what?"

"That you'll succumb to the curse his aunt put on him when he was born human. Acheron is terrified you won't be able to resist him now and that you'll want to sleep with him too."

Simi screwed her face up and bared her fangs at the very gross thought. "That's disgusting! Ew!" Jumping around the room, she made all kinds of noises as she visibly cringed. "The Simi would *never* find her akri attractive. I mean ... he cute. Not Travis Fimmel or demon cute. But he's cuter than most. People tend to notice and watch him. But not the Simi! Not ever! Ew!" She was so grossed out, she might never eat again.

Okies, that was not trued at all. She could always eat, but still.

Ew! Ew! Ew! She couldn't stop saying that one word at the thought of being attracted to akri.

Laughing, akri-Lexi shook his head. "Remind me to tell that to Ash when he comes back. He definitely doesn't need to worry about Simi chasing him around the sofa."

Leave it to her akri to be so stupid about stupid things. Though she understood. It'd happened to him before when a little girl he loved grewd up and had made a pass at him. That had traumatized her akri. But those were with human people.

Not Charonte. They were different beasts entirely and the last thing she'd ever want to do is bed down with her akri.

Yuck! Yuck! Yuck!

Still grossed out, Simi left them and went to her room so that she could be alone for a bit and try to do something to get the awful thought of out her mind before it made her vomit.

Pulling her cat to her, she kissed its head and sighed. "The Simi is so sad, Cat. I don't like being sad." Most people didn't. She'd hurt those she loved and hadn't meant to do it.

No wonder akri-Savitar stayed on his island. That way, he knew he'd never cause harm to anyone. She'd just wanted a new experience.

Akri was right.

Growing up sucked, and she wished she never had. Why couldn't she stay a little demon? What was the point of being an adult?

When she'd been little, she'd thought it would give her more freedom.

It didn't. Just more responsibilities and more people to watch out for. As a child, others were quick to help.

That stopped with adultness. No one was eager to step in anymore. They wanted her to handle it on her own and then got mad at her when she did.

Yet she still felt as confuzzled by life as she always had.

For the first time ever, Simi wasn't looking forward to anything. She just wanted peace.

The only problem was, she didn't know how to get it.

"Why we coming to an old stupid club, akri? The Simi wants to shop."

Without a word of response, akri led Simi and Xirena toward the building at the corner of the block. It looked like all the other buildings in New Orleans ... basically.

"Well, Simi, it's a special club."

"Special how?" Xirena asked irritably. Like Simi, she wanted to shop and eats. "Is there food there?"

That was why she loved her sissy. She thought just like Simi did. Belly first.

Akri nodded. "Pretty sure it does since the name of it is Club Charonte."

Stunned, Simi stopped in the middle of the sidewalk to gape. "Did akri buy his Simi a club?"

"No, I didn't."

Well, that didn't make sense. "Then how did it get named that?"

"You'll see." Akri gently tugged her forward.

Simi and her sissy picked up their pace as they neared the club that wasn't open for business at this time of night. Also weird that akri would bring her here before it opened.

A screaming pink neon sign flashed *Club Charonte* over the door.

Akri used his powers to unlock the door before he led them inside. The moment he did, Xirena let out an ear-piercing shriek. "Xedrix!" She ran across the room to tackle a tall dark-haired man to the floor.

When she did, he changed to a swirling blue-skinned Charonte for a few seconds before he turned human again.

Could it be? Was it possible?

No ...

Still not sure, Simi scowled. "Is that the Simi's Xedrix, akri?"

He nodded with a smile. "Yes, Simkey, it's your brother."

Simi bit her lip but was more cautious as she went toward her siblings. She didn't know really what to think. Her brother looked so different than how she remembered his human form. Not that she'd seen it often. It was a game they'd played when she was little. One that was supposed to teach her how to hide among the humans who were afraid of them.

Xedrix was trying to push Xirena off, but the moment he saw Simi, he froze.

"Xiamara?" he breathed.

Tears filled her eyes. "Rik-rik?"

His human body changed immediately back to his demon form as he shot out from under Xirena to pull Simi against his chest and hug her tight. "You're alive! I can't believe it. I thought for sure that you were long gone."

Simi wrapped her arms around him and squealed. "Rik-rik! I've missed you so much."

Tears flowed down her cheeks as her brother rocked her like he used to. "What are you doing here, Rik-rik?"

"We broke free from Kalosis and the portal closed before we could go home. We're trapped here with the humans."

Laughing, Simi looked at her akri and smiled. She could tell he made the other Charonte demons in the bar nervous, including her Rik-rik. Since they were servants of the Atlantean gods, and Apollymi in particular, it made them servants to akri as well.

"Akri won't hurt you, big bro. He a good god."

Xedrix was still suspicious. He leaned down to whisper in her ear, "You know the Atlantean gods still own us, right?"

Technically, maybe. But akri wasn't like that. "Poo! Akri would never do that, especially not to us."

"She's right, Xedrix. I didn't believe her at first, either. But akri is a good akri. I've been very happy living with them."

Still looking uncertain, Xedrix held her hand. "Come ... both of you. You have to meet my wife."

Simi gasped. "You gots married? No!"

Nodding, Xedrix took them to a tiny blond demon who was beautiful and very obviously pregnant.

"And a baby!" Simi was excited excepting for one thing that caused her to draw up short. "You know she not a Charonte, right?"

Xedrix laughed. "Yes. I know. She's a Dimme demon. She came here for protection, and I've been in love with her ever since."

That made Simi's heart soar. Her brother had love in his heart and a little baby to come out soon. "Now we need to find a good mate for our sissy."

The way Xirena was looking at the other male Charonte, Simi could tell her sissy didn't need much encouragement. She looked like she might already have one or two in mind.

Xirena leaned in to whisper to Simi, "We'll find you a suitable one too."

As Simi looked over them, she realized that she wasn't attracted to them. They was okies, but they didn't make her heart speed up the way akri-Thorn did whenever he came to check on her.

Or yell at her.

What is wrong with me? How could she enjoy someone yelling at her? Maybe 'cause he'd been so adorably frustrated when he did so.

No. There was something wrong with her.

She needed more food and barbecue or hot sauce.

Something definitely wasn't right. No one liked to be yelled at.

And she had hated being the only Charonte. Now she wasn't. She had plenty of them in this club, and while she was happy she'd get to speak to them about demon things and practice even more Charonte talking, she would rather visit with Thorn in his dark, dismal castle.

That would be stupid though. Especially after what akri had done to Nick …

Akri would kill Thorny. Beat himself senseless if he had any idea Simi liked her god-demon.

No, she could never chance it. Besides, Thorny treated her the same way akri did.

The Simi was hands-off.

And that just made her feel all the more isolated and lonely.

Simi sat on akri-Styxx's bedroll in his tent, waiting patiently for him to feed his animals and return inside. She shouldn't be here with akri's twin brother, but given the way she'd treated him before, she had to come back and apologize.

Styxx wasn't the awful monster man she'd thought him to be. And he was akri's twin. Family was important.

Even family they was sometimes mad at.

The moment Styxx returned inside his tent, he froze. Not that she blamed him. The last time she'd met akri's copy had been terrible. She'd been furious because akri-copy had hurt her akri.

He'd stabbed her akri in the heart and almost kilted him.

So, she'd done what she was supposed to. She'd made akri-Copy pay, only to learn that things weren't always what she thought.

There had been a lot more to akri-Styxx than just bad actions. He actually loved her akri enough to risk his life for him. He'd gone and saved akri's wife and almost gotten kilted by the bad Daimons.

All to help a brother who was mad at him.

That made her feel terrible for what she'd done, and she wanted to make it up to akri-copy.

Though the suspicion in his steely blue eyes said that it might not be possible. He was very cautious about Simi and why she'd come.

Moving as slowly as he could, he put his hand on the .38 he kept in a holster at the base of his spine which she found amusing. A human weapon wouldn't hurt her. It'd only make her very angry.

Akri even more so.

So, she smiled, trying to make him understand that she had no intention of harming him. "Hello, akri-copy."

His gaze narrowed on her. "What do you want?"

Feeling awful, she sighed heavily. "The Simi come to say she sorry for what she did to you. But see, you hurt my akri and the Simi loves her akri so anyone who attacks her akri gets eat, even those who look like akri, see?"

His expression said that he didn't.

She stood up.

Akri-copy immediately backed away.

Well, this was just awful. He wasn't really listening. He was too busy being scared. Akri was right. She needed to think more before she acted.

Cocking her head, Simi frowned. "You look so strange like that. Why you wear eye makeup, akri-copy?"

He shrugged. "Protects my eyes from the sun."

"That's why you gets sunglasses, silly. Don't nobody tell you that?" She bent down and picked up her red heart-shaped backpack that had black demon wings spanning out from it. She wrinkled her nose at him. "Itn't it cute? Akra-Danger gived it to me at Christmas. Now less see ..." She rummaged around until she pulled out a bottle of barbecue sauce with a ribbon tied around it. "Happy birthday, akri-copy!"

When he didn't move to take it, her smile faded. She stepped toward him, and he quickly took two steps back.

Her shoulders and wings dropped as she pouted. "Why you so skittish of the Simi?"

"I don't know. Call me stupid, but the last time we met, you killed me."

Her wings drooped even more as shame and regret filled her heart. "I know. It was wrong to do that to you. But that was before you saved akri and akra-Tory and gave Baby Bas his horse he loves to play with. So, the Simi glad you didn't stay dead, and the Simi promises I won't kill you again. Friends?"

He gave her an incredulous stare.

After a few seconds, he let go of the gun and reached for the barbecue sauce. "Thank you, Simi."

Her wings shot back up as a smile curved her lips and happiness filled her. "It the Simi's favorite that she only give to special quality people. See ..." She pointed to the label. "Hot, hot ... though it hot here in the desert, you might not need it. But it's good on everything." She beamed a giant smile at him.

He inclined his head to her. "I appreciate it. Thank you very much."

Simi scowled. He didn't mean those words. Not really. And here all she wanted to do was apologize. "Why you so sad, akri-copy? You got aches in your heart?"

"I'm fine, Simi."

No, he wasn't. He was far from fine, and she knew it. Her frown deepening, she glanced around the tent. "Who you gots coming to celebrates with you?"

Styxx sighed. "I don't celebrate birthdays."

Eyes wide, she gaped. "No! Birthdays are always special cause they's the days when you were welcomed to the world and people be all happy when babies are born."

Akri-copy set the barbecue sauce down next to his pack. "You should probably go back to Acheron before he misses you."

Instead, she sat down on his bedroll.

"What are you doing?"

Determined to make him feel better before she left, she opened her backpack. "Akri got lots of people who celebrate with him on his birthday, and akri-copy got nobody. That makes Simi sad for akri-copy. Nobody should be alone on their birthday so ..." She pulled out a package of Ding Dongs and held them toward him. "We have birthday cake!"

He smiled sheepishly. "I've never had birthday cake before."

"Never?" She couldn't believe it. How could anyone go without birthday cakes? They was some of the bestest.

He shook his head.

Simi pressed her index finger to her lips as she thought about what to do to make his birthday extra special. "We need candles, but you so old that we'd have to have cakes the size of a ... battleship ... Hmmm ... that's okay." She reached into her pack and pulled out a glowstick. "Less pretend this is one. But you can't blow it out, but we pretend you do. How's that?"

"Sure."

"Okays. Now akri-copy sit."

A bit reluctantly, he sat down across from her while she carefully opened the package and left the cakes on the wrapper.

Then she snapped the glowstick and shook it.

"Now you make your wish and blow out the candle." She held the glowstick up in front of his face.

With a smile, akri-copy blew on it.

Suspicious, she narrowed her eyes at him. "You didn't make a wish, did you?"

"I don't have anything to wish for."

Simi knew that wasn't true. "Everybody has wishes, akri-copy."

"I'm not everybody."

He thought he was nobody, but she knew better. He

was akri's brother, and he'd done his best to help akri even though they hadn't gotten along in a very long time.

That made him extra special. He'd admitted he was wrong and had tried to make amends.

So, she wanted to make amends, too.

Simi took his hand into hers and placed a cake in it. "Then the Simi will make your wish for you. The Simi wishes you will be happy like the Simi and her akri."

He gave her a gentle smile. "Thank you, Simi."

She touched her cake to his then ate it. "You gots to eat yours all in one bites," she said with her mouth full. "'Cause we gots no candles to blow out, you have to eat in one gulp for the wish to come true."

Laughing, he shoved the cake into his mouth and ate it all in one gulp like she said.

Nodding, Simi licked her fingers. "Good, right?"

He swallowed the cake. "The best ever."

Happy that she'd given him a wish, Simi got up on her knees and kissed his cheek then hugged him. "If you want, akri-Styxx, the Simi can love you, too. 'Cause hearts are amazing things. They get lots bigger to make room for new people to love alongside the old people you love."

She patted her chest. "The Simi gots lots of room to love you, too, if you want."

Sadness darkened his eyes before he nodded. "I should like that very much."

She hugged him again and patted his back. "Okay, the Simi have to go now, but she'll be back to see you soon. And remember akri-Styxx that wishes are powerful,

powerful things that come true when you believe in them. And the Simi believes you will be very happy, very soon." Because she was going to make sure of it.

People deserved to be happy, especially one who looked so much like her akri. Akri had found his Tory, and they loved each other so much.

Everyone should have that, especially akri-Styxx who still ached for the goddess he'd lost.

Bethany had been particularly kind. And Simi knew where she was. She just needed to wake her up, and Styxx would never be sad again. It might make akri angry, but she wanted to repay akri-Styxx for what he'd done. He'd given her a new matera and a little brother named Sebastos.

Now it was his turn to be happy.

"Simi ... Are you sure this is a good idea?"

"Absolutely." Simi grinned at her sissy as they entered the basement of akri's temple on Katateros. "Now where's a light switch."

"There's not one." Xirena breathed fire onto an old spider web-covered torch. As soon as one lit, it spread light to all the others in the dark marble room.

The flames danced along the wall, adding creepy shadows to the already creepy environment.

Simi stepped back to stare at the number of statues that were housed here. While she'd known they'd been placed here centuries and centuries ago and had gone over them with akri when he'd first comed to live here, she'd never again visited them, especially since they made her akri very unhappy. "The Simi didn't remember there being so many ... Akra really broke bad on all these non-quality peoples."

"I remember." Xirena's tone was low and breathless. "It was not a pretty day."

Simi arched a brow. "You were there, Big Sissy?"

Xirena nodded. "Xedrix, too." Their brother had been Apollymi's most favored Charonte after their mother's death. But Rik-rik had deflected ... no, defected when akri-Styxx opened the portal in New Orleans and let him out on the night he'd tried to kill akri.

That was what had made Simi so mad at akri-copy.

"Ooo, so what happened, Big Sissy?"

"The bitch-goddess Apollymi was furious. They all died screaming. Except for two."

Simi started to correct her sister, but she knew Xirena would never warm up to Apollymi anymore than Simi would ever warm up to Artemis.

So, she ignored her sister's insults and asked the question that was most dear to her heart. "Who two?"

"Dikastis and Bet'anya. Bet tried to keep the bitch goddess from killing her baby, but the bitch goddess didn't listen. She yanked it right out of her belly and then turned her into one of these."

Simi touched her own stomach in sympathetic pain. Poor Bethany and akri-Styxx. "Why was akra so mean?"

Xirena shrugged. "The bitch goddess was always mean. She only likes you and her son ... and akra-Kat and Mia-Mia." Kat was akri's other daughter he'd had with Artemis. Akra-Mia was Kat's daughter and akri's grandbaby Simi loved to play with.

While the Simi didn't like change per se, the Simi did love the fact that her family had grown a lot over the last few years.

It was why she wanted it to grow some more with akri-Styxx and his goddess.

Simi climbed up on the woman closest to her and poked at her stone eyeball. She'd called her meanie witch. But she wondered what her real name was. "Which one is she?"

Xirena spat on the ground at the statue's feet. "Epithymia. She an even bigger bitch goddess. She used to pull the wings off Charonte who made her mad."

Simi cringed, then poked harder in the goddess's eye, hoping she could feel it. "Who the one who lost her baby? She's the one the Simi needs."

Xirena walked around them, looking at them, up and down, until she found one in the back. "This is Bet'anya."

Or Bethany as akri-Styxx called her.

Simi headed over, then gasped. "She look just likes akri-Styxx's drawings. She the one he loved so much."

Biting her lip, she met her sister's gaze. "Was she nice?"

Nodding, Xirena touched Bet'anya's hand. "She was always very sad though. Even when she was happy, she looked so sad. Like something wasn't quite right in her heart. Chara goddess used to say it's because they took something from her long ago they shouldn't have."

Simi gave her sister a knowing look. "That's 'cause she didn't have her akri-Styxx. He loves her and so this is the

Simi's Christmas present to him. I told him on his birthday that wishes come true and his wish is for his akra to come home to him."

"Yeah, but Xiamara, this ..." Xirena shook her head. "I don't think we should."

"We gots to, Big Sissy. This the only time them portals things open. If we don't do it now, akri-Styxx will have to wait a long, long time, and he already waited a long, long time. The Simi don't like to see him so sad. He don't get prezzies, and the Simi wants to get him the best prezzie ever."

The ground beneath their feet rumbled. Simi's eyes widened. "What's that?"

Bug-eyed, Xirena shrugged.

Simi's watch tingled, letting her know it was time. She had less than one minute to free the goddess. Using her wings, she hovered and placed the sacred anti-aima to the goddess's lips. When akri had been frozen that time in New Orleans, she and akra-Kat had used this to free him so she was hoping it would work on Styxx's akra, too.

Hmm ...

Another rumble went through the room. Something akin to a dark shadow shot out and flew past Simi's head.

Suddenly the other bitch goddess Xirena didn't like opened her eyes.

And so did Archon ...

Uh-oh.

Simi ran to her sister. "Go get help. The Simi will hold them off!"

Sissy left and Simi realized that it wasn't that easy.

Them gods were waking, and they were angry.

Most of all, they didn't like Charonte.

Simi tried her best to fight them off, but quickly learned one Charonte against a pantheon was just a bad idea.

Archon glared at her. "Xiamara! Where's Apollymi?"

Uh-oh. He thought she was her matera. Simi let loose her leathery battle wings.

She wanted to fight but knew better. There was only one thing to be done.

Simi grabbed the goddess she'd come for and teleported to Savitar for protection and help because she knew akri would be furious over her waking up all of the gods and not just the one.

For a second, she considered going to Thorny. He'd definitely help her, but if the mean gods learned Bethany was in Azmodea ...

No, Savitar was better.

'Sides, Savitar might be able to keep akri from killing her for being so stupid while he was busy.

WELL, at least akri hadn't pulled her wings off. That was a plus, but he was really mad. So mad that pulling her wings off was still a possibility.

Right now, he was off with Savitar and Urian,

discussing what they needed to do to keep the Atlantean gods from destroying the human realm.

Simi was in New Orleans with akra-Tory and their baby boy, Bas. "The Simi's so sorry, akra-Tory. I didn't mean to make such and awful mess."

With her long brown hair in a ponytail, Tory smiled at her. "It's okay, Simi. You were only trying to help. What you did was sweet, and once Ash calms down, he'll know that, too."

"I feel terrible."

Akra-Tory gave her a hug, then kissed her head. "Eat more ice cream and you'll feel better."

That was one of many reasons Simi loved Tory. Like Simi, she believed food could make everything better.

"Do you think Savitar can get akri-Styxx to help this time?"

"I'm sure, Simi. Just be patient."

That was awful hard given that she'd made a mess of everything. Simi wasn't sure what to do.

But as she looked at baby Bas and his cute face, she hoped that she hadn't messed up everyone's life.

Tory picked up her phone and answered it. She listened for a few minutes, then nodded. "You sure?"

Simi arched a brow, wondering what had happened.

Tory turned the phone off, then picked up baby Bas. "Ash wants us to go to Savitar's island."

"Why?"

"He wants us safe. It's the one place the gods won't be able to reach us."

That made sense. But it also made the ache in her belly stronger.

Please don't let me have destroyed everything by trying to make it better.

imi sat at a table in Savitar's kitchen with Tory who was feeding crackers to baby Bas. Akra-Danger and akri-Lexi were here, along with Xirena, akri, and akri's daughter Katra and her husband Sin, and their little girl, Mia.

Urian, an ex-Daimon akri had saved, walked in and sat down beside Katra. Ever since akri had returned Urian to life, he'd been part of their family, too. He even lived in the temple in Katateros with them. Simi thought of him as another big brother, even though she was pretty sure he was younger. There was just something about Urian that seemed older than he was.

And he was old. Almost as old in ages as akri.

It'd been a long time since they were all together like this. Sin and Katra lived in Las Vegas where Sin had a casino. And though Simi was glad they were happy there, she wished she saw her baby sissy more, 'cause Kat was a lot of fun and so was her little girl, Mia.

Sadly, they mostly spent holidays together.

Or, like today, plotting ways to avert the end of the world.

Savitar appeared in the middle of the room with akri-Styxx by his side. He looked around their group and shook his head.

"They're not going to wait all day," Savitar warned akri. "We need to get moving."

"I know, but as I was reviewing the situation with everyone and trying to come up with an alternate plan that didn't leave Styxx hacked into little bloody pieces, Urian reminded me that we were missing a most vital member of the team." Akri pinned his gaze on Styxx. "The quarterback who actually went up against the Atlantean gods centuries ago and beat the shit out of them."

Styxx shrugged at the group. "Since no one has bothered to tell me what I'm heading into, I've got nothing. I still don't know why I'm here."

Akri looked at Simi who blushed and grinned sheepishly. Poor Styxx had no idea what she'd done. Or that she'd done it while trying to make him happy.

Pursing her lips, Simi tried to explain everything. "Well, see, akri-Styxx, it all started when the Simi decided she was gonna give you the promise for your birthday for Christmas. See?"

He scowled. "Clear as a two-hundred-mile-an-hour sandstorm."

Akri gave a low, sinister laugh. "Simi decided to wake up the Atlantean gods for you."

Styxx's jaw fell open. "Wait ... what? Why?"

Simi sighed heavily as she still regretted everything that had happened. Nothing had worked out the way she intended. "Well see, it wasn't supposed to be all them gods who woke up. It was only supposed to be the one. But she won't get up. Lots of them others got up and got ugly, fast, and the Simi still don't know why the only one I tried to wake keeps sleeping when it's so important she get up and talk. It's all so confusing."

Before Styxx could comment, Sin turned toward Savitar. "I have two gods and a demigod requesting permission to enter your home and join our planning session. Can I let them in?"

Savitar gave him a look that questioned his sanity. "Who?"

"My brother, Seth, and your least favorite god of all time."

Savitar arched a brow. "Noir?"

"Second least favorite," Sin quickly amended.

Savitar made a sound of supreme disgust. "I thought that bastard was dead."

"Apparently not."

A tic started in Savitar's jaw. "Why?"

Sin shrugged. "I have no idea why he's not dead. But they say they can help with this."

Hands on his hips, Savitar glared at akri and then Kat. "Apollymi owes me. Big. And so do you." He looked back at Sin and gave a curt nod. "Tell them fine. They can enter, even if it chafes me to my soul."

Simi wasn't exactly sure what was going on as the god Set appeared beside akri with a man identical in looks to Sin—only with longer black hair. Oh! She'd had no idea Sin was a twin like her akri.

Those two also had a third man with them with curly, red hair. His features were very similar to Set's. So much so that she wondered if he wasn't the son who'd been held in Azmodea long ago. The one akri-Jaden still had guilt over.

The Sin twin laughed and nudged Set to look at akri-Styxx. "Now there's a photo op expression if ever there was one."

With a wry grin, the god Set transformed into the form of another man. One akri-Styxx seemed to know. "Over four thousand years ago, Apollo and his whore mother used my son Seth," he indicated the red-haired man with them, "to trap me in the desert without his knowledge of what was being done to him and why and restricted my powers so that the Greeks could take over my pantheon and hand my son over to my bitterest enemy. But for you, Styxx, I'd still be there, chained in the desert, fighting off vultures—human and animal." He glanced to his son and his gaze softened instantly. "And my son would still be hating me for something I tried my best to spare him."

"Why didn't you tell me it was you when I freed you?" akri-Styxx asked.

"You were in enough anguish over Bethany. I didn't want to make it worse when I didn't think I could do anything to fix it or help you. Especially after you did me such a massive favor by setting me free."

Set inclined his head to Sin's brother. "Zakar and I were allies back in the day, which was why I had you take me to his place to recuperate after you found me in the desert. Since you left, we've been trying to find a way to revive my daughter without awakening the other Atlanteans."

Oh ...

Simi cringed as she realized that they would have done what she tried to do. Only they would have probably succeeded and not bungled it so badly.

Styxx scowled at them. "But Bethany was Egyptian, not Atlantean."

"From me, yes. Her mother is Symfora."

The Atlantean goddess of sorrow. Simi remembered her well. She was one of the nicer Atlanteans. Mostly because she was always so sad that she left everyone else alone.

"Bethany is Bet'anya Agriosa?" Styxx asked.

Set nodded. "For an obvious reason, she was scared to tell you the truth. She was so afraid you couldn't forgive her for what they did to you without her knowledge or approval, that she was planning to give up her godhood entirely, in both pantheons, to live a mortal life with you in Didymos. Her aunt had already mixed the serum that would have stripped her of everything so she could be with you and not hurt you."

Simi gaped as she heard those words. Giving up a

godhood was no small thing. Akra-Bet must have really loved Styxx to do such a thing.

"I wouldn't have cared about that." Styxx's voice trembled. "I would never have held the actions of others against Bethany."

"Good," Seth said. "Because if you want her back, you're going to have to bleed Apollo and battle the worst of the Atlantean gods for her."

"And you're not going to fight without us." Maahes and Cam flashed into the room, next to Savitar who cursed at their appearance.

Stunned, Simi stepped back. The last goddess she expected to appear here was Cam. Although, she was Set's sister and Bethany's aunt. Still …

What have I done?

Cam had gone by many names over the centuries. The worst was Menyara where the goddess had set up Cherise Gautier to birth Nick. Cam had ruined the poor woman's life and caused Cherise to die horribly at the hands of Daimons.

Poor Nick. He'd never get over the death of his mother. No more than Simi had ever gotten over hers.

Savitar growled. "Anyone else you want to bring to the party?"

Maahes grinned insolently. "Mother, may I?"

The look on Savitar's face said that Maahes was barely a step away from becoming a lion throw rug on Savitar's floor.

Cam stood up on her tiptoes to place a kiss to Savitar's cheek. "Remember, you like me."

"I don't like anyone who barges into my home uninvited, Mennie."

"You'll get over it." Tiny and thin, Cam had long black braids and beautiful dark skin. She turned her attention to the group. "All right, children. Catch us up?"

"From what I'm hearing ... screwed." Styxx crossed his arms over his chest. "I'm going to be dense for a moment because I'm having trouble wrapping my head around this.... Bethany can be brought back. Yes?"

Cam and Set nodded.

Simi winced at the agony that appeared in his blue eyes. It was obvious that akri-Styxx was angry over all the centuries he'd been forced to live without his Bethany.

He turned to glare at akri. "Why didn't anyone tell me this before?"

Akri held his hands up in surrender. "I had no idea your Bethany was Bet'anya or that she was in my basement garden of statues. That's the truth. I was a little distraught and disoriented eleven thousand years ago when my mother took me to Katateros the first time. After I teleported their statues to the basement and Simi told me who they were, I locked the door and never went near that area again."

Styxx looked at Set and Cam. "Why didn't one of you tell me?"

Cam tsked. "Sugar, every one of us thought she was

dead. Believe me, had we known she was frozen in Katateros, we'd have freed her for all of our sakes."

"Well, we would have tried." Set sighed. "Probably would have failed. It was the alignment on the twenty-first that made this possible. That, and the demon." He turned his gaze to Simi.

Hating to be put on the spot, Simi flashed a happy smile at akri-Styxx. "I told you wishes can come true, akri-Styxx, and not just at Disney World. The real world does a good job, too, sometimes."

Akri frowned at Simi's familiarity with his brother. "When did you two become friends?"

She wrinkled her nose at him. Little did akri know, she kept a lot of secrets. "On your birthdays, akri. Did you know akri-Styxx don't gots no one to spend his special day with? He all alone on it, and so the Simi went to apologize and make him her friend, too, so he won't be alone on his special days anymore. But he done broke the Simi's heart so now he my other akri-baby like Baby Bas and akra-Kat. The Simi has officially adapted him ... no ... adopted him." She grinned so wide, her fangs flashed.

Instead of being angry, akri laughed and kissed her cheek. Then, he turned back toward his brother. "All right, Styxx. Your show. How do we do this?"

Styxx glanced around the room at them. "Still the sole human here. I don't know what we're up against or who we're fighting. I need more details."

Akri spread his hands out and a schematic of his

temple appeared on the wall that showed the basement and the statues housed there.

As he spoke, the animation illustrated his words. "A dozen gods woke up while Simi was in the basement with Xirena, looking for Bet'anya, apparently as a birthday present for you. Since I was in Vegas with Sin and Katra fighting off gallu demons, and Tory was with my mother in Kalosis, the Simi and her sister were left alone to create well-intentioned mischief. As soon as the gods began to stir, Xirena ran to tell Alexion and Danger. The three of them grabbed Simi and escaped here to Savitar to let him know what had happened."

"That's when they called me in Minnesota," Urian said. "And told me not to come home for a few days as we had ancient interlopers in Katateros who most likely would not host me a Welcome Back party. And none of them had better be playing on my Playstation."

Akri sighed. "We're also flying blind." He motioned to his wall decoration. "We have that tidbit based on Simi's recollection. After Simi and crew vacated the premises, Archon and the others have blocked out our sforas. None of us can see where they are or anything inside the main temple. We don't know exactly how many gods are awake or what they're doing."

"Do we know who we're up against at all?" Styxx asked.

Akri glanced to Simi before he answered. "We're not one hundred percent sure. Because Simi was an infant when they ruled, she's a little iffy on some of their identities and she was the only one who got a look at all of them.

Best we can figure, it's ..." He again turned to the images on the wall—one of which looked more like Wreck-It Ralph than an actual god. "Dikastis, Ilos, Isorro, Asteros, Epithymia, Diafonia, Nyktos, Paidi, Teros, Phanen, Demonbrean, and we know for a fact Archon is with them as he's the one we've been talking to. And of course everyone's favorite dickhead, Apollo."

Styxx let out an exasperate breath. "Beautiful. My ideal guest list ... for a fete in hell."

Simi felt terrible for him, but she understood. They were horrible gods.

Styxx went over them for the others so that they'd know who they were fighting. Unlike Simi, he knew the names and faces of every one of them ... even Wreck-It Ralph AKA Demonbrean. Though to be honest, Simi preferred calling him Wreck-It Ralph.

Styxx used akri's diagram of the gods he'd named to highlight each one. "Apollo's not a problem. He's an effing idiot when it comes to things like this. And he's a bully with no courage who will back down to someone more powerful. He won't be leading a charge but will stay back until he can land a punch from safety. Unfortunately, Archon isn't any of that. He's sharp and deadly. Vindictive as hell. Brutal. But out of the list, Epithymia and Asteros"—he highlighted them—"are the two we have to neutralize immediately. Do not underestimate them, especially Epithymia. She is absolutely lethal."

He swept his gaze around the room's occupants. "And whatever you do, do not let her touch you ... Demonbrean is even dumber than Apollo, but he's also the size of an effing house. His skin is armored, and he lives to crush things. Treat him like a python and don't let him get his arms around you. Dikastis will hang back to get the lay of the situation and might not fight us at all. The rest are followers. Lethal, but pawns nonetheless. They were servants for Misos in war and only did what they were told to do. You take out Archon and they will stand down ... Now what do we know of their demands?"

Savitar laughed bitterly. "Because I was their Chthonian, Archon contacted me, not knowing my relationship with the Grom. They want Acheron as a sacrifice so that they can use his blood and heart to bring back the rest of their merry band, except for Bethany. Archon blames her for this, as if he wasn't the one who caused Acheron to be cursed ... what were you telling me about his intelligence?"

"Steadfast denial is not the same as intelligence." Styxx rubbed at his eyebrow. "Just out of curiosity, what was the game plan you had once you sent me in to die, and they discovered my blood and heart couldn't bring back their dead?"

Savitar shrugged nonchalantly. "Buy us time to gather enough Chthonians to take them down."

Simi was aghast that Savitar had planned to sacrifice poor akri-Styxx. That was awful!

And Styxx didn't look very pleased either. "Thank the gods none of you were among my military advisors. We'd have had our asses handed to us," he mumbled under his breath. Then louder, "Are they at full strength?"

Akri shrugged. "No idea."

"Let's assume yes." Styxx ran over the facts. "So our numbers are basically even. The weakest link in our group is me.... What are our strengths?"

Simi opened her coffin purse and pulled out her barbecue sauce. "Demons ready to eat, Sir Akri-Styxx! Gimme!"

Laughing at her enthusiasm, akri jerked his chin toward his other daughter. "I don't want Katra in harm's way, but she's a siphon."

"I'm also a trained soldier, Dad." Kat rolled her eyes at akri then looked at her husband, Sin, and warned him with her gaze not to say a word. She turned toward Styxx. "I was my mother's primary kori, and unlike my seriously overprotective father and husband, she—"

"Put her ass in harm's way all the time with a blatant disregard for her safety that still pisses me off," Sin growled.

Kat smiled and cupped his cheek. "Yes, baby, but had she not been so careless, I wouldn't have you. Now would I?"

He grumbled under his breath.

"What else do we have that they won't know about?" Styxx asked.

Set folded his arms over his chest. "For thousands of years, my son was the High Guardian for Noir in Azmodea."

Seth nodded. "I'm used to battling angry gods. I can

also get us a bird's-eye view of anything you need. What I use, they can't block."

"We also have this." Urian held up a shiny necklace Simi had never seen before.

Set's eyes widened with recognition. "How did you get that?"

Urian snorted. "My enemy's enemy is my best friend. We borrowed it from my father who was more than happy to lend it and wants us to tie it in a bow around Apollo's neck."

Simi was surprised by that. Urian's father was Apollo's son that akra-Apollymi had saved all those centuries ago.

"What is that?" Styxx asked.

Set laughed, low and evil, and made no moves to touch it. "The Eye of Verlyn. That will deplete the powers of any god it comes into direct contact with."

Yikes! Simi didn't like the sound of that.

Styxx looked at it with a new respect. "For how long?"

"As soon as it touches them, they're wiped. Then it depends on how long it's on their body and how strong they are. Too long, it'll kill them."

Styxx smiled. "Does it work on just full-bloods or any other species?"

Set shrugged. "I don't know."

Well, there was only one way to find out. Simi grabbed her sister and put her hand on it.

"Hey!" Xirena snapped. "What are you doing?"

Finding out the answer. "You still gots power, sissy?"

Xirena shot a blast of fire at her.

Grinning and ducking, Simi looked at Styxx and let go of Xirena. "It don't work on us."

Urian laughed. "I'm only a quarter demigod, and it doesn't seem to affect me."

"I think I'm the only true demi here." Seth bravely took it into his hand and waited. After a couple of minutes, he shook his head. "No effect on me, either."

Styxx hesitated. "Since my powers are borrowed from Apollymi, I'm not chancing it. We'll assume I need to stay clear of it. Urian, let's leave it in your custody."

As Urian tucked it away, Styxx looked at Set. "Can the stone be broken apart or duplicated?"

Set shook his head. "Not without destroying it."

"Would the stone just suck out your god powers and leave the rest intact?" Styxx asked akri.

"That's what usually happens. Why? You thinking of giving me an early Christmas present?"

"Don't distract or tempt me." Styxx swept his gaze over all of them. "My most important question of all ... Where's my Bethany?"

As AKRI-STYXX REACHED for the doorknob with Simi by his side, Katra placed her hand on his arm. "I know we're not friends, Styxx, but I'd rather you not go in there alone. Someone should be with you."

"How are you Artemis's daughter?" he asked in a quiet tone.

Kat smiled. "She's not as bad as you think... Apollo, however, is probably worse."

Standing on his other side, the Simi leaned in to whisper in his ear, "We'll be super quiet. Akri-Styxx won't even know we're there."

Urian put his hand on Styxx's shoulder. "Don't worry. What happens happens, and we won't think anything about it. We'll just be here for you if you need us."

Because this was the first time akri-Styxx would see his Bethany. And he didn't need to do it alone.

With a grim nod, he offered them a tenuous smile. "Thank you both." Then, he opened the bedroom door.

The floor-to-ceiling windows were open, letting in the soft ocean breeze. But it was the huge, canopied bed in the center of the room that was most important. White linen drapes were pulled back with gold cords, obscuring the woman in the bed.

This was where Simi had brought Bethany when the Atlanteans had rushed her on Katateros. She figured this was the safest place for the goddess to stay until they found a way to wake her for akri-Styxx.

His hands trembling, Styxx pulled the covers back and saw the blood that was still on her white gown from where Apollymi had taken their baby from the goddess's belly all those centuries ago.

Throwing his head back, he howled in pain, then gathered her body into his arms. "Beth?" he breathed against her cheek as he cradled her head to his shoulder. "Please come back to me. Please. I need you so ..."

The goddess didn't move or breathe and that made Simi ache for both of them. How terrible to need someone so much and not be able to have them. She couldn't imagine anything worse.

Tears choked Simi. Why were those other monster gods up and around and not her? It didn't make sense.

And it wasn't right.

Why couldn't she wake the goddess for akri-Styxx? He was a good man who deserved to be happy. Simi didn't like the rules of this game.

It should be fair and it wasn't.

Her heart breaking, she sniffed as akri joined them.

Without a word, he went to his brother and placed a gentle hand on his shoulder.

Kat took her hand and led her from the room so that akri and Styxx could be alone.

She didn't really want to leave, but Katra was right. Styxx needed his brother and akri needed his. This was a time for them to come together again and be a family.

Katra returned to her husband while Simi stayed out in the hallway. She wanted to help but didn't know how.

Especially when she heard Styxx's angry bellow. "I hate you."

Akri answered those words with a heartfelt sorrow that made her tears fall down her cheeks. "I know, brother ... I know. I wish more than anything that I could take it all back. Everything. That I'd listened to and followed the advice I gave to others. I hurt you and I abandoned you and it was wrong. I was wrong and I am so incredibly sorry for everything I've done."

"Why can't I just hate you?"

"Because you're a better man than I am. You always were."

But that wasn't true, and Simi knew it. They were family. Even in pain and grief. Even when the world did its best to break them, they were brothers.

Family stuck together. Through thick and thin. Just like her and her siblings. Sure, they fought. Sometimes they were really nasty to each other.

But in the end, they knew that they'd fight and bleed for one another.

Forever.

That was family, and that was the most important thing in all the world.

And akri confirmed that. "I will never turn my back on you again, brother. I—"

"Don't make a promise you might not keep."

It would kill akri if he did. As an Atlantean god, he had to keep all his promise.

She heard Styxx's low laugh through the door. "But at least you finally got a decent haircut."

Simi shook her head. While Styxx might like akri's shorter hair, she didn't. He'd worn his hair long for centuries.

Even though he'd done it for charity to celebrate Bas's first birthday, it was still strange-looking on him.

The two of them kept talking to the point that Simi felt

awkward standing alone in the hallway. Maybe she shouldn't be eavesdropping.

Just as she started away, she heard a peculiar crackling sound as if someone else had teleported into the room.

"I think we startled her more than she startled us," Styxx said in his deeper tone.

Akri sighed. "What are you doing here?"

Simi gasped as a woman answered and not just any woman.

The heifer goddess, Artemis. "That's just ... not right. Say something else so I know which of you is Acheron."

"What, Artemis?"

"There's that irritated tone I loathe." She paused a moment before she spoke again. "I have brought you presents."

Simi's brows shot up at those words. *Always beware a Greek bearing gifts, especially when it was a god.*

"Why?" akri asked.

"You're going up against my brother and the rest of those animals ... I want you to win, and make him bleed. A lot. Buckets and buckets full until it gushes and fills the entire hall."

"Should I be afraid of the bloodlust?" Styxx asked.

"I'm terrified of her. What did Apollo do, Artie?"

"He attacked Nicholas while he was weakened. I will not have it. Since I'm not powerful enough to harm my brother on my own, I want you two to kick his leg."

Kick his leg? Simi repeated silently as she tried to make sense of that.

"You mean ass, Artie?"

Oh ... Simi shook her head. The heifer could never get her sayings right. She messed them up all the time. So much so that it made akri crazy.

"Whatever body part pleases you. You can't kill him, but you can make him suffer. Long. Hard. Pitifully. I gave Savitar an assortment of weapons I dipped in the River Styx. It will weaken Apollo to the point he'll be as a mortal. If I were you, I'd castrate him slowly and with a great deal of—"

"Grammy! Grammy!"

Simi laughed at the sound of Mia breaking in. Amused, she cracked open the door to see the dark-haired four-year-old leap into Artemis's arms. She was so beautiful. The top of her frou-frou dress bulged with pink-and-white cloth flowers, some of which decorated the long, poofy, yellow tulle skirt. Her legs were covered with matching pink leggings and pink patent leather shoes. Mia was even wearing a pair of munchkin-sized, pink tulle fairy wings that Kat had made for her so that she could match Simi's resting wings.

Her rant instantly forgotten, Artemis gave the child a giant hug as she picked her up. "Mia Bella! How is my precious today?"

The little girl squealed. "Gamma, Gamma, Gamma, guess what? Guess what! The Simi gonna put hornays on my head like hers and Pappas's. And she said that I could pick any color I want and that they'd be on all the time, and they can glow in the dark, too."

That was true. Simi had offered to do it so that Mia would have beautiful hornays like hers.

Bug-eyed, Artemis looked horrified.

Akri laughed and rubbed Mia's back. "How about if Simi makes you a pair that can come off?"

Pfft on that. Akri always spoiled her fun.

Mia wrinkled her nose at him. "Pappas! No! I want real ones. Like you and Simi and Xireni."

Artemis screwed her face up at Mia. "You know Pappas only has those when he's mad, right?"

Mia's eyes widened. "Really?"

They both nodded.

Mia's attention finally went to Styxx. Her eyes widened. "Who cloned Pappas?" she whispered loudly.

Akri smiled. "He's my brother ... your grand uncle Styxx."

Mia launched herself into Styxx's arms so that she could kiss him. "You look just like my Pappas." Then she put her hands on his cheeks and rubbed noses with him. "That's how Charonte say hello. But only if they like you. Otherwise, they eat you with ketchup or barbecue sauce, or if they're like my uncle Xed, jalapenos which are really hot, too."

Simi gasped as she realized how much attention Mia paid to her whenever the Simi ate with the little cherub angel. She knew exactly how Simi and her sibs likes their foodies!

Aww! It caused her heart dance in her chest. She'd always loved Mia before, but this ...

This made Simi want her own baby.

Artemis pulled Mia back into her arms and tickled her. "Don't scare your uncle the first time you meet him, silly belle."

Kat and Sin came into the room making irritated, yet relieved parental sounds.

"Sorry." Kat took her daughter from Artemis. "She got off the chain when we took our eyes away from her for three seconds. She must have sensed you were here, Mom." Hugging Artemis, she gave her a kiss on the cheek as Sin took his daughter from Kat.

Mia made an adorable face at her father. "Am I in trouble, Daddy?"

"No, baby girl. But you shouldn't vanish like that without telling us where you're going. You scared me and your mom terribly."

Those words reminded her of Thorn all those centuries ago when Simi had gone to visit him, and he'd been afraid akri would be angry.

Some things never changed. And for that, she was grateful.

Sin kissed the top of her head. "You do have to go back to Aunt Tory and Aunt Danger and stay with them for a bit, okay?"

She pouted adorably and nodded.

Artemis stopped Sin before he could leave with Mia. "Grammy will be by in a little bit to read her baby belle a story, okay?"

Mia grinned and bounced. "Can we ride in your deer chariot, too?"

"Only if Mommy and Daddy say it's okay ... and you'll have to put on a sweater." Artemis gave her a big hug and kiss. "I'll be there as soon as I can."

She nodded then went rigid in Sin's arms. "Wait! Wait! Pappas!"

Smiling, akri gave her a tight squeeze. "I, too, will be back as soon as I can."

"Then we'll watch *Megamind*!"

Simi cringed at the thought. While she loved that movie, they watched it at least four times a day whenever Mia was with them. She just couldn't get enough of the blue alien.

"Sure, baby."

Mia planted a loud, wet kiss on akri's cheek. Then Kat took her back from Sin. "I'll return her to her closet and lock her in."

Sin kissed the top of Mia's head before he turned back to them. "Really sorry for the intrusion." He followed after his wife and daughter.

Simi stepped back and closed the door, then headed toward the kitchen where the others were. They had a lot to do and time for them was running out.

30

OCTOBER 23, 2012

"You know this isn't going to work, right?" Styxx asked akri as they were getting ready to attack the Atlantean gods.

"I've had worse odds."

Simi had seen them, too. Some, she'd barely survived.

"So have I, but most didn't work out well for me."

Simi went with them as they teleported to akri's bedroom in Katateros.

Way back before akra-Tory, the room had been sparsely decorated in black and brown. Now it was powder-puff blue with dancing circus animals on the walls and a canopied crib within easy reach of the large king bed. That was because of akri's paranoia over the awful Apollites killing akri's sister in Greece.

To this day, akri hadn't gotten over it. And because he was terrified of losing baby Bas, akri never let Bas sleep alone. In fact, Bas had been almost a year old before akri had allowed him to sleep anywhere other than akri's chest.

Which was funny but also made Simi very sad. It wasn't until Bas was born that she realized exactly how paranoid her akri was, and it made her regret all the times in her life that she'd vanished and scared him.

Can you hear me?

Simi nodded at akri so that he'd know she could hear him while he spoke to her and Styxx with his thoughts.

Good. I think it best if we communicate like this for a while.

That made sense given that if they spoke the Atlantean gods might hear them.

Styxx went to the door and listened. Seth's "bird" spirit that he normally wore as a tattoo on his chest had shown them that the gods were all gathered in the throne room, where they bragged about what they intended to do once they had her akri in their custody.

Simi would eat them all if they dared harm him. It infuriated her to listen to them. They were horrible gods, and Simi was glad that akri and Savitar had reconsidered sending Styxx in as his double.

Akri let out a sigh. *They've sensed our powers.*

Ready? Styxx asked.

Absolutely not.

Styxx rolled his eyes at akri's humor.

Locking gazes, akri held his hand up in offering to Styxx.

Styxx took akri's hand and let his brother teleport them into the throne room.

Once inside, Styxx let go of akri's hand and took his position at his back. He faced Archon, Apollo, and Epithymia while Acheron faced the rest.

Archon rose to his feet. "Well, isn't this unexpected?" He smirked at Apollo. "We don't have to play chase, after all. How kind of them to save us time." He glared at Styxx. "Which of you is Apostolos?"

"I am," they said simultaneously.

Simi giggled.

Archon growled low in his throat.

"Their eyes," Apollo said quickly. "Styxx's are blue."

Akri turned to stand beside his brother. When they spoke, it was as one. "Not anymore."

Archon narrowed his gaze on them. "Then we'll kill you both."

"No," Apollo snarled. "That wasn't the agreement."

Epithymia made a sound of supreme disgust. "Stand down, both of you. There's an easy way to get to the truth." She tugged at the black cord around her neck to show them a small crystal vial. She pulled it over her head and placed it on the arm of Archon's chair, then manifested a hammer. "This is the heart of Bethany. If the real Styxx doesn't step forward, I'll destroy her. Forever."

Simi gasped as she saw panic spread over Styxx's face. But somehow, he caught himself. It was only a flash and then he was calm again.

"So, you don't love her?" Epithymia hovered the hammer over the vial. "Really?"

"You do that, and you lose all leverage over both of us.

Her life is the only thing keeping you alive right now." That had to be Styxx, even though he sounded just like akri.

A light flashed in the room.

Simi expected Urian to show up.

Instead, it was Artemis who popped in beside her brother.

"Oh my!" Artemis exclaimed as she looked at them. "Am I interrupting?"

Apollo seized her arm. "What are you doing here?"

"I came to see Acheron. This is his house where he lives. I'm allowed to visit."

No, she wasn't. Simi was baffled by the lie. Akri had never allowed the heifer in his home. She wasn't supposed to be here.

More than that, Artemis wasn't part of the plan.

At all.

Why was she here?

Archon bellowed in outrage. "This is not his home! This is our temple!"

Blinking her eyes, Artemis gave the older Atlantean an innocent look. "No? Then why are you sitting on his throne? That's not yours, you know. I was with Acheron when he picked it out and brought it here."

What? Simi was so confused. The heifer goddess had been nowhere near akri when that had happened.

What game was she playing?

"Why is she here, Apollo?" Archon asked through clenched teeth.

"I have no idea."

Epithymia went rigid. "Something's not right..."

"That's because she's not my daughter."

Simi looked over to see Leto, the mother of Apollo and Artemis, entering from a side door.

And as she watched her, a horrible thought entered the Simi's mind. If that wasn't Artemis ...

There was only one person it could be. One person who looked enough like Artemis to pretend to be her.

Katra.

Covering her lips, Simi wished Thorn was here. He would know what to do.

"Mom," Apollo said irritably. "What are you doing?"

Ignoring him, Leto smirked as she approached their group. "Really, Katra? I'm so disappointed in you for this ridiculous charade. But that's all right." She looked at Archon. "We don't need the twins now. Katra is the daughter of Artemis and Acheron. She has the Destroyer's bloodline and is actually stronger than her parents."

Leto grabbed Kat and held a dagger to her throat. "So, Acheron, who do we kill? You or your daughter?"

Simi started for the goddess, but before she could take a step, a sonic blast went through the room. One so fierce, it knocked everyone off their feet and slammed Leto against the wall.

Artemis appeared instantly and pulled Kat to safety. "How dare you," she enunciated each word slowly as she faced her mother. "No one threatens my baby ever! You cow!" She attacked her mother so ferociously, Kat and

Simi had to pull Artemis away to keep her from killing Leto.

Akri took advantage of the distraction to use his powers to jerk the vial from Epithymia's hand. Using his powers, he sent it to Styxx.

Styxx carefully tucked it in his glove.

With a mutual nod, they attacked the Atlanteans closest to them.

The moment they started fighting, Simi realized why she was so important and why pantheons didn't like to war among themselves. Since the gods pulled their powers from a mutual source, they were fighting in a weakened position, and their powers weren't working properly.

It was why gods who belonged to more than one pantheon were stronger. They could call on these additional powers and not be weakened.

Being a Charonte, Simi had an advantage as her powers had nothing to do with theirs at all.

"Katra!" Styxx called as he saw Epithymia going for her back.

She turned the instant Epithymia went to touch her.

Instead of retreating, Kat pulled her close and sucked her powers out of her. "You won't be needing those anymore."

And as she pulled Epithymia's powers, her teeth elongated, and her eyes turned demonic red. Her skin began to swirl like Simi's.

"Acheron!" Artemis screamed. "The demon's taking over Katra. Help!"

His face turning white, akri met Styxx's gaze.

"She's more important than I am," Styxx said. "Get her out of here."

Simi ran cover as akri ran to his daughter to get her to safety.

"Follow us, Simi."

Unsure, Simi looked back at Styxx who'd manifested a hoplon to deflect their god-bolts as he covered their retreat.

"Shouldn't I stay, akri?"

"No."

Still not sure if this was the right thing to do, Simi teleported with them back to Savitar's island.

AKRI HANDED Katra off to Sin. "Something from the old demon bite interacted with Epithymia's powers. I drained her, but she needs to feed."

Sin nodded grimly as he took her and vanished.

Breathless from the fighting, Simi looked at the others in the room who were supposed to have been there with them, protecting Styxx.

"What happened?" akri asked.

Set growled. "We're locked out. If you're not Greek or Atlantean, forget it. Only Katra had the ability to get to you. And even then, it wasn't easy for her to teleport in."

Oh ... that explained it. Since the Charonte served the Atlanteans, Simi had been able to go.

"I couldn't get in either," Urian said. "You're all he's got, boss."

"Simi, return to me."

She immediately laid herself over akri's heart as a dragon-shaped tattoo.

Xirena bit her lip. "Me, too, akri?"

"Absolutely."

Akri glanced around at his allies. "I'm weakened. Every time I strike them, it drains a portion of my god powers—and the weapons Artemis brought might work on Apollo, but they're shite on the Atlanteans. We are in over our heads, and I won't lie, it's ugly. So, who wants to try to go in with me and save my brother's life?"

They all stepped forward.

"All right. Here goes nothing." Closing his eyes, akri summoned all the powers he could and teleported them back to Katateros.

As soon as they returned, Simi peeled herself from akri's body and flew above the blood-soaked floor. It looked like the Malachai and his army had been here.

But what concerned her the most was the sight of Styxx's phoenix shield. Twisted and bent out of shape, it was in the middle of the largest pool of blood.

Had they killed him?

Blood was smeared to the doors as if a struggling body had been dragged through them.

Simi's heart pounded as she feared for her akri-copy.

Two of them ugly Atlanteans, Demonbrean and Ilios, lay moaning on the ground near Apollo who wasn't in any better shape. Simi hoped Styxx had beat the crap out of the Greek god before they'd overpowered him.

And he better be okay, or the Simi would eat all of their heads ...

Without barbecue sauce! That was how angry she was.

Off to the side, Epithymia sobbed uncontrollably and hadn't moved from her spot where she'd fallen after Kat had drained her powers.

As Styxx had predicted in Savitar's kitchen, Dikastis stood calmly in the shadows and appeared to have not fought at all.

Akri went to him first. "Where's my brother?"

Raw anger flared in the god's eyes. "They took him to the temple arena."

Akri glared at him. "Why aren't you with them?"

The Atlantean shrugged. "I'm a god of justice. I will not participate in something that's wrong and undeserved."

Akri took a moment to consider that. "Will you fight with us then?"

Dikastis nodded without hesitation.

SIMI PAUSED at the entrance of a temple she'd never been inside before. But she knew it.

This was where akri had confined Styxx when he'd brought him to Katateros. The temple that Styxx had hated.

"What is this place?" akri asked.

Dikastis let out a long breath. "It's our arena where we held games and competitions, and where we brought those who needed to be punished and taught humility."

Simi wanted to cry. That meant that this was where akri-Styxx had been held when he was a human. How awful for him to be back here with the ones who'd abused him.

Akri swept his gaze over Simi, Urian, Dikastis, Seth, Set, Maahes, Cam, Zakar, and Xirena. "I don't know what we're about to walk into, but let's move forward with Styxx's original plan. And whatever we do, save my brother."

Simi couldn't agree more, especially because she knew how important Styxx and Bethany were.

One day in the future, their daughter, Nekoda, would come back in time to help save Nick Gautier from becoming the scary Malachai. This was more important than any of them knew.

"What do you want from me?" the Atlantean god asked.

Akri sighed. "Help us any way you can."

Simi looked around, wondering where the other gods were. How strange that none of them Atlanteans had come out to challenge them on their arrival. They should have been out here, tossing a fit and screaming.

Yet it was eerily quiet as they entered the building.

Inside the dark hall, a feral wind howled and plastered their clothes against their bodies. It was so fierce that it forced Simi to tuck in her wings.

Her sissy too.

Where was the wind coming from? It made no sense and because it was so intense it took them several minutes to make it to the arena.

Once there, Simi understood the ugly wind. It had pinned down all the gods. No one was standing.

No other than Styxx. He was held up while a ghosty woman dressed in red wrapped around him and held a dagger over his heart.

She sort of looked like Bethany, and yet Simi wasn't sure.

Set moved forward, through their group. "Bathymaas! No!"

Without the slightest hesitation, she sank the dagger deep into Styxx's chest, all the way to the hilt, then threw her head back and roared in satisfaction.

When she finally spoke, she used Atlantean only. "Take your bastard back, Apollymi. Now come and face me, you wretched dog, so that I can bathe in your putrid blood! Taste my vengeance and choke on it!"

Simi couldn't believe what she was seeing. Akri-Styxx's love was stabbing him?

How was this possible?

But Bethany didn't see Styxx. She only saw akri.

And for once, Apollymi answered Bethany's summoning. In the same ethereal shade form she used whenever she visited akri or Simi, she stood over Bethany. "What have you done?"

Bethany ran at her, and then through her. "Are you afraid to face me?"

Her expression one of deep sadness, Apollymi shook her head. "You did not kill my precious Apostolos." Tears filled her eyes as she looked at Styxx's body. "I am still trapped in Kalosis. The man you killed is Styxx of Didymos."

Recognition darkened Bethany's eyes. She turned back toward Styxx's body and paled. "You lie!"

Blood dripped from the wound she'd given him and, as it did so, it drained the powers Styxx had borrowed from Apollymi. His hair returned to blond, his skin darkened, and the scars that had been hidden, reappeared on his body.

There was no denying the fact that Bethany had killed Styxx.

Leto's laughter filled the room. "Poor Bathymaas ... you are damned again by your own hand."

The angry Greek goddess materialized behind Bethany and ripped a necklace from her neck.

Set ran for them, but before he could close the distance, Leto joined the necklace with another piece she had.

Cocking her head, Simi tried to understand what the goddess was trying to do.

"Now I will be the soul of justice, and you'll ... You'll..." Leto frowned as the two pieces fought against each other like two magnets that were repelling. "What? Why isn't this working?"

Akri met Urian's gaze and jerked his chin toward the pinned gods.

Urian nodded in understanding and made his way toward them.

Akri had just started for Styxx when all of a sudden, Styxx gasped and arched his back as if something possessed him.

The knife Bethany had buried in his chest shot through the air and landed harmlessly on the ground near Leto's feet. Light streamed out of the wound, sealing it closed.

In the next heartbeat, a shockwave went through the room, knocking everyone off their feet, except akri.

Gaping, Simi hovered over the floor as she realized that this was just like the time in New Orleans when Styxx had tried to kill her akri. Only then, Simi had wrapped around her akri to protect him.

This was what happened when a god tried to kill a Chthonian. It was a freaky rebirth they had that would bring them back from death.

The chains that held Styxx in place shattered, sending shrapnel in all directions. Simi ducked, grateful they missed her as they struck the wall right beside her and shattered glass.

Styxx rose to hover over the floor.

"What's happening?" Archon roared.

No one answered as lightning bolts shot from Styxx's body, blowing out the windows and ripping the doors from their hinges. Bolts of light pierced Styxx's eyes and mouth.

They exploded through his body like a beautiful light show.

Simi started to go to Styxx to help him like she'd done her akri, but akri held her back.

"No, Simi. He might hurt you."

She had a hard time believing that. Styxx would never hurt his Simi.

Instead, akri teleported himself to where Styxx hovered.

Simi cringed, praying her akri didn't get hurt.

Or worse, dead.

The moment Bethany saw what akri was doing, her nostrils flared with anger. "You!"

But akri caught her with his powers and held her in place. "Kill me and Styxx dies, too. Is that what you want?"

"Kill them both!" Leto shouted, still trying to put the two halves of the Egyptian heart together.

Bethany rose up as if she'd obey Leto, but then her gaze went to Styxx, and she calmed instantly. "What do I do to save him?" she asked akri in an anguished tone.

"You have to ground him. Make him aware of who and what he really is outside of his powers."

"How?"

Akri shook his head. "I have no idea. I'll try and hold him, but you have got to reach him, or those powers will rip him apart and destroy us all."

Simi wanted to help but had no idea how to do so.

Bethany stepped back and cleared the way for akri to

launch himself at Styxx. When his brother went to hit him, akri embraced Styxx with everything he had.

Styxx bellowed furiously as he tried to break free.

Bethany appeared in front of Styxx and cupped his face in her hands. "Styxx? Can you hear me?"

A hurricane blast went through the room with enough force that it knocked Bethany back and sent Simi careening into a wall.

Akri held on to Styxx and grabbed Bethany by the hand before the mean wind carried her away.

Styxx shoved akri way and turned on her with a murderous glint in his blue eyes.

Simi held her breath, expecting the worse.

Instead, Bethany kissed him.

Styxx pulled back to look down at the woman in his arms. "Beth?"

She smiled warmly up at her long-lost husband. "Are you with me, akribos!"

"I'm not sure. Am I dead?"

Bethany laughed. "I don't know. Am I?"

"No!" Leto screamed as she ran for them.

Without hesitating, akri intercepted her. But as soon as he neared her, she stabbed him through his stomach with the same Atlantean dagger laced with ypnsi sap that Bethany had used to kill Styxx.

Fury went through Simi as she saw that goddess dare to do what should never have been dared. She stabbed her akri.

While the poison was fatal to mortal beings, it was a

potent miasma for the gods, and it was the same serum Apollymi had used on the evil Atlantean gods to lock them in their deathlike limbo.

Akri staggered back and fell to his knees.

The Simi and Styxx ran to him.

"Acheron?" Styxx said, cradling his head.

"Simi!" akri called, ignoring his brother.

She knew instantly what he wanted and why he called her. What she needed to do to save him. "Simi on it, akri!"

Teleporting to Kalosis, she went to Sarraxyn so that she could get the three leaves from the Tree of Life once more. But while she did so, akra-Apollymi remained strangely quiet and reserved.

Simi paid it no attention as she quickly gathered what she needed and returned to poor akri who was completely gray and frozen on the ground. He looked terrible!

Not wanting to think about that, Simi handed the leaves to Styxx.

"What do I do with these?" he asked her.

Apollymi's ghosty form moved to stand over them so that she could make sure her son wasn't harmed. "Twist them until they're moist. Then drip nine drops into Apostolos's mouth."

Styxx hesitated. "What happens if I do ten by mistake?"

"Let's not find out."

Simi couldn't agree more. Holding her breath, she watched as akri-Styxx carefully put nine drops in akri's mouth.

As soon as the ninth one hit his lips, the color slowly returned to the whole of his body.

Simi smiled in relief.

Groaning, akri opened his eyes, then grimaced. "Next time, add peppermint flavoring somebody. That is the nastiest-tasting crap on the planet."

Simi laughed.

"You're not seriously complaining that I brought you back. Are you?" Styxx asked.

"Yes, and no. Taste it for yourself. It's worse than eating one of Urian's shoes."

Snorting, Styxx held his hand out to his brother. Akri took it and allowed him to pull him to his feet.

Simi was thrilled. This was the first time she'd seen them as actual brothers.

Forever and always. It made her happy that akri and his copy were in the same room and not trying to kill each other.

Akri hugged Styxx close, then stepped back to leave him to his Bethany.

Styxx turned and wrapped his arms around her. "I told you I'd come back for you, my goddess. That nothing would stop me."

"Yes, but did you have to drag your feet? Seriously?"

Styxx laughed. "I'm afraid you're going to have to get used to living with me right here. I will never again let you go. Just consider me a large exterior growth on your body."

Bethany nodded. "I am so glad to have you back. I just wish we had our son with us."

"I know, precious," he breathed.

"Uh ... about that."

Simi looked at Apollymi. Never in her life had she heard such a tone from the goddess. If she didn't know better, she'd swear akra-Apollymi was anxious about something.

Styxx stepped back to glare at her. "What?"

"Remember my promise to you, Styxx?"

"That you'd make everything right if I survived? Yes. I remember that."

Apollymi glanced at Simi, then akri before she spoke again. "I didn't kill your son. I wanted to. Desperately. But as I looked down at that tiny, beautiful baby, I saw my Apostolos and I couldn't bring myself to hurt him."

Bethany gasped. "He lives? Where is he?"

Apollymi's gaze went to Urian who turned around to look behind him.

Simi's jaw dropped in understanding. That was why the goddess had always been so fond of Urian.

"Urian is Galen?" Styxx asked.

Urian shook his head. "It's not possible. I was born before they died."

"No, you weren't." Apollymi smiled sadly. "Strykerius told you that because he didn't want you to know that you and your brother were the first Apollites born cursed. And that was my fault. I intentionally chose Strykerius's wife because I thought it the perfect revenge that Apollo should look after Styxx's child given what he'd done to him ... in both lifetimes. I had no idea Apollo would curse all of you over the death of a woman he really couldn't stand. Like Apostolos and Styxx, your blood mingled with that of Strykerius's real son, and that made you a part of Strykerius, too. You, child, are the only being alive who is part human, Atlantean, and Apollite ... and you carry in your veins the blood of three pantheons and gods."

Urian was as aghast as Simi was to hear that. "Does Stryker know?"

The goddess nodded. "I told him long ago—after you were grown, and he wondered about some of your heightened abilities—that you were very special to this world, but not who your real parents were. Your unique bloodline was why the evil souls you once lived on didn't infect you at all. Why you could go longer between feedings than others of your kind. It's also why Strykerius cut your throat instead of stabbing you in the heart. Unlike other Daimons, you wouldn't have died from a heart wound. Only blood loss could kill you."

Urian looked at akri. "Did you know this?"

"I knew it was odd that Stryker cut your throat instead of stabbing you, but no. I had no clue you were my nephew. My mother"—he passed a peeved glare at her—"never mentioned it to me."

Urian scowled. "Man, I'm messed up right now. My best friend is my father? The man I idolized as a kid ... whose tattoo is on my arm ... And he's younger than me. Yeah, I don't think I can handle this. Mind-wipe me, somebody ... please! Where's that dragon from Sanctuary? Simi, go get Max. I need him."

Simi laughed at his order. Though honestly, she couldn't blame him. It was hard to believe Apollymi had done something so mean.

Bethany approached Urian tentatively so that she could study him. His hair was lighter than Styxx's. He wasn't quite as tall as his father, but he had the same expression now that Styxx wore whenever he was irritated or confused. She placed a gentle hand on his cheek as she stared up at him. "I see your father in you. My baby's beautiful. Just like I knew you'd be." She pulled him into her arms and held him tight.

Simi felt for the goddess who hadn't been alive to raise her son. Urian was a good man and one Simi called friend. He was good quality people, and she was glad that he now had his real parents.

"I hate that I missed seeing you grow, but I do love you ... Urian."

In spite of what Urian had said, he held on to his mother as if she'd raised him.

Styxx wrapped his arms around both of them.

Simi looked over at her sissy and smiled. She was glad that Styxx had found his family and even gladder that akri had his brother again.

Just like she had hers.

They had saved Styxx and Bethany. She was so glad to know that they'd kept the future intact.

Because one day, Simi wanted to see Nekoda again.

Most of all, she wanted Nick to be the Malachai who saved the world. Not the one who destroyed it.

31

THREE WEEKS LATER

"You know what you needs, Thorny?"

Sitting on his throne, he looked up to find Simi in front of him, dressed in an adorable corset top with a short plaid skirt. "A doorbell?"

She laughed in that adorable way that never failed to make him smile. "Well, sure, if you wants them demons to announce themselves when they're being all intrusive. Probably good for Shadow, too."

But she didn't include herself in that, he noticed. Not that she needed to. Her unexpected visits were usually the highlight of any given day. And even at times, the highlight of his year.

"So what brings you by tonight?"

"Actually, it's day. I'd tell you to open the windows, but it don't matter here. It always blah!"

She was right about that.

"You still haven't told me what you think I need," he reminded her.

Simi smiled and flounced over to the wall across from his fireplace. "A big, gigantus TV, right here. You needs that."

"Why?"

"So when the Simi comes to visit I won't miss seeing my QVC. We coulds even watch it together. Pop some corn. Eat some chips and barbecue ..."

"We could. I could also let Paimon gouge out my eyes. Both are equally appealing."

She made an adorable face at him. "What do you do here for fun? All these centuries the Simi comes to visit and you're always in your chair, drinking. That can't be all you do."

He held up the book in his lap. "I read. It's retro and fun. Best of all, you don't have to charge it at night."

Simi came over and looked at it. She wrinkled her nose over the fact it was nonfiction. "Okies. That's fun. Simi likes to read, too. But it not the same as watching movies and shopping QVC."

"I don't like to shop."

She scoffed at his words. "The Simi sees how you dress. You shop. A lot."

And she'd done a lot of shopping with him over the years. Mostly because he loved the way she skirted about racks, looking adorable and trying to get him to wear ghastly things that should be set on fire.

"Your point?"

"You need a TV. Simple, silly."

"I profane modern technology."

"Again, we could watch movies and eat popcorn. Not have to go out to the theater all the time. I know how much you profane that, too."

He rolled his eyes, even though her argument was a good one. He did spend an inordinate amount of time complaining about people and sticky floors, especially people who eyed Simi with an interest that made him want to rip out their spines and beat them. "I'll think about it."

Simi spread her hands wide. "I'm telling you, Thorny, big TV, right here. Beautimous!"

Maybe, but he doubted if anything could be more beautimous than Simi being herself.

One Month *Later*

Thorn was again reading when Simi appeared in his room. Looking up from his book, he arched a brow.

Hands on hips, she stared at him. "Don't you be looking so surprised the Simi is here after you done texted me to come visit." She held up her phone and twisted it playfully. "Simi thought you said you profaned tech."

"I do. But not when it brings a beautiful demon to my home."

She tsked. "What am I going to do with you?"

It was sad that she thought he was kidding. Or maybe drunk. The latter was a definite. It was his natural state of being.

Still, he'd summoned her for a reason.

"There's something I want to show you."

She arched her brow. "And that is?"

Getting up, he set his drink and book aside, then used his powers to manifest a blindfold. "You trust me?"

"Always."

"Then turn around."

Putting her fists up against her shoulders, she flounced about, giving him her back.

Gah, she was adorable. Smiling, Thorn placed the blindfold over her eyes, then teleported them into a new room. One Simi had never seen before because he'd never had any use for it.

Now ...

"Remember, Thorny, akri is vicious."

He smiled at the threat. "So are you, my lady." Thorn stepped away, even though it was the last thing he wanted to do. "Open your eyes."

Giggling, Simi pulled off the blindfold. The moment she opened her eyes, she instantly sobered and gasped as she saw the room he'd made for her, alone.

"Oh, Thorny!"

Sheepish, he looked at the theater room he'd made, complete with a popcorn machine and a small fridge that held an assortment of hot and barbecue sauces he knew she loved. "You like it?"

She walked over to the dark brown wallpaper that was covered with Art Deco monkeys. "It's amazing!"

Thorn went to the dark red Bombay chest where he had two sets of glasses charging. "It even has 3D." Because he loved to watch her try to reach out and touch things whenever they saw 3D movies together.

Letting out an adorable squeal, she rushed to him and took a pair. "Can we watch something now?"

"Absolutely." Thorn opened the cabinet in the wall. He'd stocked it full of Simi's favorites. "What's your pleasure, my lady demon?"

Eyes wide, she started picking through the DVDs. "Oooo! The Simi is so happy! We have our own theater now! No more people walking through my movie and making the Simi want to eat their heads!"

"I'm surprised Acheron hasn't given you one."

Simi shrugged. "We gots a gigantus screen. But not the comfy chairs. Akri likes his throne too much." She handed him a DVD of the *Sound of Music*."

Thorn groaned in pain over her choise. "Seriously? I do this for you and you torture me? Why?"

Lifting herself up on her toes, she kissed his cheek. "It not torture, Thorny. The hills are alive."

He laughed as she flounced over to a recliner and put her feet up.

Why do I adore her?

No, he realized as he put the DVD in. He didn't adore her ...

He loved her.

Shock froze him to the spot as he realized a truth that burned him to his soul. He loved Simi.

Not as a friend.

Much, much more. Because he would never have altered his home for anyone else, nor been so happy to do so.

Ash will kill me. But as the movie started and Simi manifested a blanket and bucket of popcorn, he realized he didn't care what Ash thought. Or what he did to Thorn.

All that mattered was Simi and her happiness.

His heart pounding, he sat down next to her.

She smiled and offered him her bucket.

Thorn took a handful of the popcorn and sat back.

"We need Cokes."

Thorn manifested a big cup of fountain soda for her. It was her favorite for movies and the smile on her face made his heart pound even harder.

He'd done this as a lark and honestly had expected her to mock him for it and not really use it. But this ...

She was giddy and he was thrilled that he'd made her so happy. Which was weird. He hadn't cared this much about someone else's happiness since Brigid.

For a time, he had lived and died for the goddess. And he'd never thought to feel this way about anyone ever again. Especially not Simi.

With Brigid, she'd enchanted him the moment they met. He'd known she owned him right away.

With Simi ...

She'd snuck up on his feelings. Or had she?

Now that he thought about it, he'd adored her since the moment they first met and she'd laughed at him.

There was nothing else in this universe like her charm. Or her heart.

They'd been friends first. Best friends for centuries.

Now he wanted more. Much, much more. He wanted her here with him all the time.

And he couldn't do anything about it. Ash would absolutely destroy him.

They would never be friends again if he told her or acted on his feelings.

You have an even bigger problem.

He didn't know how Simi felt about him. Never once in all these centuries had she ever shown an interest in him as anything more than a friend.

She slept with the Malachai.

That still galled him.

No, it hurt him and that was the truth. He'd never been angry over it. He'd been gutted. Gutted to the core of his rotten soul. She had chosen someone he still wanted to slug over it.

Too bad Nick was such a decent guy. He made it hard to hate him.

Simi slurped her soda, then frowned. "You okay, Thorny? You seem distractable."

"Sorry. Not my favorite movie, but I know you love it. So here I am."

She handed him her cup. "Thank you for suffering. It is much appreciated."

"All good." And it was. As bad as he hated this movie, he loved her enough to sit through it for the thousandth time and listen to her sing off-key with Julie Andrews. Besides, it could be worse. She could have chosen *Nosferatu.* Her other favorite movie that made him crazy.

Yeah, this was love. Because there was no other reason he'd suffer through something he despised this much to make someone else happy.

And he would never be able to tell her how he really felt. Which made this so much worse than Brigid.

Because Simi was loyal. She would never denounce him, never turn on him, and he would have to spend the rest of eternity pretending to be just her friend.

Thorn froze the moment he returned home to his bleak, dark castle in the Nether Realm of absolute evil. As he entered his study to drink what he needed for nourishment, he felt a powerful presence in the room.

Why would *he* be here?

Other than to annoy him. "What are you doing?"

With long dark hair and mismatched eyes, Jaden stepped out of the shadows. "I felt that which should not have been done. Valac is dead?"

Thorn sighed wearily at the mention of the demon they'd executed. "He is."

Absolute horror darkened Jaden's eyes. "Only the Sephiroth has that power."

"Apparently your grandson has a friend who can also do it." Even though Jared was the last Sephiroth left alive, he wasn't the only one to share that power.

Thorn moved to his crystal decanter and poured himself his favorite fermented libation. "As the Chthonians rose from the Source as a counterbalance to the gods who were abusing their powers to prey on humankind, it seems we have a new species born to balance the demon races."

Jaden cursed under his breath. "Forneus—"

Thorn hated whenever someone used that name. It was the one that allowed someone to control him. "What would you have me do? Tell me what power can destroy this one?"

"The Malachai."

That was laughable.

"You want to pit the Malachai against Jared and make the Malachai all the more powerful? Is that really your plan?" He shook his head at the idea of Jaden allowing his grandson to square off against Nick. Not that it would matter given that Jared was Nick's grandfather.

He couldn't imagine the two of them ever in battle. Jared would sacrifice himself before he'd ever harm a hair on Nick's head now that he knew he was Cherise's father, and Nick's grandddad.

Cam had picked the perfect way to set up the Malachai. Jared had unknowingly fathered Cherise Gautier.

Nick was now part Malachai, part god and part Sephiroth. A unique mixture that would either save the world.

Or end it.

"Good one, Jaden. Let's set off nukes while we're at it.

At least then, the planet would be habitable again ... eventually."

Jaden rubbed his hands over his eyes. "You're insane. You should have killed your son at birth."

Thorn wouldn't argue that. It would have saved all of them a lot of trouble if Cadegan had been suffocated on arrival. But he could never do that to one of his sons, anymore than Jaden could. "As you should have killed your progeny?"

Jaden's eyes flared with his hatred. "We don't speak of that. Ever."

Narrowing his eyes on the beast he hated most—the bastard who was solely responsible for Thorn's regrettable birth—he swallowed his drink. "Ditto. What do you think would happen if Noir ever learned of my son's existence?"

He would use both of Thorn's children as tools to subjugate the gods and the world.

Well aware of that nightmare, Jaden glanced away. "What game are you playing?"

"The same game you are. Survival."

"No," Jaden growled, "I know who and what I am. What side of this conflict I clearly fall on. You dance with a darkness that will one day swallow you whole."

"For your sake ... for the sake of the human world you love so much, you better pray that never happens."

Jaden winced as he was summoned home by Azura and Noir.

His gaze dark and filled with foreboding, Jaden paused before he left with one parting shot. "I had this very conversation with your father, once, Thorn. Long before you were born. Let us pray, that when history repeats itself, your conqueror is kinder to you."

Thorn set his drink down as those words echoed in his ears. Centuries ago, the Chthonian, Savitar, had warned him of the same thing.

And Savitar had condemned the union that had brought Thorn into being.

They both walked a tenuous line between opposing forces that constantly sought their very souls. Like him, Savitar had chosen to abandon the mortal realm for solitude. It was much easier to avoid temptation when it wasn't near.

We are all the architects of our own downfall. Acheron's words haunted him now.

Yet, on the other side, everyone was also the architect of their own salvation and redemption.

Sadly, there was only one creature who could tell the final outcome of it all. And thankfully that one still remained dormant.

Sleeping.

For the sake of them all, no one needed to disturb that beast.

Sighing, Thorn moved to sit before his fire and stare into flames that spoke to him in the quiet solitude of his lonely home. He used his powers to pull his drink to him so that he could toast the noise. "Here's to the future. May it never bring to me what I deserve."

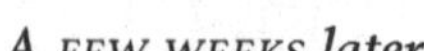

A FEW WEEKS later

THORN FROZE the moment he sat inside the back of his Bentley and closed the car door. Something was wrong. Deadly wrong. He could feel it in the air around him. It sizzled as if the particles in the air were electrified by unspent magic and energy. "Josiah?"

His driver didn't turn around. He was completely frozen in place, with blood trailing from his left ear.

Shit.

As Thorn reached for the door handle, it melted and the doors locked. He was blocked from teleporting. Furious, he knew of only one demon who would dare such with him.

"What do you want?" he demanded through clenched teeth.

A dark shadow appeared in the seat beside him. "You don't call. You don't e-mail. I'm beginning to feel like you don't like me. And that really hurts me in my inner tender place."

Thorn glared at Paimon who was currently possessed. "Didn't you get the Father's Day gift I sent you?"

Red eyes manifested to glare at him. "Yes, the hands of my best demon in a pink, bloody box, middle fingers extended. How very thoughtful of you."

"Knew you would like it. Soon as I saw him on my ass, I knew it would make the perfect gift for you."

His father, through Paimon's body, blasted him against the door. "Where is he?"

The *he* being referred to was Cadegan. His eldest son was finally free of the hell realm Thorn had unknowingly banished him to and he was being sought by those who wanted to use him for the birthright his mother had given him.

In spite of the pain, Thorn gave him a droll stare. "He's where you can't reach him."

"I know you have that little bastard shielded from me. It's just a matter of time before I find him again and take what I want."

Thorn scoffed at his nebulous progenitor. "He would die before he allowed you to have it."

"I will kill him for it. See, we can all get what we want and be happy. Why prolong the inevitable?"

"And miss out on all these fun father-son chats we have through your demons? Why would I ever do that, old man?"

Paimon hissed as if Noir had pulled out of him and left the two of them alone to "chat" in his car. "Do I have to kill you?"

Thorn burst out laughing. "Try it."

Paimon created a giant mouth with serrated teeth. Then he was stupid enough to try and swallow Thorn whole.

Oops, he'd been wrong.

Noir was still in control of Paimon.

"That was only scary when I was a young idiot, Dad. I've grown up. Deal with it."

Noir, in Paimon's body, screamed in Thorn's face. "I weep over your birth!"

So did he.

Thorn patted his heart in deep sarcasm. "Such fatherly love and compassion. It brings tears to my eyes." Sighing, he spread his hand out and examined his manicured nails as if bored with their exchange. "Why do you want him so badly, anyway? Not like you can use his powers where you are. Or his shield, for that matter."

Thorn looked up as another way to control Cadegan occurred to him. "Unless you have a body?"

"Why would I tell you if I did?"

His father was so predictable.

Thorn smiled snidely. "Good. You don't. That'll save me the trouble of having to track Paimon down and banishing him again."

Noir, in Paimon's body, pinned him back against the seat. "You think you're so clever and smart. But there's something a lot worse than me after Cadegan, Leucious. We will find him."

"No. You won't. Now begone. You're stinking up the place. And it's a six-month waiting list to get another one of these."

Paimon rushed him, then went through his body and vanished from his car.

Sighing in relief, he leaned forward to close Josiah's

eyes and whisper a prayer for the poor man. As he did so, Cadegan's rosary fell from his pocket.

He'd brought it with him today to return it to his son but had refrained. He had so few things from his son that he hadn't been able to part with it. It was literally all he had as a memento.

Thorn picked it up from the floorboard and pressed it to his lips. Cadegan was so much more than Thorn had ever hoped for in a son. For now, they were reunited.

Still as brothers.

Even now, he wasn't sure how to tell Cadegan the truth about their relationship, any more than he'd ever been able to tell Simi how he felt about her. And maybe he never would. Some truths were just too hard to face and served no purpose other than to cause pain.

33

OCTOBER 31, 2030

"Do something with your son! I'm at my end with him!"

Thorn arched a brow as Karma met him at the front door of her house, shrieking loud enough that it stopped two pedestrians on the sidewalk behind him. Once they realized she wasn't yelling at him per se, they quickly walked on.

Wow. No preamble. Just another denouncement of E.T. and his stubbornness. Which Thorn could understand. E.T. did enjoy being pig-headed.

Just like his mom.

And his father.

"Where's the boy? I'll take him out back and beat him forthwith."

Karma glared at him with the full weight of her wrath. "Just don't, Thorn. This is serious. He's been slipping out at night and—"

"He's a grown man, Karma. Almost thirty. I doubt he's slipping out to meet his friends."

"Have you met him? He might look like a grown man, but he has the instincts of a five-year-old! I don't like the people he's hanging out with. They're trouble."

Could they really be worse than his father, and the demons Thorn called friends?

Trying not to say that out loud, Thorn entered her house so that the people on the street would no longer have a free show. "Are you talking about Val and Annabelle?"

Karma locked the door and gave him a hot, furious glare. "My niece and nephew aren't the problem ... much. Annabelle could be a little more circumspect, but given her mother and father, she's remarkably stable."

She wasn't wrong. Annabelle and her brother, Valerian, were the children of Karma's sister, Tabitha, and the ex-Dark-Hunter, Valerius Magnus.

They and their cousins had been virtually inseparable since they were born and could get into more than their fair share of trouble. Thorn suspected it had a lot to do with the Devereaux blood mixing with whatever Artemis did to create a Dark-Hunter.

Just a bad combination all around.

"He's not hanging out with his cousins, Thorn. Not since he found out about *you*."

Oh ...

That made his blood run cold as it opened the door to

a much lower class of entities the boy could be seeking out to befriend. "Then who?"

"Demons."

Like father, like son. Shit. He dreaded the next question, but he needed clarity. "What do you mean?"

"It started with them hanging out at Club Charonte and that other place where demons gather. Next thing I knew, he wasn't coming home. I don't know what they're doing. But I'm worried."

She had every right to be. While E.T. was a good kid, he had enough of Thorn's blood in him to make him a target, especially for those like Paimon who wanted to control him.

"Is he at work?"

"He quit his job two weeks ago. Don't get me started on that!"

Thorn ground his teeth. "What's he been doing?"

"That's what I'm saying. He hasn't been doing anything. Just hiding out in his room or off with who knows what until all hours of the day and night. Being evasive every time I ask him where he is or where he's going. Who he's meeting with. He needs his father."

The boy obvioudly needed something. Maybe a butt kicking might be the best course.

"All right. I'll take care of it."

"Thank you." She gave him a tight hug. "And don't kill him. I have earned that privilege."

Snorting at her humor, he stepped away from her.

"You're welcome." And with that, Thorn left her alone in her house so that he could track down their errant child and see what E.T. had gotten himself into.

Simi LEFT the dance floor so that she could head to the bar and get something to drink. Dancing always made her thirsty.

Raising her hand, she motioned the green-and-yellow Charonte over to her and did her best not to laugh at the humans who all assumed their waiter was wearing a costume and makeup.

If they only knew ...

It was why she loved her bro-bro's bar so much. Here, she could let her hornays out and even her wings and no one thought anything about it. The humans just thought it was a theme.

Theme demon.

Simi's favorite.

"What can I get for you, beautiful?" Fiore asked.

Simi smiled at the demon who always flirted with her. Fiore made no attempt to hide the fact that he was most interested in the Simi. Brave considering akri or Rik-rik would gut him if they ever saw it. "Gimme one of them pretty Shirley drinks, please. Extra cherries!"

Fiore laughed, then went to get her drink.

Simi turned around to scan the bar full of dancers.

Cocking her head, she frowned as she saw Thorny's son with a group of demons she didn't know.

Tall and blond, E.T. tended to stand out even in a crowd. 'Course he looked a lot like his daddy. Eerily so at times, only he didn't have the same sadness in his eyes that Thorny did.

"Here you go, Simi."

Thanking Fiore, she took her drink and headed for E.T. and his group of friends.

As soon as he saw her approaching, he stopped laughing and cursed under his breath. Well that didn't make her happy.

Really?

"E?" she asked.

He tried to shoosh through the crowd.

Now that was just plain ole rude and honestly, it made her angry! Aggravated, she teleported in front of him so that she could cut his path off.

"What are you doing?" Simi asked, tsking at him before she took a sip of her drink through the little red straw.

"I'm out with my friends, Simi. What are you doing here?"

"Dancing in my brother's bar where I frequent a lot." Simi glanced over to the dark demons who smelled like they'd just come out of Azmodea. "Why you hanging with lowlifes? I know your mama done taught you better than this."

"They're good friends, Simi." He tried to move past her.

Simi cut him off again. "E ..."

"Stop, Simi. I know what I'm doing."

She arched a brow at his defiant tone. "Why you being so mean to the Simi?"

He had the decency to look sheepish and well he should for yelling at her like that when all she was trying to do was watch after him. "I'm not trying to be mean. I just don't feel like I belong. You could never understand."

"Of course I understand. You have any idea how many centuries I was the only Charonte in the human world? But you definitely don't belong with them riffraff." She cut a meaningful stare at the demons.

"Who you calling riffraff?" One of the demons sidled up to her.

Simi pushed him away daintily. "You, smelly demon. Why aren't you in your hole where you belong?"

E.T. pulled him back. "Don't pick a fight with Simi. It won't end well for you."

He raked an arrogant look over her body. "I'm not afraid of a Charonte."

"Then you're just terminally stupid, given the fact that her brother owns this club full of them."

Simi gasped at the sound of Thorn's deep voice cutting over the music as he appeared behind her.

E.T. cursed again. "What are you doing here, Thorn?"

He swept his gaze over the ones with E.T. and shook his head. "Visiting. And I think it's time for your friends to leave."

"I like my friends and I have no wish for them to go."

Thorn shook his head at his son. "Leave, demons. Or

you're going to regret being stupid. Which as I said is terminal. Stay and I'll show you exactly how terminal it is."

They vanished instantly.

E.T. growled. "Really? You're as bad as Mom."

Thorn's eyes turned a vibrant red. "I'm so much worse than your mother. Never forget that, Ian. She's your sympathetic parent who carried you inside her body. I don't have that attachment."

He started past Thorn, who gently took his arm. "What's going on with you, kid?"

"I want to know more about my demonic kin."

"I'll send you a scrapbook."

Simi bit her lip as she saw the defiance in E.T.'s eyes. He had a lot of his daddy in him.

A lot.

She'd never realized that before because he'd always been such a sweetie baby. What happened to that perfect little angel boy who used to sit on the floor, eating potato chips and playing cars with his Simi sitter?

The man in front of her was angry. Defiant. He reminded her a lot of Thorny when akri-Thorn had been that age.

Except E.T. wasn't nearly as scary.

"This is such bullshit!"

Thorn growled. "Enough!"

"Or what? You'll ground me, Dad?"

The look on Thorny's face was enough to make Simi take a step back. Sadly, E.T. didn't have the same level of self-preservation.

"This isn't a game, kid. There's a war coming and you don't want to be on the wrong side of it."

E.T. actually had the nerve to roll his eyes. "You sound like Mom. There's always the end of the world looming. Since we're tap dancing on a constant landmine, why can't I have fun before the Malachai or whatever destroys us?"

Thorn wasn't having any of it. "Fun comes after you grow up and stop acting like a baby. Go home, E. Don't make me have to spank you in public."

The look in E.T.'s eyes said that he was tempted to push his father to that point.

Simi understood. She'd been known to press her luck with akri a lot more than she should. Although, compared to akri sons with akra-Tory ...

The Simi was a delight for her akri. Bas and Terry had been making akri crazy since they hit their teens and turned all lippy with their daddy.

Kind of like E.T. and Thorny. Only worse 'cause Bas and Terry knew their grandmother would protect them from akri no matter how mad they made him. Akra-Polly had become exceptionally protective of her grandboys.

Even over akri.

It was funny sometimes. Scary most times.

"You two can't run my life. I'm grown!" E.T. looked at Simi as if he knew she understood his frustrations.

And she did. "I have the same argument with my akri, too. It okay, E. Growing up is hard and there were times when the Simi hated it all." She still had her issues with it, but she was getting more accustomed to being an adult ... ish.

Thorn sighed heavily. "No one is trying to run your life. We're trying to keep you from ruining. And keep you safe."

"No one is going to mess with me. Not given who I'm related to."

Simi widened her eyes. "Oh, that's not true, E. Trust the Simi. There are lots of beings out there who will mess with you exactly 'cause who you related to. Even the Simi gets messed with 'cause of akri and everyone knows akri would eat the head of anyone who hurt his Simi."

E.T. rolled his eyes again. "It's not the same thing. I want my place in this world."

Thorn scoffed. "And you think hanging with demons and acting like a two-year-old is going to give you that place?"

"At least they were planning to show me how to use my powers."

Thorn winced at those words. "Once you open that door, boy, you can never close it again."

"I want to open it. I've been begging to open it and none of you will help me."

Simi shook her head at his insistence. She knew what Thorn was trying to make him understand. But the boy wasn't getting it. "E ... powers are like taking that first bite of chocolate. Before you understand the nummy, you think you want it. But then you find out that chocolate is really, *really* good. Then you start to crave it and if you eat too much, it'll make you sick. Might even kill you."

He scowled at her. "What?"

"Don't eat the chocolate," Thorn said, slowly enunciating each word.

E.T. turned toward his father, "Whatever. I'm going home. But this isn't over."

Thorn moved closer to Simi as E.T. headed for the exit. "Should I follow him?"

She shook her head. "It'll just make him madder."

"Everything I do makes him angrier, Sim. I wish his mother had never told him I was his father. It was a mistake. All it's done is make him furious at both of us. And seek out things he shouldn't."

Simi shook her head. "He loves you. The Simi feels his heart. He just doesn't know what he is. You remember that confused feeling, don't you?"

Thorn went quiet as he considered Simi's question. He did remember that lost feeling of everything being ripped out from under him. Of the world not making sense because he wasn't who and what he'd thought.

It was why he'd wanted Karma to keep Ian's birth a secret from their son. Now that the boy knew, he was angry and bitter. Accusatory.

And he couldn't blame him. He should have been more active in his life. But how could he?

Had he played Daddy Dearest, others would have grown suspicious and figured out why. Then both E.T. and Karma would have been targets for his enemies.

It was the same reason he couldn't spend much time with his grandchildren.

No one needed to know he had *any* weaknesses.

"It'll be okay, akri-Thorny." Simi patted him gently on the back.

"I hope you're right." Because if they didn't get E.T. to calm down, there was no telling how much harm the boy could do.

34

NOVEMBER 1, 2030

Alone in his study, Thorn felt the sickly presence that never failed to make him nauseated. Why could he never have peace?

"Paimon. Come to slum?"

"Gloat, actually."

That didn't sound good. "Gloat about what?"

"The fact that you have no idea what you've done."

Thorn turned toward the demon, ready to splinter him into pieces over this imbecilic game. "I don't have time for your games. Get out."

"Suit yourself." Paimon vanished.

Thorn was happy for a half second until he allowed those words to get to him.

Had he done something he didn't know about?

Stop it. The bastard's playing with your head.

That was what Paimon excelled at. The only thing he did well, point of fact.

But what if he wasn't just messing with Thorn's mind? What if something else had happened?

Given his life, it was a good bet that he'd run afoul of something with power.

Paimon's an idiot. Ignore him.

Granted it was true, but what if he was being honest this time?

When has he ever been honest?

Rarely. Rarely didn't mean never. There had been times when Paimon had been honest. What if this was one of them?

"I hate you, Paimon," he growled under his breath. Because the sad truth was, he believed him.

GRIM CAUGHT sight of Paimon the moment he entered their abysmal castle. "Well? How did it go?"

"Idiot wouldn't listen to me. I accomplished nothing."

Grim cursed. "We need Thorn neutralized."

"I'm open for any and all suggestions."

So was Grim. "Look, Laguerre has a plan for us. Thorn is the only one who can mess it up."

"I still don't see how."

Because Paimon was an idiot. Right now, the Malachai had his powers restricted because Nick Gautier didn't want to be Ambrose. Nor did he want to end the world.

The Malachai had no idea what was coming, and it gave them the perfect opportunity to kill Nick, once and for all. Since Nick wasn't a true Malachai like the others before him, he was weak.

And Laguerre had come up with a way to create a new Malachai. One *they* would be in charge of raising. A Malachai they could turn mean and make more powerful than anything this world could handle.

They wouldn't be like Cherise, coddling and petting the Malachai. Teaching him how to love and be good.

They could create the monster the world deserved.

The monster Malachai who would actually end the world as everyone knew it. That was what they wanted. A Malachai they controlled. Then the gods would fear them, and they would be the ones in charge.

But first, they had to get Thorn out of the way. And Grim knew exactly where to put him.

"**H**ey, Ma! Can I get extra credit in your class if I tell the story about how Simi helped you find Atlantis?"

Thunder clapped through the small shotgun home where Simi lived sometimes with akri, akra-Tory and their two teenage sons, Terry and Sebastos.

Simi laughed as she added more syrup on her pancakes 'cause she was out of barbecue sauce. "You done made akri angry, baby Terry! You needs apologize before Daddy whups your butt."

With bright blue eyes and dark brown hair, Terry looked an awful lot like akri and akri-Styxx. But then so did their cousin, Ari who was sitting beside him at the breakfast table.

'Course a lot of that had to do with the fact that Ari's daddy was Styxx and his mom, Bethany. Since the two of them were only a few months apart in age, Terry and Ari hung out together a lot.

A lot, lot.

Bethany and Tory said that they were the twin brothers akri and Styxx should have been when they were little.

And that was okay. Akri and Styxx had learned to be twins and even friends over the years.

Akra-Tory set more pancakes down between them before she brushed the hair back from Terry's forehead and kissed his brow. "How many times do I have to tell you not to tease your father about Atlantis?"

"I know, but I want to graduate early and get on with my life."

She snorted at his answer. "You're seventeen, a senior in college, and you're immortal. Slow down. You have eternity to get on with your life." Tory handed Simi a bottle of barbecue sauce. "Not sure how that'll taste with the syrup mixed in, but ..."

Simi smiled as she gladly accepted the bottle, then she poured it over her stack.

"Besides," Terry pointed at Ari, "it was *his* idea."

"Hey! Don't throw me under the bus. I said we should try to get extra credit and graduate before the spring so we could get jobs with the Squire's council. Atlantis was all your idea."

Akri appeared in the room so that he could glare at Terry. "Why do you want to torment me in the morning when you know how much I hate mornings?"

Terry smiled. "Simi told me to."

Blinking, Simi swallowed her bite. "Uh-uh! Why you want to lie on your sissy like that, Ter-bear? And after all the times the Simi done helped you when you were little and hid things from akri you thought he'd kill you for doing." She tsked at him. "I even removed the hornays from your bitsy head that I put there when you were two."

"I know, Simi. I was just kidding. Besides, Dad knows you'd never do that. It's why he's still scowling at me."

Akri ruffled Terry's hair while Ari laughed at them.

Simi didn't speak as she watched them go through their normal morning routine. The only thing missing was Sebastos, but he'd spent the night with a friend.

And, of course, Xirena who'd left them a few years back. Her sissy had decided to move in with Drakus. Xirena's favorite Charonte. They were extremely happy together and Simi prayed that her sissy never regretted leaving them.

But Simi regretted it. Everyone was getting older and going on to new things.

She hated that.

Thorny was right. Change sucked. Although akri seemed completely happy with the change Tory had brought into his life, especially their sons. They made him happier than Simi had ever seen him.

So maybe some change was good?

She watched as Ari and Terry pulled out their phones and started making plans for the weekend. Even in a room with people, they were off by themselves again. Just like when they'd been babies who babbled together.

Something she missed so much.

So no, she decided. Change made the Simi's heart ache. She missed when they were little and ran through the house like shrieking demons, chasing her and her sissy. They never did that anymore.

They were too grown now.

Akri pulled his phone from his pocket, then turned it on to read it.

"Everything okay?" Tory asked as she set a plate of crispy bacon in front of akri.

"Not sure … It's from Fang. He's asking me if I've seen Thorn. For some reason, he's not responding to Fang or anyone else."

Fang was married to Aimee Peltier, one of the owners of Sanctuary, but he was also one of Thorny's Hellchasers.

Normally, the Hellchasers could find Thorny easier than Simi could. Thorny always kept an eye on them in case they needed help.

"He was at Club Charonte on Halloween." Simi took another bite of her pancakes.

"You saw him there?" Akri reached for the bacon.

Simi nodded. "He was fighting with E.T. 'cause E.T. was hanging with some no-good demons. Not high-quality demons like the Simi."

Terry arched a brow. "Girl demons?"

Narrowing his gaze on his son, akri cleared his throat.

"You're not old enough to be inside the club." Then he looked at Tory. "Remind me to talk to Xedrix about letting the kids in there. I know he's trying to be nice, but they don't need to be hanging out in that club until they're ... eighty, at least."

Terry and Ari began laughing together.

"Busted," Ari snickered. "And just to be clear, we didn't even do anything more than dance with Xedrix's daughters who were told to report to their dad if we did anything wrong."

Tory gave him a loving, but firm glare. "No more letting your cousins slip you in when you're sleeping over with them. Kerryna knows to watch y'all now. And she will."

Yes, she would. She was a fierce mama-demon. And Simi found it funny that akri was so stern with the boys and yet let his Simi flounce off wherever she wanted to go.

'Course the Simi would eat the heads off anyone who annoyed her, while the boys were much more cautious. They didn't like the blood the way Simi did.

Even so, they still laughed, completely unrepentant about getting into the club last year.

Akri dialed his phone, but after a few minutes, he shook his head. "Thorn's not answering."

That was strange. He always took akri's calls. Just like he always answered Simi when she sought her Thorny-man.

"Want me to go sees if the Simi can find him?"

Akri fidgeted with his phone. "Normally, I'd say leave it be. He's a big PITA who can fend for himself. But ... I have a bad feeling. If you could check and see, I'd appreciate it."

"Okies, akri." Simi finished her breakfast and then went to Azmodea.

Nothing was out of place. Thorny's office was crisp and clean. Just the way he liked it. His bed made up.

But there was no sign of the big guy. Weird. It didn't look like he'd been here in days.

"What are you doing here?"

Simi paused in the bedroom at Misery's mean demand. "Where's Thorny?"

Crossing her arms over her chest, Misery glared at her. "Obviously not here and you need to leave."

"I'm looking for Thorn, heifer demon. It's important."

"I don't know what to tell you, Charonte. He hasn't been here in a week. I've no idea where he is or when he'll be back. He doesn't exactly confide in me. I'm just the servant he hates."

Well, that wasn't good, and it wasn't true, and Simi knew it. Thorny didn't hate Misery. He felt sorry for her, which was why he'd taken her in. But she'd betrayed everyone, and that was why Thorn kept her at a distance.

Trusting for him was impossible when he knew someone had betrayed others.

Yet even so, he helped a demon who couldn't be trusted.

That was why Simi loved him. Like akri and Styxx, Thorn had a unique heart and the last thing she wanted was to see her Thorny hurt.

Where are you, Thorn? It wasn't like him. He didn't just go away …

Maybe he was at Karma's?

He might be staying there to help with E.T.? It was as good an idea as any.

Without a word to the smelly girl demon, Simi headed back to New Orleans where Karma lived not all that far away from akri.

Her little pink house looked normal and pretty. Nothing unusual about it at all.

Simi headed to the door and knocked.

She heard Karma fussing under her breath as she came to the door and opened it. Surprise darkened her eyes. "Simi? What end-of-the-world apocalypse is happening now?"

Simi shook her head. "Akri's looking for Thorn. Last time the Simi saws him, he was with E.T., so I was wondering if he came here?"

Karma scowled at her. "I haven't seen him since Halloween when we went after our boy."

That wasn't good. Where could Thorny be?

"Is E.T. home?" Simi asked.

"Yeah." Karma let her in the house, then hollered for her son to come to the living room.

After a few seconds, E.T. left his upstairs room in the back of the house. "Geez, Mom! I'm on an open mic. Do you mind?"

"Yeah. All the time. Just not when the orders come from my kid." She winked at him.

E.T. rolled his eyes, until he realized Simi was there. "Hey, Simi."

"Hey, baby E. I'm looking for the Thorny-man. I haven't seen him since Halloween. Have you?"

"No. And I wasn't hoping to see him again anytime soon given how mean he was at the club. I can do without being chewed out all the time." He cut his gaze in the direction of his mother.

Ignoring what E.T. implied, Karma duplicated his frown. "Thorn's missing?"

Simi nodded. "If you hear from him, please lemme know, okies?"

Karma looked as worried as Simi felt. "Absolutely. Let me know when you find him."

"Will do." Simi left them and went back to her room in Katateros. Here, she could be alone in the quiet and listen to the ether for Thorn.

Yet for once, she heard nothing. Felt nothing. It was as if he didn't exist.

"Where are you, Thorny?"

It wasn't like him to vanish, especially not from Simi. All these centuries, Thorn had been there. Like akri. He was stable and dependable.

But Halloween was always a dangerous time. Things came into this world when they weren't supposed to.

And one creature in particular used that time to increase its powers.

Wanting to check on him, Simi teleported over to Bourbon Street. It was a huge, dark-gray mansion where she'd spent many years visiting. Her favorite times here had been when Cherise Gautier was still alive. The petite blond had always greeted Simi and brought her some of the best handmade eats. This was where Simi discovered hot sauce-covered Oreos—one of her favorite nummy treats.

Cherise had been amazing. No wonder Nick still missed her.

They all did. Even akri often visited her grave to put flowers on it. As did Nick.

Sighing over the tragedy of losing someone so precious, Simi knocked on the door and waited.

It took a couple of minutes before Nick opened it. He was dressed in a black t-shirt and jeans. His dark-brown hair was a bit shaggy, and he hadn't shaved today. Still, he was incredibly handsome, even with the heifer goddess's double bow mark on his cheek. "Simi? What are you doing here?"

"I'm looking for akri-Thorn. Have you seen him?"

Shadow appeared instantly beside Nick and nudged him aside. "What do you mean you're looking for Thorn?"

"He vanished on Halloween, and no one knows where he is."

Shadow looked up at Nick. "You didn't do anything to him, did you?"

Nick shoved playfully at Shadow. "You're such an idiot. I'd rip your head off before I would Thorn's. He's one of my protectors and has done me a lot of solids." He looked at Simi. "I'm not my father."

That was certainly true. In spite of being the Malachai, Nick helped protect humans. He'd always been a good guy.

Even though it was hard for him because the Malachai blood inside his veins wanted to destroy the world. But his mother's love counteracted it. That was the one thing Cam had done right. She'd found a way to suppress the Malachai and teach him how to love, and be decent.

Nick's eyes darkened as he searched the ether. "I can't find Thorn. Anywhere."

Shadow went pale. "Neither can I."

Nick brushed his hand through his dark-brown hair. "How is this possible? Is he dead?"

That word made Simi's heart stop. Thorn dead? She couldn't even bear the thought. Thorn could never die. It would destroy her. "No one would dare kill Thorny."

Would they?

Panic set in as she realized how many enemies Thorn had. Like akri. So many wanted him gone. Even his own father was known to threaten him. Thorn liked to joke about it, but Simi didn't find it funny. Especially right now.

Shadow rubbed at his arm. "Let me go see if I can find something out with the powers that be. Maybe they know what happened to him."

Simi nodded as he vanished.

Nick stood awkwardly in the doorway. "Want to come in? I think I have some Tabasco sauce. We definitely have pizza."

She laughed. "Normally the Simi would never turn

down such an offer, but I'm worried about Thorn. Not even hot sauce will help."

"We'll find him, Simi. Don't worry."

She wanted to believe that. But something about all this seemed wrong.

Thorn needed her. She could feel it. She just didn't know where he was or how to help him.

36

NOVEMBER 9, 2030

T horn growled as he felt his control slipping. There was no light or sound other than the fierce beating of his heart. Everything here was torture. Especially the darkness that seemed to infiltrate every part of his being.

He was losing his mind, and he didn't know how to fight this.

Damn you, Paimon!

How could he have let his guard slip?

I underestimated him. Not his powers. Paimon's viciousness. It was arrogance really. He'd correctly thought of Paimon as a parasite. His problem was that he forgot how destructive something as innocuous as a parasite could be.

The smallest thing could be lethal, especially when you turned your back on it.

Effing weasel.

Now he was trapped in a dismal ten-by-ten room with no window. No furniture.

No light.

Nothing except his thoughts. That was a dangerous combination. All his regrets were first and foremost. Every nasty moment of his life played out in his mind.

All there to torment him.

Time was terrifying when there were no distractions. All those *would haves*, *could haves* and *should haves*. They were the worst tormentors of mankind.

And especially demons.

His mind spun with every mistake he'd ever made. The greatest mistake being that he hadn't helped raise his sons. That Cadegan still didn't know he was his father.

And that E.T. was rebellious because he knew Thorn had fathered him. It made his youngest bitter and resentful. Angry. At least, as his brother, Cadegan had forgiven him and held not grudges.

No, he decided.

His biggest mistake was Simi. Why had he never told her how he really felt? How much he loved her. They'd lost all this time together where they could have been happy.

And for what?

"Enough!" he roared, wanting all those recriminations to stop. "Let me out of here!"

As expected, nothing happened. No one answered.

This had to be one of the lowest pits of his father's dungeon. Why he'd been trapped here, he had no idea. Was it his father's plan?

Azura's twisted madness? Or had Paimon done this on his own? They wanted to make him crazy, and it was working.

Calm down. Don't let him win.

Easier said than done. Thorn was surrounded by shadows. He should be able to reach through them and find his allies or friends.

"Where are you, Shadow? Why won't you answer me?"

But again, no one responded. It was as if the entire universe had ceased to exist.

For the first time in his life, he was absolutely alone.

Like Cadegan. Was this his punishment for sending his child to a realm that had been a nightmare for centuries?

The guilt of that alone was enough to justify his being here.

Maybe this *was* justice.

Maybe I deserve it.

No, he definitely deserved it for what he'd done to Cadegan. One act of stupidity. He should have had more faith.

I should have been a better father.

Regret was the hardest thing to live with. So many things he should have done differently. He needed to make amends.

What if I'm stuck here and never have the chance to apologize?

To tell Simi that he loved her.

Actually, that wasn't an if. He was definitely stuck, and he had no way out.

He wanted to scream in frustration. Wanted to kill everyone involved. But that was most likely why he was here. What they were trying to do.

Turn him into the weapon he'd been born to be. A weapon that had no mind and no conscience.

One that would destroy the entire world.

37

DECEMBER 9, 2333

"We failed ... again."

Noir did his best to ignore his sister while he stared out the window, into the darkness that made up the realm he despised passionately. "Perhaps we're not supposed to succeed."

Azura curled her lip. "Since when are *you* fatalistic?"

"The word is maudlin, Azura. And I'm tired of all the scheming that comes to naught. Face it. We're stuck here." They were always going to be stuck here.

It'd been centuries and everything they had tried had amounted to nothing but disappointment.

He was tired of it all.

Azura curled her lip. "We're not stuck here. The prophecy promises us a way out."

"Ambrose will never free us. You know that. Even if he did, Apollymi is going to make sure we never stop suffering." Noir growled low in his throat. "We should have never sided against her and demanded the life of Kissare or her son." He couldn't blame Apollymi for her hatred.

They'd earned it.

Out of sheer ignorance, he'd allowed Azura to talk him into something profoundly stupid. Apollymi had been their greatest ally.

Now, she was their greatest enemy.

And he couldn't blame her. But then he'd never understood what it meant to love in those days. It had been an inconceivable emotion.

He'd assumed that she would put the death of her Sephiroth and child behind her and move on.

I'm such an idiot.

One stupid momentary decision made out of spite, and he'd screwed up his life. No, his eternity.

Azura continued to glare at him. "We can't change what we did. We just have to find a way out."

He rolled his eyes. "How do we do that, my love? Flag down a motorist? Send Apollymi flowers?"

That didn't please his sister at all. "Cam created her Malachai and raised him ... what if we do the same?"

Noir arched a brow at a novel concept. "Pardon?"

"You heard me. What if we send one of our agents out to seduce the Ambrose Malachai?"

It was a nice plan, but there was one serious flaw to it. "Seduction won't create a Malachai." They were conceived in violence to do violence and die violently. That had been the curse they'd laid on the entire Malachai line.

And it was why Apollymi hated them so much.

Still, Azura wasn't to be daunted by something as trivial as reason or common sense.

"We'll send him a nightmare then ... something he'll attack without knowing it's real."

Noir rose from his throne as he considered what she was saying. It was one heck of a plan.

Don't even get excited. When have any of her plans worked out?

Even so, he wanted out of this hell hole with every fiber of his being. Oh, to be back in the world again ...

To be able to come and go. It was all he wanted. All he craved. So, he allowed her fantasy to draw him in. "I'm beginning to follow your logic. Who do you have in mind?"

Azura gave him a wicked smile. "We'll use someone the Ambrose Malachai won't see coming. Someone he won't be able to deny."

SIMI AND SHADOW walked through Thorn's castle for the babillionth time. Cobwebs covered everything.

Her heart was broken by the shell of a home that used to be filled with Thorn's huge personality. Even now, she could picture him in front of his fireplace, making snarky comments. Or the two of them together in the theater room, watching movies where Thorn constantly stated his opinions and picked the movie apart.

What she wouldn't give to see him there again.

"Where can he be, Shadow? Why can't we find him?"

Shadow sighed heavily. "I don't know, Sim. We've looked everywhere. There hasn't been a single sighting of him anywhere in centuries."

It was as if Thorny had vanished into another realm. Or another time.

"He's not dead." She would know if he'd died. She'd feel it. "Where could he be? Where haven't we looked?"

Shaking his head, Shadow used his powers to return the room to how it'd been when Thorn had lived here. It was clean and shiny again. "I don't know. But I miss my brother-in-spirit. I've searched every realm I could think of and there's nothing. It's as if he'd never been born."

Those words seared her because she couldn't imagine him not having been a huge part of her life.

Shadow met her worried gaze. "And I've tortured everyone I could think of to get information about his location."

"Even Paimon?" she asked.

"Especially him. He said he has no idea."

Of course he did. "I don't believe that evil demon. Do you?"

Shadow snorted. "Not even a little bit, but it doesn't give us anywhere to look."

No, it didn't.

Aching over the loss, Simi went to sit on Thorn's throne. For some reason, this made her feel closer to him. But not as close as it would if he were here, staring at her in a pique because she'd interrupted his reading.

Thorn was her bestest friend of all time. Had been so for most of her life. He'd always been there for his Simi. She missed him so much.

Closing her eyes, she tried to remember the exact sound of his voice.

Normally, she could duplicate any voice. But it'd been too long since she last heard Thorn's pleasant accent. Too long since he'd been here to make her laugh.

Where are you, Thorn?

He'd become a ghosty that lived only in her memory.

And her heart.

I won't forget you, Thorny. Most of all, she would never stop hunting him. Not until they found him and brought him home.

FORNEUS HEARD the sound of his power crackling all around. It echoed off the dark walls surrounding him. Gone was any care for anything.

Even his own life.

All he felt now was hunger. Soul deep. A need inside him to bathe in blood. He didn't care whose blood or even why. It was that part of him that wanted only destruction. The part inherited from both his fathers.

The craving was insatiable. Worse, it had control of him. Nothing else mattered. Only destruction and blood.

Unable to contain that thirst or the surge of his powers

as he yielded to the demon that he'd spent centuries bury-ing, he blew the door from his prison cell.

Akantheus Leucious Forneus was back, and he would not be contained.

Not by anyone for any reason. Thorn was gone now. He was the tool Noir had wanted him to be, and he was ready to destroy any- and everyone who came near him.

As soon as he was free of his cell, he saw a demon who shrank back, cowering at his approach. That was mother's milk to him. He drank the demon's fear like a fine brandy.

"Where's Paimon?" he growled.

"I don't know, my lord."

Too bad. Thorn ripped him to pieces and smiled at the sound of his dying agony. That was what he needed. The sound of misery to keep him company.

But he was far from finished.

There were more victims waiting for him. Many, many more.

First though, he had one in particular he wanted to beat.

One who'd created him and left him to wallow this state.

Determined to rip apart his father, he headed for Noir's throne room.

His wings sprang out from his back as he flew into the room where his father was busy plotting with Azura.

Both of them turned toward him with a stern glower.

His father came to his feet "How dare ..." His voice trailed off. "Thorn?"

"Forneus," he growled. "Thorn's dead."

Azura and Noir exchanged a confused stare an instant before Forneus rushed his father.

Noir sent a god-bolt at him, but it didn't do any good. He caught the bolt and sent it straight back at Noir.

"You wanted a weapon ... I am one." And he was done being controlled. Grabbing his father, he threw Noir through a wall.

Azura shrieked as she came at his back.

Forneus caught her, then backhanded her. She fell away from him.

When Noir started toward him, Forneus hit him with another god-bolt. "Don't," he growled. "For once, you're going to do *my* bidding."

And he was about to show the gods what a real warrior was capable of.

38

OCTOBER 31, 2334

Shadow popped into the living room of akri's New Orleans house where Simi was lying on the floor with her legs stretched up along the wall. Simi frowned as she realized Shadow stood between her and her barbecue-flavored popcorn.

That was never a good place to be.

So she arched a brow. "Problem?"

"I've found Thorn."

Oh! In that case, she'd forgive Shadow for blocking her popcorn since he brought such happy news. "Where is he?"

"Raining hell all over the human world."

"What?" she gasped, sitting up and tucking her legs under her body.

Shadow used his powers to conjure an image of Thorn and his army as they were fighting against humans, Daimons and Dark-Hunters on what appeared to be the

Vegas Strip. Simi hadn't seen anything like this since the Primus Bellum.

There were bodies everywhere.

How could that be her Thorny? Yet there was no denying his demon form that she'd only seen when he was extremely upset or angry. "What's going on?"

"He's aligned himself with his father."

No. That made absolutely no sense to her. "Thorny hates Noir ... I don't understand."

"No one does. Nick and the others are heading to Las Vegas where Thorn is systematically tearing down everyone and everything he can."

Her heart pounding, she went to the kitchen to check on akri. He was with his brother, akri-Styxx. Bethany and Tory were with them as they discussed the best way to deal with Thorn.

Why hadn't one of them told her that Thorn had been found?

Worse? Simi was terrified by their plans that included killing him. "You can't hurt Thorn, akri."

"I'm not sure if we have a choice." He gave Styxx a sad stare. "He's more powerful now than he's ever been and let's face it, he was never weak."

Bethany scratched at her neck as she stared at wall where the PC had all their plans laid out for them to review and discuss. "We could always try and bind his powers."

Akri sucked his breath in sharply. "It's a good thought, but I don't think we can."

"Then the Malachai can stop him," Styxx reminded him. "He definitely has the powers."

Simi wasn't sure about that either. It sounded good except for one thing. "The Malachai almost killed Thorn the last time they fought."

"That was Adarian," akri reminded her. "Not Ambrose."

"True, but what if the old Malachai takes control of Nicky? Nicky might not even know he's hurting Thorn. He might just do it." That was her fear. How could they save Thorn without killing him?

Akri arched his brow. "We can't let him continue to destroy humans, Simi."

"Why not?"

His gaze turned droll. "You know why."

It was wrong. That was what akri always said. Humans needed to be protected.

Pfft on that!

Worse? Thorn would most likely agree. But Simi couldn't stand the idea of Thorn being harmed because of some smelly humans.

Everything came back to them. Why were they so important anyway?

Even so, she would respect akri's opinion. Most of all, she'd respect Thorny.

"Fine, akri. I want to go with you."

Akri arched a brow. "I'd rather you stay, Simkey."

If it was anyone else, she might. But this was different,

and she wasn't listening. "This is Thorn. I won't stay behind."

Not for anything.

She loved her Thorny, and she wasn't about to let them kill him if she could help save him.

Akri nodded as he finally relented. "We need to head out. I don't want to leave my kids fighting alone."

True. While Sin and Kat were great warriors, Simi had no idea how Mia or her little brother Karadin would do in a massive battle. Even though they had impressive powers, they weren't the seasoned fighters that their parents were. Mostly because no one wanted them to fight.

It was too scary.

Without waiting on the others, Simi used her powers to locate Thorn and teleported to Vegas. Akri and the others would catch up.

But first, she had to find her best friend and see what was happening.

Not that it was hard to find him. His army had laid waste to the entire Vegas strip.

There were bodies and fires everywhere. It looked like the whole place had been firebombed.

Simi paused as she finally understood why akri said and did the things he did. Humans were frail, and no one was prepared to deal with the ferocity of an army of demons coming at them. She actually felt sorry for the poor people who'd died and especially the ones who were wounded, trying to find shelter from an army bent on their deaths.

I will never joke about eating humans again.

Because this wasn't a joke.

Biting her lip, Simi flew to where the worst of the fighting was taking place. Demon fire and god-bolts rained down from the battle. Demons flew overheard, screeching and dipping toward their victims.

Because it was daylight, there weren't any Dark-Hunters on the street. Instead, their army was made up of Daimons who were now able to tolerate the sun. Most of them she remembered from her visits to Sin's casino. They were good Daimons who took care of their patrons.

Simi paused as she saw Karadin fighting a demon on the street. Fury darkened her gaze. How dare anyone attack her baby! Karry was precious!

Okies, she admitted he was a grown man who was a carbon-copy of his father, but still …

Karry would always be her baby no matter how old he got.

Her gaze narrowing, she changed from her black feathered wings to her leathery battle wings and headed straight for them.

"Get off him!" she snarled as she dove for the demon who looked up at her in shock.

Without hesitating, Simi grabbed him and tore a chunk from his neck. Blood soaked them both, but she didn't care. Her only goal was to protect her nephew.

Panting from the fight, Karadin looked at her incredulously. "Wish I could do that, Aunt Simi."

She wiped at the blood on her face with the back of her hand. "You don't need to. It's why the Simi's here."

Another demon started for Karadin, until he saw the demon at her feet. Eyes wide, he turned and ran.

Normally, Simi would have given chase, but right now, she had to make sure her babies were all right. "Where's your sissy?"

"At the casino, holding back a group that was trying to break in."

"Why did you leave them?"

"I didn't mean to. One of the demons picked me up and carried me off."

She gaped. "What?"

"I stabbed him, and he dropped me. I was trying to get back to the casino when you showed up."

Her stomach lurched at his news. "Were you hurt?" She lifted his shirt, looking for wounds.

Protesting, he backed away with a smirk. "I'm fine, Aunt Simi. Unless they cut my head off, I'm immortal." He rubbed at his back. "But it wasn't comfortable being air dropped. A gentle landing would have been nice."

Fury consumed her. "Show me the demon who dared!"

He gestured at the one she'd bitten and killed.

Oh. "Wish I'd known. I'd have made him suffer longer."

Karadin laughed. "You sound like Mom."

The Simi had no doubt about that. Katra was fierce when it came to her children. It was a family trait.

"Let's get to them."

Nodding, Karadin headed back to the casino while Simi made sure no demon came near him. She was the mother duckie protecting her duckling.

By the time they reached the casino, akri and the others were there.

The moment akri saw Karadin, he grabbed him into a tight hug. "Your dad told me what happened. I was just going to look for you. Are you all right?" He stepped back to examine him.

"He's fine, akri. The Simi already checked." She looked their group over. Akri, Sin, Kat, Mia, Tory, and Urian. "Where's akri-copy?"

Kat pointed to the doors. "He and Bethany took off to fight demons."

Oh ...

"I'll go join them." Simi left before anyone could stop her. Her plan was to route demons until she found the big guy she was wanting to see more than anything, but she'd barely gone outside before she saw the main demon she'd come to see.

Thorny.

Wings spread, he flew after two Daimons.

Simi cut him off.

Thorn started to hit her, then paused as he recognized her. Disbelief swept across his face. "Simi?"

"What are you doing?" The question was barely out of her mouth before he grabbed her and vanished.

〜

By the time Simi could see again, she was in Thorn's home, inside his throne room. She expected him to let her go, but instead, he continued to hold her.

Simi savored the sensation. "Thorny?"

"Is it really you, Simi?"

His question confused her. How could he not know. "Of course it's me. Why am I here?"

"Because ..."

She waited for him to continue.

He didn't.

"Thorn?"

Instead of responding, he leaned his head against hers and took a deep breath. He'd never behaved like this before. It was so peculiar to her.

"What is wrong with you?"

Thorn wanted to answer, but too many emotions rushed through him. The beast inside wanted blood.

No, it demanded blood. Craved it.

And yet ...

He remembered her. This was Simi. *His* Simi. The only creature in the world who had made him deliriously happy while knowing exactly who and what he was.

She didn't judge him. Or care that he was the son of Noir.

In his mind, he struggled to think of the last time he'd seen her. She'd been wearing red. A short skirt and boots. Her hair had been in pigtails.

Today, she was dressed in purple. No horns, but her wings were now feathery—a sign she wasn't going to fight him. And that she felt comfortable with him even though he was a monster.

He'd missed her so much. For so many reasons. And now she was here.

With him.

"I won't let you go, Sim."

Simi gasped at his words. "We can't stay like this, Thorny. How in the world will the Simi be able to eat her barbecue?"

He laughed at her primary concern. "We'll find a way. I'll even make it extra spicy."

Instead of letting her go, he tightened his hold on her.

"What are you doing, Thorny?"

He had no idea. He'd told his father that he would lead his army. His rage against the world had been absolute.

Until he saw Simi.

Now that he was holding her ...

He didn't care about anything else. "Stay with me, Sim. Stay with me because you want to."

"Have you lost your senses or thrown them away?" Simi asked. "Akri was planning how to kill you just a little while ago and that was before you kidnapped his Simi. Now, he'll be even madder."

And Thorn didn't care. "Please, Simi?"

Simi placed her hand against his cheek. "Tell me where you've been?"

"In hell."

"Thorny—"

"I'm serious. I was held prisoner until the demon inside took over me."

"Why you want to fight for your daddy? The Simi thought you hated him."

"I do." And he had no good reason for what he'd done. Now that his rage was gone ... "I don't know what they did to me."

Why was he attacking the world he'd spent centuries protecting?

None of it made sense.

Whatever had possessed him was gone now. He even turned back into his human form.

"I can't remember anything, Simi." Nothing more than attacking. But again, he didn't know why. There was just a huge hole in his memory.

It seemed like just yesterday he'd been in the theater room with Simi. And at the same time, it seemed like an eternity ago.

Nothing made sense. The world had gone insane.

No, he'd gone insane.

"How long as it been?"

Simi scowled at his question. He was serious. He had no idea. "Centuries, Thorny. Shadow, akri ... all of us have been hunting everywhere for you. Where have you been?"

"I just remember darkness and anger."

Simi pulled him against her for a hug. "You're safe now."

He nodded against her shoulder. "What have I done?"

"You made everyone mad."

Thorn winced. Of course he had. "Can you forgive me?" He didn't care if the others did. All that mattered was his little demon.

Simi stared at him aghast. "Always."

That wasn't the problem. The problem was akri might not. He wasn't the most forgiving of beings.

He picked her up then and held her so tight that she could barely breathe. "I want to keep you here."

She gasped at those words. "You know you can't."

"I know. I said I wanted to. But I could never hurt you, Sim. I think it's why I came back to me when I saw you. You're my touchstone."

Simi didn't understand. "Your what?"

"Anchor is what Nick would call it. You keep my beast tamed."

For reasons she couldn't name, that made her heart flutter. "The Simi keeps you tame?"

He looked away from her, then back. "I love you, Simi. I always have."

She smiled. "I know."

Thorn was aghast at her nonchalant tone. "What do you mean you know?"

"The Simi knewed it when you builted us the theater room. It was obvious."

"Really?"

She nodded.

"Then why did I wait so long to tell you?"

"Because you knew akri would be furious." Wrinkling her nose, she leaned against him. "And you were skeered."

He laughed at the thought of him being scared.

Then again ... he wasn't exactly scared of Acheron. Just cautious. Only an idiot would piss off someone that powerful on purpose.

But he'd lived centuries without her. Centuries.

And he'd hated every single moment they'd been apart. "Do you think Acheron will kill me?"

"Well ..."

39

A cheron watched as all the demons fled Vegas. While grateful for that fact they were going, there was one demon in particular he searched for. "Where's Simi?"

With a bad cut on his forehead, Styxx looked sick to his stomach. "Thorn took her and vanished. I'm sorry. I tried to get to her and failed."

Ash could feel his blood rush through his veins. More than that, he felt his horns rise from his head and knew his eyes must be glowing. "He did *what*?"

Styxx winced before he answered. "Took her. I would assume to Azmodea."

One of the few places Ash dared not go. Unmitigated fury tore through him. "Shadow!" he roared.

Shadow appeared instantly, then froze when he looked at Acheron in his full demonic form. "Whoa ... you look like a blue Charonte. What's up, boss man?"

Styxx answered for him. "Thorn took Simi."

"Okay, let's define some terms. I know Thorn. I know Simi. What do you mean he 'took' Simi?"

"He flew off with her while we were in battle." Acheron enunciated each word slowly so that Shadow would understand them and the amount of anger he was holding back.

Shadow nodded. "'Kay. We're still mad at Thorn. Got it. He did something profoundly stupid."

"I'm thinking they flew to Azmodea," Styxx said.

"Good bet. And I now see why I'm here. You"—Shadow looked at Acheron—"want me to go retrieve her."

"Or take me in."

"Yeah ... no. Not a good idea. The blue lady and major asshole don't need to get their hands on you in their Private Idaho. That would be worse than this Strip littered with bodies."

"You know what would be worse?" Acheron asked.

"Me wasting any more time. I'm going to retrieve your demon." Shadow vanished.

Styxx looked up at him. "You doing all right?"

"Am I still blue?"

"Yeah and fully horned."

"Then why did you ask?"

"Stupidity." Styxx pointed to his bleeding forehead. "Pretty sure I took one too many hits to my head and it knocked loose my last remaining brain cell."

"I thought you said I knocked that out centuries ago."

Styxx laughed until Bethany appeared by his side.

"You're hurt? What did they do to you?"

Styxx dodged her hands. "I'm fine. Simi's the one we need to worry about."

Bethany froze. "Simi?"

"Thorn has her." Just saying those words made Acheron want to choke the demon with his own entrails. When he got to them ...

He would make Thorn regret ever being born.

"Yo! Thorn? My demon ... where are you?"

Thorn froze as he heard Shadow's voice calling out through his castle.

Simi's eyes widened. "He sounds pissed," she whispered to Thorn.

Yes, he did. And Thorn knew why.

"We're in the theater room."

Shadow appeared instantly, then pulled up short. "I see the 'we.' Have you any idea how stupid and reckless that is?"

Thorn sighed heavily. "Yes, I do. And I'm pretty sure Acheron is the reason you're here."

"You know it."

"On a scale of one to ten—"

"He's ninety."

Thorn cringed. He could just imagine. "Over my attack on the humans?"

"Screw that. Over Simi."

That was what he was afraid of. Acheron didn't play when it came to his children. Especially his eldest daughter.

"*And* because of the bodies," Shadow added. "He's *really* unhappy about those. More pissed over Simi. But the body count just makes it all the worse. Why did you do it?"

"I don't know."

"Thorn—"

"No, Shadow. I mean it. I don't know what happened to me. I lost something."

He scowled. "How do you mean?"

"I ... I can't even explain what happened. I was me and then I wasn't. It's like a fever dream I had until I saw Simi and brought her here. Then I found myself again and had clarity."

"That is not going to save your ass. You know that, right?"

Sadly, he did. He'd screwed up in a major way.

"You have to send Simi back to Acheron."

No! That word resonated in his soul. "I can't do that, Shadow."

"If you don't ... There's no telling what Ash will do to you. But I do know that I wouldn't want to be you."

Simi pushed Shadow back two steps. "Tell akri that his Simi is safe."

Shadow let out a nervous laugh. "Oh, I'm not about to do that. I like my body parts in their current location, and I have no desire to turn Acheron into Picasso."

His heart breaking, Thorn glanced to Simi, then back to Shadow. "How do we resolve this?"

"No idea. Your killing spree was quite impressive."

"I don't even know how it happened. I went to kill my father and the next thing I knew ... I don't know if it was something they did to me or the insanity of being trapped for centuries."

"Where were you?" Shadow asked.

"The lowest pit of the dungeon. I didn't even know they went that far down. I couldn't hear or see anything ... I just went insane."

Shadow nodded. "Look, I'm going to give you two some room, but you need to decide what you're going to do. And you need to decide that fast."

"Are you planning to tell Acheron?" Thorn asked.

"About the two of you? Hell no! That's your job. I'm going back to lie to him. I have no idea what I'm going to say. But I will give you both some advice. The longer you wait, the worst this will get. Tell him soon. Rip off the band-aid."

Thorn knew he was right. They needed to face this.

He inclined his head to Shadow before he returned and left him alone with Simi.

"What are you planning, Thorny?"

"Nothing really." Because he just realized that while he'd confessed his love for her, she hadn't said it back.

A part of him was tempted to keep her regardless. But that wasn't fair to her, especially if she didn't love him in turn.

No, he could never hurt his Simi.

Fine then. He'd go to Acheron and, if he was lucky, the Atlantean might finally put him out of his misery.

ASH PACED the small living room of his daughter's condo while he waited for Shadow's return. And he better return hauling a demon in his wake.

Otherwise, Acheron was going to go into Azmodea, consequences be damned.

"It'll be okay, Poppy. Shadow's got this."

Ash offered Mia a smile. "Thank you, Miakey."

Smiling back, she flounced off toward her bedroom. Thorn was lucky neither of his grandkids or daughter had been harmed in the fighting.

"Ash?" Tory asked in a chiding tone. "What are you doing?"

He hated that his wife could see through him so easily. "I'm on the verge of taking a trip."

"Don't you dare! Not unless you want me to go with you."

And she would, too. He knew that for a fact. Tory was the most obstinate person he'd ever met.

Suddenly, a flash lit the room as Shadow returned.

Ash stood up. "What happened?"

"Simi's safe."

"But?" Acheron asked.

"No buts. She's safe and Thorn will return her. He promised."

"You sure?"

Shadow nodded. "Give them a little time."

Those silver eyes turned red. "I'm not a patient being."

"I know, but rushing this will only play into the hands of the two gods your mother hates most."

He was right and Ash hated him for it. "Fine. But they better not make me wait too long."

"How long can I keep you before Acheron gets stupid?"

Simi snorted. "Akri probably passed that point two seconds after you grabbed me."

He had a feeling she was right.

His common sense begged him to return her. But he'd never had much sense. In fact, he profaned it as it often impeded him in the past.

Before he let her go though, there was one thing he had to know. "I told you I loved you, Simi. You didn't—"

"I love you, too, Thorny-man."

The relief inside him was palpable. He hadn't realized until she said those words how much of his sanity was tied to this ...

Demon. Precious, precious demon.

His heart pounded as knelt before her. He had never felt quite like this—so vulnerable and strong. All at the same time. Her eyes shone with an intensity that took his breath away.

"Simi," Thorn said softly, his voice heavy with emotion. "I've loved you for centuries—" *Literally.* "Even when I didn't fully realize it."

She looked at him, and he didn't think. He closed the distance between them, pressing his lips to hers. The kiss was soft and sweet at first, but as they both fell deeper into the moment, it became bolder, and more passionate ... less clumsy, intense.

Simi's fingers tangled in Thorn's hair, gripping lightly as their tongues danced, and she moaned deep and low in her throat, the sound thrilling him to no end. It sent his heart into a skitter and he deepened the kiss, encouraged by her reaction.

Every graze of their lips ignited a burning desire that spread through his body like wildfire.

His breathing ragged, Thorn pulled back slightly, his hands still roaming Simi's body, exploring every curve and dip. "Simi ... I don't want to be without you. If you stay, we can find a way to make this work ..." His voice was desperate, his eyes pleading.

She cupped his face with her hands, her voice scarcely more than a whisper, "I want to stay, Thorn. I do."

He knew it was the truth ...

But there was a "but" hanging in the air.

He didn't want her to say it out loud. He found her lips again, pressing his mouth against hers, insisting. That kiss heightened the intensity of his desire and his love for her.

Gods help him. Their kisses were like a never-ending feast, each more delicious than the last. The taste of her lips, soft but insistent, was the sweetest thing he had ever experienced. It was like ambrosia, leaving him craving more. But as much as he wanted this ... wanted her ... a part of him knew they couldn't continue.

Acheron would kill him. Plain and simple.

Even so, he couldn't stop himself as she melted into his kiss. He reveled in it, ignoring the small voice at the back of his mind reminding him of the reality of their situation. Reminding him of what this kiss might ultimately cost him.

She closed her eyes, her long lashes brushing her flushed cheeks, and he drew her fully into his embrace, like a starving man at his last meal. Her body molded perfectly against his, soft curves meeting hard planes. Thorn's hands roamed over her back, tracing the delicate outline of her wings. Simi shivered at his touch, a soft moan escaping her lips.

"Thorny ..." she breathed, her voice thick with desire, and he kept going, wanting to savor every moment, every sensation. His hands skimmed her body as if memorizing every curve and plane as she returned his fervent kisses with equal passion. The heat between them was electric, sparks of desire crackling in the air. Her body pressed against his, her arms wrapping about his neck as their lips moved together in a long, passionate dance.

Their heartbeats pounded in unison, a primal rhythm that echoed in their ears.

Simi's body felt like a river of molten heat at the touch of Thorn's lips, but as she gave in to his passion, a nagging voice in the back of her mind reminded her of the harsh reality that threatened to tear them apart.

Her akri would never approve of this.

Even so, this was a moment that suspended time itself, their souls merging and their hearts beating as one.

Simi never wanted it to end.

The air, mixed with Thorn's familiar musk, created a heady aroma that consumed her.

Akri will be so mad. But for once she didn't care. Simi craved this intimacy with her precious demon. Thorn was everything to her and she was willing to upset her akri to have this one special person.

Forever ...

Pulling away, Thorn looked up and captured her gaze with his. "Simi ... I know Acheron is going to kill me and I won't be able to stop that. But I can't go the rest of eternity without you. I'm willing to give up anything to spend the rest of my life making you happy. Marry me?"

Never once in all these centuries she'd been alive had she ever hoped to hear those words.

But ...

"I can't, Thorny."

The disappointment in his eyes shredded her heart. "No, listen," she said quickly. "This is not because of you. The Simi doesn't want akri to destroy you." Tears filled her eyes as panic consumed her. "Don't you see, Thorny? He kilted Nick. Granted he didn't mean to, but he did. I can't let akri do that to you. The heifer might not bring you back. Then what would I do? How could the Simi live without her Thorny?"

His grip tightened as he brought her hands to his lips and kissed them. "Okay. I get it. But if I can convince Acheron—"

"No, no, no. No! You can't talk to him about this. Akri a little nuts, and the Simi doesn't want you hurt."

"I don't want me hurt, either. But I don't want to be here without you, Simi. I'd rather be dead."

Tears stung her eyes. "The Simi couldn't live if you were kilted because of me."

Rising to his feet, he flashed her an adorable grin. "Trust me, Sim. I'm charming. I'll win him over."

While she agreed he was charming, she doubted if it would ever work on akri. "What if you don't?"

"I have to. My heart depends on it, and I swore that I would never make you unhappy. That starts with dealing with Acheron."

Before she could say another word, he vanished.

Simi gasped as she realized what he was going to do which was the stupidest thing he could.

"Akri's going to kill him." And she wasn't sure if she could stop it.

40

Acheron froze at the last thing he expected.

Thorn, in full demon form and armor, appeared in the middle of Kat's condo.

What was he thinking after what he'd done?

Acheron immediately threw up a shield to keep his family safe. "Come to surrender?"

Thorn shook his head. "Where's Styxx, Kat or Tory?"

"My family doesn't concern you."

Clearing his throat, Thorn ignored him. "Styxx? Kat? Tory? Hell, even one of the grandkids," he called out. "Could one of you come out here for a minute?"

Ash's eyes turned vibrant red. "They need to stay put."

"I'm not going to hurt them."

"You damn right about that." Horns shot out of his head.

Thorn took a deep breath to settle his nerves as Ash's family came out from a door behind the Atlantean god.

"Something wrong?" Kat asked.

Before Thorn could answer, Simi appeared by his side. The moment she saw Acheron turning blue, she gasped. "It okies, akri! Your Simi is fine. See?" She turned around to show him that Thorn hadn't hurt her.

"Then get behind me."

Instead of doing as Acheron ordered, she stepped in front of Thorn. "I will if you promise me that you won't hurt him."

Thorn had never seen eyes boil before, but he would bet his rotten soul that Acheron's boiled as his lips curled.

"This isn't a game, Simkey."

"No." Thorn gently nudged her toward Kat. "It's not and I'm here to ask you something important."

Styxx scoffed. "Are you kidding? You just laid waste to a good portion of prime Las Vegas real estate. There's a body count out there that warrants the governor calling out the National Guard."

Thorn cringed at that. "I would say I'm sorry, but we both know it would be insincere. And I'd tell you that I don't remember it, except I doubt you'd believe me. Even if it's true."

"Then what happened?" Ash asked.

"I really don't know. My last memory is fuzzy. All I can recall is being stuffed in a room and left there after I had a bad conversation with my son." He gestured toward Simi. "I really lost myself. Paimon and Noir knew what they were doing when they trapped me. I can't handle what I damned my son to. Something inside me broke and it unleashed the demon. I had no control over myself. I never would have attacked humans had I been in my right mind."

Styxx scowled at him. "So what? You're here to apologize?"

Thorn turned toward Acheron. "Well, yes, and I'm here to ask for Simi's hand in marriage."

Faster than anyone could blink, Acheron exploded. His skin turned a swirling blue. Black horns jutted from his head at the same time a pair of black wings sprang out.

One second, he was in front of Thorn, the next, he had him on the ground in a choke hold so tight, that Thorn actually feared dying.

"Akri, no! Stop!" Simi grabbed Acheron's arms. "Let him go! Don't you dare hurt him!"

For the first time in his extremely long life, Thorn didn't fight back. The last thing he wanted was to hurt Simi, and of all people, he knew how much Simi loved her akri. If it meant his life to keep from breaking her heart, he would.

He felt the demon drain out of him. All of it. He was in human form, on the floor and he was pretty sure he was turning the same shade of blue as Acheron.

The moment he was no longer a demon, Acheron returned to his own human form.

But he didn't release Thorn.

"Would you kindly remove your hands from my throat, Acheron?"

His grip tightened for a moment. Then Ash let out a

fierce roar, released him and stood up. "I should rip your head off your shoulders."

"I would not enjoy that."

"And neither would the Simi." She moved to stand between them.

To Thorn's shock, she turned toward him and scowled as she saw his neck. "No! You damaged my Thorny! How could you, akri?"

Acheron's nostrils flared. "How could you, Simi? It was bad with Nick, but *Thorn*? Seriously? Thorn?"

Wow. No one had ever used his name as an insult before. It was quite impressive.

Thorn pushed himself to his feet. "Let's be clear, Blue Man Group. I haven't touched Simi."

That took some of the bluster from him. "What?"

"I love her, Acheron. I want to marry her. But I haven't touched her ... other than a kiss."

A myriad of emotions played across Acheron's face. With an astonished expression, he turned toward Simi. "No?"

"No. Thorny always been a gentle demon. That why the Simi's in love with him. 'Cause he's not only quality. He's the bestest. So, don't you hurt him, akri. The Simi would never forgive you."

Styxx let out a low whistle at that. "So ... how do we proceed?"

Kat clapped him on the back. "Bad news, Dad. Simi grew up."

"Would you all stop!" It was obvious Acheron wasn't

enjoying their teasing. "I'm trying hard to process this without committing murder. And none of you are helping." He turned back toward Thorn. "You have more nerve than anyone I've ever known."

Not sure if that was a good thing or bad thing, Thorn shifted his feet. "Do we have your blessing?"

Acheron turned back toward Simi. "Is this what you want?"

She shrugged. "The Simi's heart is a complicated thing, akri. It's lubbed him since he made me laugh 'cause he was trying to scare me."

Shaking his head, Ash let out a long, tired sigh. "Fine. I won't stand in the way, but you cannot take her to Azmodea. Ever. Not for *any* reason. You understand? Those are my terms. I don't want her near your father or Azura."

"Understood and for the record, I wasn't going to take her there."

"Good. So, where are you going with her?"

Thorn grinned. "I was thinking of a temple in Katateros ..."

He expected Acheron to protest or insult him. Instead, he nodded. "There are dozens that are unoccupied. Sounds like a plan."

Thorn felt the color drain from his face as his ploy backfired. "That was a joke."

Laughing, Styxx put his hand on his shoulder. "Nope. My brother has spoken. Looks like we'll be neighbors. But don't worry. Ash only visits when the human world is about to end."

Great. Thorn wanted to protest, until he looked at Simi.

The happiness in her eyes was too great. She seemed to love the idea. "Is that where you want to live?"

"Oh absolutely! Then the Simi won't have to rearrange her room. I can leave it as is and all things Simi will be nearby, but we can decorate the new place all scary like you like. Maybe even move your bony throne there."

Thorn actually felt Ash's stare on him. It hung hard and heavy. Almost the same as when Ash strangled him.

Only worse.

It was a good think he loved Simi enough to tolerate his future father-in-law.

Thorn offered Simi a smile. "We can live wherever you want."

Clapping her hands, Simi threw herself into his arms.

Thorn caught her against him and closed his eyes at how good she felt there. It was incredible.

Until he saw the look on Acheron's face as the Atlantean god cleared his throat.

Sin laughed. "You'll live, Thorn. But you will never be comfortable around him, and he will *never* stop glaring at you."

"And now you know why we live here in Vegas," Kat said. "Dad might be able to pop in whenever he wants, but we're just far enough away to where he usually has better things to do than make us crazy."

"Fair point. And note taken." But there was one major difference.

Kat agreed to live away from her father. Simi ...

The happy look she had said that he was trading a private mansion with no interference to a temple right up under a god he knew wanted to skewer him.

Joy. Oh joy.

But one look at Simi's happiness and Thorn realized he'd rather live there than anywhere else.

"We are going to be one weird family, aren't we?" he asked.

Ash looked over at his daughter and Sin, then to his brother. "We've been that for a long time, brother."

Simi smiled. "Well, y'all know what the Simi says... We have three kinds of family. Those we are born to, those who are born to us and those we let into our hearts."

Akri gasped. "Wait! I'm the one who said that."

Simi tsked at him. "You might have said it first, akri. The Simi made it famous."

41

ONE YEAR AND SIX MONTHS LATER

Thorn let out a long breath as he finished tying the skull bow tie around his neck. Only for Simi would he wear something so garish.

Ash knocked on the door behind him, then pushed it open. "You ready?"

"Sure." Thorn grimaced at Ash, knowing he wore the same pirate-styled tuxedo. A long black cutaway jacket and vest with tan knee breeches, and black riding boots. White silk shirt with the black skull and crossbones bow tie.

Ash gave him a droll stare. "I hope that pained expression isn't from wanting to marry my daughter."

"You know it's not."

"Good, because I still feel like I should kill you over this."

Thorn snorted. "As long as you promise to dress me in something else for my funeral, I'd probably be all right with that."

Laughing, Acheron clapped him on the back. "You are way too obsessed with clothes, my friend. Besides we dressed like this a lot ... centuries ago."

Scoffing, Thorn adjusted his cuffs. "I promise you, I have never dressed like this. But it's fine. For Simi, I'd walk naked down the aisle, over broken glass."

"Good answer."

And he was grateful that he wouldn't be the one walking down the aisle in front of that crowd. There were be hundreds of people on Simi's side, and he was dreading it.

But the worst was the knowledge that his side would be practically empty.

Okay, it would be completely empty. The only one who was here for him was his best man, Shadow. Simi, on the other hand, was loved by everyone.

I love her more than all of them together.

Why hadn't he seen it sooner? All the centuries they could have been together. That was on him for being so stupid.

Or maybe it was scared. Loving her was terrifying. Especially since she came with an almost seven-foot-tall, angry god.

Another knock sounded on the door.

It was Shadow who stuck his head in. "Showtime. Y'all ready?"

"Yes, I am." No regrets. What he felt for Simi far surpassed anything he'd ever felt for anyone else.

Thorn couldn't wait to let everyone know that special demon was his significant other.

No, she was his heart and soul. The best part of him.

Inclining his head, he crossed the room and let Shadow lead him to the outdoor garden they'd rented.

Weird that he'd never once thought about getting married after his twenty-first birthday. Not really. Yet here he was on a warm April day in New Orleans, tying his eternity to Simi's.

There were no butterflies in his stomach. No hesitation.

Just immense relief.

As they headed toward the flower-covered arch, Thorn slowed down. His side wasn't empty.

His breath caught as he saw how many of his Hellchasers had shown up for him.

Damn. It looked like all of them. Past and present. To his complete shock and delight, his side was every bit as full as Simi's. Fang Kattalakis was there, along with his wife Aimee and their three kids and their grandkids. Devyl Bane and Marcelina, along with their children. William Death, Jake ... all of his Deadmen and their spouses and children.

Thorn couldn't believe how many were here.

For him.

Granted, Simi still had more on her side, but not nearly as many more as he feared.

He couldn't believe how many of her "friends" he actually knew. Kyrian and Amanda Hunter and their kids.

Talon and Sunshine and their army of children. Valerius and his brother Zarek.

But the ones who meant the most to him were on his side of the garden. Cadegan and Jo, along with Thorn's grandkids and E.T. who sat beside his mother.

My kids came. He'd sent them an invitation with no expectation of their joining him for this.

His chest tightened at the sight of them, and of the men and women Thorn had known for centuries.

All here to watch him tie his life to Simi's.

Clearing his throat, he moved to his position in front with Shadow by his side.

With his hands folded in front of him, he heard the harpist begin to play the Macarena. Still Simi's favorite.

Thorn bit back a laugh at Simi's choice of wedding procession music. Why would she have chosen anything else?

God, I love her.

She was the most unique creature to ever grace this earth. Her sister Xirena's four-year-old daughter, Mara, came down the aisle first, scattering rose petals and bird seed.

Her mother followed behind in a vibrant red dress, carrying black roses that had been sent to them from Apollymi. The goddess had wanted to make sure that at least a part of her was here for the ceremony which she was watching from her pool in Kalosis.

Xirena made her way to her spot that was opposite of Shadow.

Then Thorn saw Acheron. But that wasn't what mattered to him. It was the little demon goddess standing at his side, dressed in a black Goth wedding dress, complete with a black veil.

Never had he seen anything more beautiful. Simi's long black hair was curled to perfection and her eyes twinkled as she looked at him.

As they stopped by his side, he saw a moment of hesitation in Acheron's swirling silver eyes. It looked as if the Atlantean was thinking of picking Simi up and running with her.

But after that, resignation descended over his features, and he placed Simi's hand on Thorn's arm. "Take care of her."

"Always."

Ash placed a hand on his shoulder and gave him a fatherly squeeze before he headed toward Tory.

Thorn kissed Simi's hand as they turned to face Savitar who was officiating the ceremony. While this might not be legal in a human world, it was in theirs.

Savitar, who was actually wearing pants for once and not board shorts, smiled at them. "Dearly beloved, we are gathered here today because hell has apparently frozen over."

Thorn glared at him. "Could you please be serious?"

Making a face, Savitar sighed. "Everyone here knows how hard that is for me, but for Simi's sake, I'll try." Clearing his throat, Savitar began again. "We are gathered here today to honor Thorn and Xiamara who are creating a life together ... gods have mercy on you."

"Seriously?" This time, it was Acheron calling him out.

Savitar held his hands up. "All right. All right. You have made the conscious decision of commitment to one another, and today you will begin your future as a wedded couple."

He looked out at the huge crowd. "To those who've come to witness this union, and there are a bunch of you, you are the most important people in Simi and Thorn's lives. We've assembled here from near and far to celebrate this wonderful moment. You are the ones who know them well, and you are an integral part of their lives and this ceremony."

Savitar looked over to where Nick Gautier sat with Artemis. "And we are all deeply grateful that Acheron didn't kill our groom."

Thorn didn't speak as he imagined the looks on both Acheron and Nick's faces.

Savitar paid them no heed. "Your love for Simi and Thorn fills this ceremony with meaning, and we're grateful that so many of you have joined us for this. Makes me wish I'd prepared a better ceremony. But that's okay. I'm told our couple have prepared their vows." He inclined his head to Thorn.

Thorn smiled at her. "Sim ... you are the light in my darkness. Before you ... well, I can't really remember a time in my life before you. But what I do remember are all the times when I needed a friend and you were there, without hesitation. You are the air I need. The only thing to keep me going, and I promise to love you for eternity and to trust you with my credit card. Even when you're watching QVC."

Simi laughed at the most wonderful thing she'd ever heard. She still couldn't believe this moment was real, but she was grateful for it. "My dearest Thorny-man, the Simi has loved you since the first time you made me laugh. Which happened to be the first day we met. I can't believe that you will be my husband. Mostly, I'm glad akri didn't hurt you. You have given me your hand and I promise to give you my forever. The Simi will always love you and I will protect you and make good use of all your credit cards."

Everyone, especially Acheron, laughed.

Thorn kissed her hand.

Savitar sniffed before he cleared his throat. "By the powers vested in me by me, I now declare you married demon and demon. Thorn, gently kiss your bride and remember that Acheron is watching and scowling. Let's not end this in carnage."

"I'm sure he's scowling more at you at the moment." Thorn cupped her cheek in his hand and quickly kissed her lips.

Even that light touch was enough to thrill her. This was her husband. Now and forever.

No one would ever divide them. And hopefully akri wouldn't kill him.

Thorn stepped back as everyone cheered. It was a

perfect moment, and Simi was grateful to everyone who was here to share it.

They rushed down the aisle to where the tents were set off to their left. Their reception was extra special. Catered by Fang and Aimee and the staff at Sanctuary, it was her favorite barbecue and fixings, along with a chocolate fountain for dessert.

At this moment, she had everything she'd ever wanted and one thing she'd never planned on.

A demon of her own.

Laughing, she hugged Thorn. "Thank you."

"For what?"

"For being mine."

EPILOGUE

Simi bit her fingernail as she walked through the temple that had been her home with Thorn since they'd married six months ago.

While this had never been her favorite building in Katateros before, it had become the best one ever. Mostly because it had everything she loved.

And it was where she spent lots of time with Thorny.

At the moment, however, he was angry and yelling on the phone at someone.

He hung up, then glared at her. "You know what I miss most?"

"Newspapers?"

"What?" He snorted at her arbitrary comment, and shook his phone at her. "No. I miss when you used to slam a phone down in anger. Madly pressing a button just doesn't have the same satisfaction."

"Well, that's just a weird thing to miss. You must also hate that you don't have doors to slam, either."

"Exactly! That's half the problem with kids today. No effective way to convey their fury."

Sure. Why not blame it on that? It made as much sense as anything.

"Well, it's interesting that you brought that up."

Thorn scowled. "What? Old phones? Or anger?"

"Kids."

"Why?"

Pressing her lips together, Simi glanced around sheepishly.

It took Thorn a few heartbeats before he realized what she was trying to say without saying it. His face went pale. "Oh my God! You're having a baby?"

She nodded.

Shouting out in happiness, he picked her up and swung her around.

Until the joy went out of his eyes. "Oh, dear gods ... Ash is going to kill me."

"No, he won't. Kat has babies. His sons have babies. He used to this."

Thorn didn't really hear those words as his head reeled. Finally, he was going to have a child that he could raise. One he could watch grow up.

He couldn't believe it. He was going to have a real child. With the woman or demon that he loved.

Unbelievable joy tore through him. His hand trembling, he reached out to touch her stomach that was still flat. "Are you sure?"

"Positive."

He couldn't believe this. After all these centuries, Simi had given him everything. She kept him sane and away from his manipulative father.

Even living here had been much better than he'd ever dreamed. Acheron never really bothered them.

This was the home he'd never had. The one he'd gone to Azmodea seeking and hadn't found.

Everything would be perfect except for the one thing that worried him.

Noir and Azura had succeeded in breeding a new Malachai and none of them could figure out where the boy was.

He and Simi were bringing a child into an uncertain, terrifying world. One filled with danger and enemies out to end them.

Even so, he was delighted.

"I won't let you down."

"You've never let me down, Thorn."

That wasn't true and they both knew it. But the most beautiful thing about Simi, she never brought up anything from the past. Her focus was always on the future.

And the miracle was that she'd taught him to be the same way. The past was the past. There was no way to change.

Every day was a brand-new chance to make a better future. A clean slate.

Simi had been his tabula rasa.

And no matter what life threw at them, they would meet the challenge. Hand-in-hand. Together.

For all eternity.

ALSO BY SHERRILYN KENYON
(LISTED IN CORRECT READING ORDER)

NICKCHRONICLES

Infinity

Invincible

Infamous

Inferno

Illusion

Instinct

Invision

Intensity

SHADOWS OF FIRE

Sabotage

Last Christmas

Savage

Simi

NEW TITLES

Eve of Destruction

Born of Blood

Dark Places

Dark-Hunter®

The Guardian

The Dark-Hunter Companion

Time Untime

Styxx

Dark Bites

Son of No One

Dragonbane

Dragonmark

Dragonsworn

Stygian

Deadmen Walking

Death Doesn't Bargain

At Death's Door

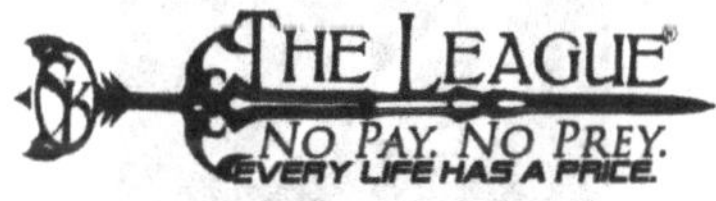

Born of Night

Born of Fire

Born of Ice

Fire & Ice

Born of Shadows

Born of Silence

Cloak & Silence

Born of Fury

Born of Defiance

Born of Betrayal

Born of Legend

Born of Vengeance

Born of Blood

Born of Trouble

Born of Darkness

<u>Lords of Avalon</u>

(written as Kinley MacGregor)

Sword of Darkness

Knight of Darkness

ABOUT THE AUTHOR

Defying all odds is what #1 New York Times and international bestselling author Sherrilyn Kenyon does best. Rising from extreme poverty as a child that culminated in being a homeless mother with an infant, she has become one of the most popular and influential authors in the world (in both adult and young adult fiction), with dedi-cated legions of fans known as Paladins–thousands of whom proudly sport tattoos from her numerous genre-defying series.

Since her first book debuted in 1993 while she was still in college, she has placed more than 80 novels on the New York Times list in all formats and genres, including manga and graphic novels, and has more than 70 million books in print worldwide. Her current series include: Dark-Hunters®, Chronicles of Nick®, Deadman's Cross™, Black Hat Society™, Nevermore™, Silent Swans™, Lords of Avalon® and, The League®.

Over the years, her Lords of Avalon® novels have been adapted by Marvel, and her Dark-Hunters® and Chronicles of Nick® are New York Times bestselling manga and comics and are #1 bestselling adult coloring books.

Join her and her Paladins online at QueenofAllShadows.com and www.facebook.com/mysherrilyn.

www.ingramcontent.com/pod-product-compliance
Lightning Source LLC
Chambersburg PA
CBHW011142100726
47899CB00010B/3146